The
Hangman's Row
Enquiry

ANN PURSER

BERKLEY PRIME CRIME, NEW YORK

THE BERKLEY PUBLISHING GROUP
Published by the Penguin Group
Penguin Group (USA) Inc.
375 Hudson Street, New York, New York 10014, USA
Penguin Group (Canada), 90 Eglinton Avenue East, Suite 700, Toronto, Ontario M4P 2Y3, Canada
(a division of Pearson Penguin Canada Inc.)
Penguin Books Ltd., 80 Strand, London WC2R 0RL, England
Penguin Group Ireland, 25 St. Stephen's Green, Dublin 2, Ireland (a division of Penguin Books Ltd.)
Penguin Group (Australia), 250 Camberwell Road, Camberwell, Victoria 3124, Australia
(a division of Pearson Australia Group Pty. Ltd.)
Penguin Books India Pvt. Ltd., 11 Community Centre, Panchsheel Park, New Delhi—110 017, India
Penguin Group (NZ), 67 Apollo Drive, Rosedale, North Shore 0632, New Zealand
(a division of Pearson New Zealand Ltd.)
Penguin Books (South Africa) (Pty.) Ltd., 24 Sturdee Avenue, Rosebank, Johannesburg 2196,
South Africa

Penguin Books Ltd., Registered Offices: 80 Strand, London WC2R 0RL, England

THE HANGMAN'S ROW ENQUIRY

A Berkley Prime Crime Book / published by arrangement with the author

PRINTING HISTORY
Berkley Prime Crime mass-market edition / May 2010

Copyright © 2010 by Ann Purser.
Cover illustration by Teresa Fasalino.
Cover design by George Long.
Interior text design by Laura K. Corless.

ISBN: 978-0-425-23473-0

BERKLEY® PRIME CRIME
Berkley Prime Crime Books are published by The Berkley Publishing Group,
a division of Penguin Group (USA) Inc.,
375 Hudson Street, New York, New York 10014.
BERKLEY® PRIME CRIME and the PRIME CRIME logo are trademarks of Penguin Group
(USA) Inc.

PRINTED IN THE UNITED STATES OF AMERICA

10   9   8   7   6   5   4

One

"IF YOU ASK me," said Ivy, lifting the teapot lid and peering inside, "he's got something to hide. Moved into Hangman's Row, so they say, and living on his own. A bit smarmy. I wouldn't trust him as far as I could throw him."

"That's not very far, then," said her cousin Deirdre, with a smile, knowing that Ivy belonged to a generation of country families whose first reaction to a newcomer was suspicion.

Ivy scowled at her. Anybody would think she was having tea with the Queen, she thought acidly, observing Deirdre, well groomed from top to toe.

Former lifelong scourge of the village of Round Ringford, Ivy Beasley had moved, under considerable pressure from Deirdre, to Springfields luxury retirement home in Barrington, in the county of Suffolk.

As Ivy had yet to admit, Barrington was a beautiful village, each house a jewel, with its ornamental plasterwork and ancient timbers, originally built to serve the folk at the Hall. It was an estate village, and had all once belonged to the squire, but recently Theodore, the latest in a long line of Roussels, had raised much-needed money by selling off most of the houses. He told friends he felt a traitor to his ancestors and vowed his descendents would always own and live in the Hall itself. As he was a bachelor with no apparent intentions of marrying, the village was sceptical.

"They say Theodore Roussel has upped the rent for this new man," Deirdre said. "What's his name, anyway?"

Ivy shrugged. "Don't ask me," she answered. "I'm not one for gossip, as you know."

Deirdre swallowed a sharp retort, and said, "He won't have much fun with his neighbours." She helped herself to another biscuit from Ivy's tea tray. "You can't get much drearier than old Mrs. Blake and Miriam. Sometimes you can see Miriam peering out from behind the curtains. I feel sorry for her. She's not that old, and had a good job once, so they say."

"I've seen her in the shop," Ivy said. "Only time she gets out."

"She should take a stand," said Ivy, pushing back into place a strand of iron grey hair that had had the temerity to stray from under her "invisible" hairnet. Her sharp, beady eyes behind steel-rimmed glasses clouded as she added, "My own mother was similar, and I left it too late. Had me under her thumb until she passed away. And even then she used to come back and haunt me. I don't think she approves of Barrington, though. Haven't heard from her since I arrived."

"That's one good thing, then," said Deirdre promptly. She was finding her plans for caring for her elderly cousin more tricky than she had supposed, and her daily visits to Springfields were more of a duty than a pleasure.

* * *

HANGMAN'S ROW, A small terrace of three cottages, was still in Roussel hands. In spite of its gruesome name, the lane was leafy and shade dappled. It was half a mile or so from Barrington Green, where the local gibbet had once stood as a warning to transgressors. A young farm-worker, his wife and baby, lived at one end of the row, with widow Blake and her spinster daughter in the middle cottage. The new tenant was at the far end of the terrace, and had yet to be seen long enough for the locals to pronounce judgement.

Rumours of Roussel's rent increase were true. A few new coats of paint had smartened up the cottage, and Theodore had found at the local dump a surprising supply of little-used bathroom and kitchen fittings to bring the place up to standard. Satisfied with this, he had advertised the cottage for what he regarded as a more realistic rent than the other two.

It had taken a while to find a tenant, but then curious eyes had seen a tall, middle-aged man with sparse, sandy hair and a hunted look, appear with his grey whippet and a small amount of furniture in a Thrifty self-drive van.

Augustus Halfhide had so far avoided Miriam Blake, though she had made several approaches to him over the garden fence. Now he watched her return from a visit to the shop. He sighed. She peered into his window and gave a little wave, accompanied by a hopeful smile. "Oh, God," he said to his little dog Whippy, "it's just my luck to move in next to a predatory female."

It looked as if his hopes of having a period of peace and quiet were under threat.

Recently, after his wife had finally left him, he had taken a hard look at himself and decided to begin again. After a life so far filled with action-packed missions in foreign lands, nothing, he had decided, would be better than a remote village, in a community that would not regard him as one of their own for at least twenty-five years. He could spin them a good story, and they would leave him alone to adjust to a different way of life.

Augustus Halfhide, Gus to his friends, could not have been more mistaken.

Two

GUS MET IVY Beasley in church. It was an unlikely place for him to be, but he had felt a sudden urge to observe some of his fellow villagers without necessarily being accosted. He planned to slip into the back pew in the darkened interior and indulge himself by inventing identities for the people in front. Although he wouldn't admit it, even to himself, he was missing congenial company.

There were very few in church for the service, and among the mostly elderly parishioners his eye was taken by a woman in a solid black coat covering her broad shoulders, and topped with an extraordinary black felt hat like an upturned pudding basin, reminiscent of photographs of his grandmother in a distant past.

When the service finished, he hung back until nearly all had gone, and saw with alarm that he was being approached by the vicar, who held out a welcoming hand.

"New to the village?"

Gus nodded, and said he had moved in a few weeks ago, and was beginning to find his way around. The vicar said

how good it was to see him in church, and began a lengthy
history of the ancient building. "We have our very own
martyr, you know," he said with a keen smile. "Taken away
by the Roundheads in the civil war. The village never saw
him again."

"And you'll never see our visitor again, if you don't let
him get home to his lunch," said a sharp voice behind the
vicar.

Gus peered gratefully at the figure emerging, and saw
that it was the woman with the black hat. She was not smiling, and had a stern and disapproving expression. Now,
here was a challenge! Gus prided himself on his way with
women, and judged this one was much too old to be predatory. He could safely practise his charm, sadly unused for
too long.

"Good day, madam," he said and bowed his head in
greeting.

"Not good. It's raining," Ivy Beasley said flatly. "And
I've forgotten my umbrella."

"Allow me," Gus said, stepping forward and offering
his arm. In the church porch he put up his city umbrella,
picked up from habit at the last minute before leaving
home. "Now, which way? And do tell me your name,
Mrs. . . . um . . ."

"Beasley. And it's Miss. I go up that way, past the
shop."

As they stepped out briskly, Gus discovered that Ivy had
come from the village where his old school friend Richard
Standing lived.

"Fancy that," Ivy said caustically. "They were above
me, of course. Lived up at the big house. We'd see them
driving about in one of them limousines."

Anxious not to seem patronising, Gus hastened to assure
her that he had known the Standings only casually—
a lie—and he himself had been in very much lowlier circumstances. By the time they reached Springfields, Ivy had

warmed up a little, and Gus was intrigued by her past life in Round Ringford. He asked if he could visit her at some time convenient to her. "You could tell me things about Richard that I'm sure I don't know," he said jovially. "And anyway, it must be dull in there for you, missing all your old friends," he added.

"All dead," Ivy replied bluntly. "Anyway, please yourself. I'm always at home—if you can call it home. Thanks for keeping me dry." With that, she disappeared, and Gus returned home, feeling unaccountably cheered.

Three

THEO ROUSSEL LOOKED out of the window. He was still a handsome man, neatly put together and with a good head of pepper-and-salt grey hair. But he had a gloomy air, as if his life had become a sad disappointment, as in some ways it had. Rain fell steadily across the park, and his prize Manx brown sheep were huddled under one of the big chestnut trees planted by his ancestors. Roussels had lived in Barrington for generations, going back, so they said, to the Norman conquest. Others said half the village had Roussel blood in them as a result of Theo's grandfather merrymaking his way around the girls of the village, some willing and others obedient, but most in time producing offspring with a remarkable resemblance to the squire.

"There must be some way," he muttered to himself. He had been examining his accounts, and was depressed. The Hall and its estate cost far more to maintain than ever the farm could support. He had to find some way of increasing his income, and whichever way he took would, he knew, have to meet with approval from Beatrice Beatty.

She had been with him for years now. When she first came, she had acted as housekeeper and kept her place. Now, he realised too late, she had taken over. Was he frightened of her? Only in small matters, he comforted himself, turning away from the window. At this moment, Beattie came into the room with coffee and a handful of letters for Theo.

"All junk," she said. "I've been down to the post office to collect them. I've opened all except for the one from the bank. I've left the bad news for you. And," she continued, "we really must get round to doing something about the Blakes. I have a plan, but you'd better know about it before I take action."

"Better get your breath back first. Did you hurry? Anyway, fire away when you're ready, Beattie," Theo said, reflecting that it wouldn't make the slightest difference what he said, she would go ahead with her master plan anyway. The only thing he had been able to resist was her often hinted at desire to become his wife. He knew that she could probably hold out longer than he could, but so far he had managed to deflect all her attempts.

After she had told him what she intended to do about the Blakes, and he had recovered from shock at her hard-heartedness, he sat at his desk and found the rent books of the three cottages in Hangman's Row. It was true that the new tenant with the ridiculous name had been quite willing to pay the increased rent, and so the Blake cottage with new tenants could in theory produce the same. He should probably have moved out Miriam Blake and her appalling old mother long ago.

The late John Blake had been one of the estate workers, and a pretty idle one, too, but Theo had a vague notion that the law might step in if they summarily ejected his widow and daughter. But what would happen when the old woman died? It shouldn't be long now. They would surely not be morally obliged to allow Miriam to remain there at such a peanut rent?

Young David Budd, his farmworker, lived in the remaining cottage in the Row. He and his wife and small child were a breath of fresh air on the farm. He was a good worker, and vital to the running of the estate, so nothing to be done there, except perhaps creep the rent up bit by bit.

The telephone on his desk rang, and Theo swore. Somebody wanting to be paid, no doubt. He would leave it to ring, and Beattie would answer it.

Sure enough, Beattie was by the telephone in the kitchen in seconds. "Mr. Roussel's residence," she said. "Who is it speaking?"

It was a policeman who announced himself as Detective Inspector Frobisher, and his voice was solemn. "I would like to speak to Mr. Roussel, please," he said.

"I'm afraid that is not possible at the moment. I am his assistant, and shall be happy to give him a message."

"I must insist, Miss, er . . ." Frobisher had heard of Miss Beatty, and was not to be fobbed off that easily.

Beattie sniffed, and said if the inspector would hold on, she would see if Mr. Roussel was receiving calls. She walked through to the study, and saw that Theo was pretending to be asleep.

"No good, Mr. Theo," she said flatly. "It's the police. You'd better speak to them." She picked up the receiver and handed it to him, then retreated hastily to take up her listening post on the extension in the kitchen.

Theo sighed. "Good morning, Inspector," he said. "What can I do for you? Miss Beatty handles everything, you know. You'd be better speaking to her."

Now the policeman's voice was irritated. "We have a job to do, and try to do it as tactfully as possible, Mr. Roussel, but you are the owner of the estate, and it is a matter for your ears only. I have to tell you that one of your tenants has been found dead on her cottage floor. Hangman's Row. Mrs. Winifred Blake. Her daughter is being cared for by us at the moment, but she asked that you be informed. She is naturally distraught. She had been to the shop and returned home to find her mother lying there."

Theo heaved a sigh of relief. "Oh, that old woman," he said. "She's been on the blink for some time, Inspector. Natural causes, you'll find. Nothing to worry about except funeral arrangements. Miss Beatty will of course be helping Miss Blake. Meanwhile, please let me know if there is anything I can do."

"Not as simple as that, I'm afraid, sir," Frobisher said. "A bread knife stuck in the heart does not normally come under the category of natural causes. Questions to be asked. We shall be in touch very soon. Oh, and please tell Miss Beatty that we shall be along to talk to her as well."

Theo put down the telephone with a shaky hand. For God's sake, did the man think he was capable of creeping in with a bread knife and helping Nature to send her on her way? He got up, and shouting "Beattie!" made his way into the echoing corridors of the Hall. He had to keep up the fiction that she wouldn't already know the contents of the call, and so descended to the kitchen to tell her.

IN HER COTTAGE, Miriam sat in a chair by the window, dry-eyed. From habit she peered round the edge of the curtain and saw Gus Halfhide walking down his garden path and out into the road.

"He's coming here!" she exclaimed in alarm, and ran out of the room to hide in the kitchen. What could he possibly want? Surely he wouldn't be so insensitive as to call on her at this moment. But there was a sudden firm knock at the door, and although she was still genuinely shocked, she could not help her heart beating a little faster. She opened the door a couple of inches and said, "Yes? Can I help you? I have had a bereavement and can't ask you in. At the moment," she added hastily.

"Just came to pay my respects," said Gus. "I saw the

police and the ambulance and realised that you must have had a serious illness or loss. Please forgive me for intruding. I will leave you in peace." He turned to go, but Miriam said quickly that it was her mother who had died. He turned, his interest caught.

"And in suspicious circumstances," she added, with some pride at having found the right phrase. "Thanks for coming along." She shut the door apologetically as he was about to say something more.

Four

SOME DAYS LATER, Gus thought seriously of doing a runner. But then he reconsidered. Was it merely bad luck that right next door to him, in a deserted lane leading to a tiny village in darkest Suffolk, chosen by him because he was sure absolutely nothing would ever happen there, an old woman had breathed her last with a bread knife stuck through her heart? He could not deny that all the old instincts had immediately reappeared, just when he had renounced them forever.

"I rather wish," he said aloud, "that there was some old chum who could put me right." His little whippet jumped out of her basket and stood shivering in front of him. "Sorry, sorry!" he said, and tickled behind her ears. "You are quite right." She made a small grumbling sound, and looked longingly towards the door.

"Right, message taken," Gus said. "We'll go for a walk. Clear our heads. I must forget all about it and concentrate on the Great Novel."

This was one of the reasons why he had come to

Barrington. He intended to free himself from all unwanted questions, and to escape the temptations of the casino and the race course. He would settle down and write a lively fictionalized account of some of his more lurid adventures.

It had begun to rain, a very light misty rain, and Gus put a small waterproof jacket on Whippy to keep her dry. She was in fact quite tough, but he felt that with so little flesh on her bones and such a thin smooth coat, he should cosset her. Anyway, he loved having the small creature dependent on him, and reflected that he would probably have made a very fussy father.

"Not too late, Gus," he said to himself as they walked down Hangman's Row and out into the main street of Barrington. All he needed was a tall, willowy blonde in her broken-down car languishing by the roadside, when he would leap forward, fiddle about under her bonnet—ahem!—and fall headlong in love. She would, of course, reciprocate.

A figure approached him, walking slowly with a stick, and he was sadly sure that this was not the girl of his dreams. An old woman, with a black coat, a hat like an upturned flowerpot and steel-rimmed glasses, bore down on him. His new friend, Miss Ivy Beasley. He had given the Standings a call, and asked them about her. "Guaranteed to find out all about you, Gus," Richard had chortled. "You'd be safer in the middle of London!" But Richard's warning had only sharpened his curiosity. Could an old woman in a retirement home still be a fearsome tyrant?

Ivy fixed him with her beady eyes. "Good afternoon," she said firmly. "Getting to know the area? That's a funny little old creature you got there, I must say. Is it a greyhound? Must have been the runt of the litter."

Gus bridled. "She's meant to be that size. Whippets are small. And she's not old, you know. Quite young, in fact. She'll be two in August. She's a dear little thing, aren't you, Whippy?" he said, and patted her light-bulb head. "It

is nice to see you out for a walk, Miss Beasley," he continued. "But aren't you going to get wet again? Do let me see
you back to Springfields. The weather forecast was not at
all good."

Ivy stared at him. In all her long life, nobody had ever
before offered to see her home, and now it had happened
twice. She was about to assert her independence and refuse,
but her curiosity got the better of her and she accepted.

"Very kind of you, I'm sure," she said, and took the arm
that he proffered.

"You've heard the news, I expect. Living next door, that
is," Ivy said, as they walked on towards Springfields. "If
you ask me, that daughter of hers should be asked some
hard questions."

"My neighbour?" Gus asked innocently. "Do you know
the Blakes?"

Ivy cupped her hand to her ear. She was a little deaf
now, but refused to have her hearing tested, claiming that
there was nothing wrong with her ears that a good syringe
wouldn't put right.

"The Blakes," Gus repeated. "I heard that the old lady
next door had died. I called to pay my respects, but her
poor daughter was obviously very distressed. Do you know
more than that?"

"Huh!" said Ivy. "Distressed! I can't think why. Miriam
Blake has been wanting her old mother to kick the bucket
for years. So you haven't heard about the knife? The bread
knife, sticking straight into the old woman's heart?" Ivy's
voice was full of disgust and disapproval, and Gus felt her
hand tighten on his arm. My goodness, Richard Standing
was right! He must be very careful with this one.

"How on earth do you know that?"

Ivy glanced sideways at him. "I have my sources,
Mr. er . . . er Halfhide, isn't it? My memory is not as good
as it used to be, I'm afraid."

Gus doubted this. He could recognize a put-down when

he saw one. They were nearing Springfields, and Miss Beasley left him at the gate, shutting it firmly against him. "Thank you," she said. "I expect we'll meet again. It is a very small village, you know. Very difficult to keep anything private here, I have found." Gus judged it was not the time to remind her of his intention to visit her, and started off back home.

Whippy chose this moment to squat on the verge and Gus dutifully found a poo bag. He pondered on Miss Beasley's last remark. Was it a warning? And what secrets had she found it difficult to protect? "We must find out more," he said to Whippy as they set off again at a brisk pace. "And who knows, we may meet the blonde on the way back."

Five

GUS WAS OUT of luck. So far no blondes. But he was curious to see a muddy four-by-four slowing down as it came towards him. It stopped, and the nearside window was slowly lowered.

"Good morning." The voice was low, and came from a distinguished-looking, grey-haired man sitting in the passenger seat. Next to him, driving the vehicle, was a fortyish woman, with hair scraped back in an old-fashioned bun, and eyes like ripe sloes, blue black and blank in expression. "Mr. Halfhide?" continued the man. "I'm Theodore Roussel. Settling in, I hope? Anything you want, ask Beattie here. She runs everything." He leaned forward until his head was close to the window. Gus walked forward until he was close. "Including me," the man said sotto voce.

Gus smiled. It wasn't the time to mention numerous faults in his little house, including the gap wide enough to post a parcel between the back door and its split frame. Nor would he complain about the old-fashioned flush lavatory that took at least three desperate attempts to make it work.

First, he should be on good terms with everyone in the village, and especially with this interesting Roussel landlord. Not so sure about Beattie, he said to himself. Can't see the old Halfhide charm working on this one. Still, give it time.

"Oh, everything is fine, I'm sure," he replied. "Charming little cottage. Just what I was looking for."

"Shut the window, Mr. Roussel," Beattie said sharply. "You'll be getting a chill."

Roussel made a face at Gus, and began to shut the window. Then he stopped and said, "Nuisance about the Blake woman. Beattie'll get the daughter moved on. Hardly pays any rent, you know. Old John Blake used to work on the estate until he died. Useless when he was alive, and even more useless now he's dead. Don't let the daughter bother you, Mr. Halfhide. Beattie'll get rid of her." He closed the window, and the car moved off with a jerk.

Gus walked on home and thought hard about what Roussel had said. He had seemed extraordinarily unconcerned about having a murder in his property. Did that mean he had had a hand in it? Or had Beattie? Gus's experience of murders in villages was much influenced by the crime novels of Agatha Christie, and so he was sure that under the tranquil surface there were secret family feuds and hatreds. A large bagful of twenty pound notes under the mattress might be quite enough to trigger a violent death! Money problems at the Hall? It was common knowledge that members of the aristocracy were poor as church mice.

Gus shook himself. This was pure fantasy! Maybe the old duck was holding the bread knife and conked out, falling on the knife as she went. But no, in his experience, such things seldom happened without a helping hand.

As he approached the terrace, he saw a police car parked outside the Blakes' cottage. Damn and blast! He hoped they hadn't arrived to arrest Miriam Blake. His meetings with Ivy Beasley and Theodore Roussel had fed

his curiosity, and during his walk home he had again felt
that need to *know*. He had given in, and now had all the
excitement of being back in business. After all, there was
damn all to do in this place, and Gus had quite decided that
a satisfactorily long investigation would fill his time when
not writing. Now he had to think quickly how he proposed
to make a start.

First, he must have a way of talking to all kinds of village people. He had quickly realized that he had no hope of
keeping himself to himself, so he might as well make use
of village nosiness.

What would give him easy access into their lives? He
could apply for a job as newspaper delivery man, going
every day to village houses. Or relief postman? No, neither of those sounded convincing. He would be instantly
under suspicion. He looked around his sitting room for
inspiration, and saw where a triangle of plaster had already
fallen off the corner of the wall by the fireplace. A cheap,
bodged job by a local, he thought. But that was it! He would
advertise in the local shop as an experienced painter and
decorator. The fact that he knew very little about either
did not bother him. It surely could not be too difficult to
slap a coat of paint on a wall. And he was good with his
hands. He could easily manage the fiddly bits, like window
frames.

With relief, he watched the police car depart with no
Miriam Blake inside. It would be neighbourly, he convinced himself, to pop along and see that she was not too
upset by a visit from the law.

Miriam answered the door straightaway. She looked
warily at him, and said, "Hello."

Gus gave her his most charming smile. "Gus Halfhide,"
he introduced himself. "Next door. But I am sure you know
that. I couldn't help noticing the police car, and wondered
if you would like a restoring cup of tea with me?" He hadn't
meant to say that at all, but she looked so unhappy that he

could not suppress his natural kindness. After all, he had many times comforted the bereaved.

She hesitated. "Um, well, I'm not sure," she said.

"Don't worry," Gus reassured her. "I am quite safe in taxis." She looked puzzled, and he realized the old phrase used by flappers in the twenties meant nothing to her. "I can't prove it," he said, holding out his hand, "but I assure you I am a perfectly trustworthy and honest citizen."

He was relieved when she shook his hand limply, and gave him a faint smile. "Well, thank you, Mr. Halfhide," she said. "Just a small cup, then. I can only spare a few minutes. So much to do after a death in the family." Her chin wobbled, and he nodded. "Off we go," he said. " 'The cup that cheers but not inebriates.' "

"Mother used to say that," Miriam said, and locked her cottage door behind her.

COMFORTABLY SETTLED, MIRIAM looked over the top of her glasses at Gus Halfhide. "Now then," she said, putting down her mug of strong tea. "If we're to be neighbours and friends, I shall have to know a bit about you."

Oh no you won't, thought Gus. But he was practised in dissembling, and was relaxed about answering her questions with lies and half lies. "Fire away, Miriam," he said. "I do hope I may call you Miriam?" Without those dreadful glasses, she would be quite good-looking, he decided. Good skin, thick wavy hair. A little carroty, but nicely done.

Miriam looked doubtful. He was definitely attractive, she considered, and someone a lot worse might have moved in next door. "Well, I suppose it's all right," she said.

"And you must call me Gus," he continued. "Perhaps you'd like a potted biography? Or should it be autobiography?"

Miriam frowned. What on earth was he on about. "Go on, then," she said, and waited.

Gus gave her a big smile. "Born thirty-five years ago," he said, having knocked off ten years for luck. "Out in India with parents until aged five, then home to Surrey. Series of unpleasant nannies, and finally boarding school. Harrow, actually." No need to add the grammar school bit. He could see she was looking mightily impressed, and he continued. "Married twice, divorced twice. Not the marrying kind, I have decided. Still on good terms with both ex-wives. No children, fortunately." He paused for breath.

"What work do you do?" Miriam asked. This was the most important question as far as she was concerned. They had had enough advertising executives, film producers, aging actors, and so on, buying up all the village properties.

"I'm a best-selling writer," he said. He put his head on one side and smiled winsomely at her.

Miriam looked at him, then burst out laughing, a surprisingly raucous sound. "Pull the other one," she said.

"Absolutely true," he said, joining in the laughter. It always worked, he thought happily.

Six

AFTER MIRIAM HAD gone, Gus cleared away dirty crocks and found himself a glass. All the glasses in the cupboard were straightforward tumblers, thick and not too clean. He rinsed it under the tap and poured himself a whisky. Adding a teaspoonful of water, he took it into the sitting room and settled down with a pad of paper and a pen. Time to make plans.

He noted down his intention to become a painter and decorator. He must make an attractive poster for the shop. His computer would do that for him, with two or three images of paintbrushes and efficient looking men up ladders. Then there was Miriam to cultivate. He felt he had made a good start there. And probably the most important of all was to develop a friendship with the all-knowing Miss Ivy Beasley at Springfields. Once he had got a foot in the door there, he reckoned he could tap in on several of the old folks' memories. But most usefully, he would gain Ivy's confidence so that she would tell him all her secrets and continue to glean information around the village. He must also get to know her cousin. Quite an attractive woman. Probably a goer in her youth. And moneyed. He laughed. Must be well worth listening to a conversation between Ivy and Deirdre!

Right, no time like the present. He would walk up to Springfields and ask about being a volunteer. All these retirement homes had Friends groups. He could offer to read to them, play cards, push wheelchairs. . . . All good opportunities for gathering information. He reckoned that he would, in record time, find the assassin who had done for old Mrs. Blake. No need for PC Plod! Never fear, Gus is here!

IVY BEASLEY WAS in her room, which she preferred to spending useless hours in the communal lounge, listening to boring reminiscences from old people. She did not consider herself a typical candidate for a residential home for the elderly. And why "elderly"? "Old" was a perfectly good word, wasn't it? She narrowed her eyes. Labels were ridiculous, anyway. It was all Deirdre's fault she was here, going on and on and forcing Ivy to agree. Deirdre had mustered all the support she could find in Ringford, including the Standings', in order to convince Ivy that Springfields was the answer.

Her reminiscences were interrupted by a girl with duster and a basket of cleaning materials peeping round her door.

"Please knock before you open the door!" Ivy said sternly. "And I am not ready for you to come in, anyway. Come back later." The girl swore under her breath, but shut the door quietly, as instructed.

Back in her reminiscences, Ivy remembered that it was those leaflets of Springfields that Deirdre had sent her that had softened her up. "Comfortable rooms and all residents' privacy requirements respected," she had repeated to the vicar of Round Ringford. He was one of a campaign to get rid of her, she reckoned. But she had finally reluctantly given in, with the thought that perhaps a new start would be a challenge. With the best of her old friends in Ringford graveyard, Ivy decided she had little to lose.

Now her room was beginning to be a familiar and pleasant retreat. She looked out of her window, and could see down the drive and as far as the road. Wasn't that the lanky figure of Augustus Halfhide approaching? He must be coming to see her, of course. There was nobody else in this dump worth speaking to. She got up from her chair and swiftly closed the romantic novel she had been reading. There had been only one romance in Ivy's life, and that had gone horribly wrong. It had been a long time before she could even think about it, but now she could look back and despise herself for being so stupid. Much better to rely on novels. If the romance went sour, you could get another from the library and hope it would be different.

Half an hour went by, and Ivy frowned. Where had he got to? Probably that wretched woman had intercepted him and kept him talking. Well, she still had the use of her legs, and she would go and rescue him. She left her room and went purposefully down to the hallway. As she thought, there he was, trapped by Mrs. Spurling. He saw her coming, and smiled broadly.

"Ah! There you are, Miss Beasley. I do hope you have time to talk to me for a while? I have been offering my services as a volunteer to Mrs. Spurling, and would like to become a friend to all at Springfields." Is this really me? he thought to himself. Gus Halfhide, man about town, gambler extraordinary—friend of Springfields Home for the Elderly? Yes it is, he told himself firmly.

"You'll soon get fed up with that," Ivy said, with a prim

smile. "Why don't you come and have a cup of tea with me, and I can set you straight."

"Wonderful!" said Gus. "If you'll excuse me, Mrs. Spurling. Now don't forget, I am at your service. Lead on, Miss Beasley."

Ivy gave her orders to Mrs. Spurling for a good pot of tea and two pieces of window cake.

"Window cake?" Gus said. Ivy laughed. "Dear me," she said, "you're still wet behind the ears, Mr. Halfhide."

He followed meekly as the old woman stumped back to her room. She ushered him in and shut the door firmly. "All eyes and ears, the residents of Springfields," she said. "And that includes me. Sit you down, and you can tell me what you've really come for."

Gus hesitated. Should he enlist Miss Ivy Beasley straightaway? Tell her that at the moment he was a one-man detective agency, but could use a partner? She would laugh in his face. Still, nothing ventured, nothing gained.

"My line of business, Miss Beasley," he began, "before I came to this village of Barrington, was investigation. I am not at liberty to tell you the nature of this investigation, but I have now retired. However, as I have been unfortunate enough to move next door to a house where there has been a violent death that looks like murder, I can hardly forbear to use my skills to help Miss Blake and obtain justice for her poor old mother."

Ivy looked at him, her head on one side, weighing up what he had just said. "Now, Mr. Halfhide," she replied, "let's put it like this. You were in some dodgy line of business that probably meant poking your nose into other people's affairs. Now you've given it up, or it has given you up, and you're here in Barrington, in the middle of nowhere, to keep your head down and hope that whatever it is you're escaping from will go away and be forgotten. Am I right?"

The old devil! Gus dearly wished he could tell her how near the truth she had guessed. But it wouldn't do. He had to be consistent, and he laughed rather too loudly and said she couldn't be more wrong.

"The only part of it that is correct is that I was in the investigating business," he said, looking at her seriously now. "And I am sure you will appreciate that I have sworn an oath of secrecy."

"Don't be ridiculous," Ivy said. "That may wash with Miriam Blake, but not with me. Anyway," she continued, "I don't care a fig what you were in the past. It is what you do here that is important. As for the Blake affair, if you ask me," she added, "you don't have to look no further than the daughter. I can't say I care for her much, but she did have a time of it with that old mother giving her the runaround. And I'll tell you this for nothing. From what I've heard, that Miriam Blake is no better than she should be. Don't let her give you all that innocent spinster stuff. Ah," she added, "here's tea."

She looked at the tray brought in by a young girl, and said slowly and loudly,"You forgot the window cake!" The girl looked frightened, said she was sorry and vanished to fetch it.

"Foreign," Ivy said in explanation. "Polish. They're everywhere these days. I don't know I'm sure, what is this country coming to, Mr. Halfhide?"

"We can fix it," Gus said with a smile. "Shall I pour, or will you?"

Gus and Ivy sat talking amiably in her room for a few minutes when there was a tap at the door. Without waiting for an answer, Mrs. Spurling bounced in.

"Just popped in to see if you two dear things would like a small sherry? Such a gloomy day . . ."

Ivy stared at her. "What are you talking about?" She looked at her old clock brought from Ringford and put safely on the chest of drawers where she could see it, even if she was in bed. "Drinking at this hour?" she said bluntly.

Gus said quickly, "A small sherry is very acceptable at any hour. Most kind of you, Mrs. Spurling." He gave her the full blast of his charming smile. She giggled. Not a pretty sight, he thought. Then she said, "Would you like me to join you, possibly?"

"That won't be necessary, thank you," said Ivy firmly. "And if Mr. Halfhide would like a sherry at such a daft time of day, then please send that girl up with one. Nothing for me, of course. What an idea! Mother would turn in her grave."

When Mrs. Spurling had retired scarlet-faced with annoyance, Gus attempted to calm the atmosphere. "Tell me about your mother, Miss Beasley," he said. "She sounds a most interesting woman." An evil old bag, more likely, he thought, but settled back in his chair prepared to listen.

Ivy looked at him, frowning. "You don't want to hear about my mother," she said. "You want to know some more about the Blakes, don't you. D'you know what I really think about you, Mr. Halfhide?"

Oh Lord, now what, thought Gus, but he nodded bravely.

"I'm sure you're up to more than you've said, young man," she said. Gus was quite happy about the adjective, until Ivy added that most people looked young to an old lady like herself. "No doubt you have a good reason for living on your own, and you don't seem one of those."

"One of whats?" Gus said, knowing perfectly well what she meant.

"Fancy men," Ivy said flatly. "I've always liked to call a spade a spade, and Mother always said she'd have no truck with fancy men."

"Ah," pounced Gus. "Your mother. Now do tell me more

about her. She must have been a great character . . . like mother, like daughter, would you say, Ivy?"

Ivy wondered whether to point out that she never allowed people she hardly knew to call her by her Christian name, but decided to ignore it. Actually, she quite liked it from Augustus.

"Yes, she was a character. Very forceful. Boss of our house, no doubt about that. My father was a good man, but not as strong as she was. Came from farming stock, and had been brought up to work on the farm from an early age. I was an only child, Mr. Halfhide, but that didn't mean I was spoilt. Oh no. 'Spare the rod and spoil the child.' That was my mother's favourite saying."

"You mean she hit you?" Gus said in a shocked voice. No wonder the old thing was so sharp-edged.

"On occasion," Ivy said. "But not with a stick. Flat of her hand on the back of bare legs. That was her way. My father used to go out of the room. He couldn't stay. Didn't hold with smacking girls, I heard him say once to my mother. But she just laughed."

"Now, that's quite enough about Mother," she went on, conscious that Gus Halfhide was looking a bit green about the gills. "Let's talk about the reason you're here. It's finding out who killed old Mrs. Blake. And my guess is that you're nothing to do with the police. Right?"

Gus nodded firmly.

"And you want me to help you. Right?"

Gus nodded.

"Very well," Ivy said. "I like the idea of something to occupy the brain. It can go to mush, you know, if it's not exercised. But Deirdre has to be in on it, too. She's a pain in the neck, but not stupid. And she has money. We might need that. Add to that the fact that she's fit and well and has nothing to do, I reckon she'd be useful."

"Can she keep her mouth shut?" Gus said meekly.

"Like a clam," Ivy said. "She's had plenty of practise,

spending her husband's money without the rest of his family knowing," she added, smiling grimly.

Gus stood up and extended his hand. "A deal, then, Ivy?" he said.

"A deal, Augustus," she said, shaking his hand vigorously.

Seven

DEIRDRE BLOXHAM HAD married money, but not class. But then, she hadn't been exactly classy herself, not upper class nor even upper middle, but good solid working class, eminently respectable. She was a bright schoolgirl, and went on to improve herself in adulthood with all kinds of further education courses. It was on one of these, a basic introduction to motor maintenance, that she met her future husband.

Bert Bloxham had planned out his future as a successful garage owner. Included in his plans was an attractive, capable wife, who could rise with him up the social ladder.

In Deirdre, he saw the perfect partner. She was lively, ambitious, and capable, and, what is more, he fancied her. Luckily, she fancied him, too, and after a decent interval of courtship, they were married, had two small girls, and settled in a small terraced house in the suburbs of Thornwell, a large town near to Barrington.

By retirement age Bert and Deirdre had amassed

a considerable fortune, selling the now large chain of garages for a handsome sum and moving into a large house in Barrington. Unfortunately, Bert was not suited to retirement, and within two years had died of inactivity and boredom.

Deirdre, apart from loneliness after Bert had died, did not pine. Once grief had been dealt with, she set about making a different, but satisfactory, life. She was good at spending money and bossing people around. Ivy had not been her only project. Her proudest moment had been the presentation to her of an MBE for dedicated services to the local community.

Now she sat in her elegant drawing room, as she had learnt to call it, enjoying a large gin and tonic, and wondering if it would be a good idea to invite Ivy to tea to meet some of her club's members. She weighed up the pros and cons and decided that on balance it was a bad idea. The old thing could be very tricky, and deliberately tactless, and it would probably be best to have Ivy for a cup of tea along with Deirdre's next-door neighbour, who was ninety-three and deaf as a post.

GUS, MEANWHILE, HAD returned home a happy man. With Ivy on his side, he reckoned he could have a great deal of fun playing detective and sorting out Miriam Blake, who was rapidly becoming an object of considerable interest. No better than she should be, did Ivy say? Ah ha! Just the kind of thing he loved to investigate.

Then he remembered one thing Ivy had stipulated. Her cousin Deirdre must be involved. Deirdre had money, said Ivy, and they might need some. Gus could second that heartily. He always needed money, and if this was a way of making some, all to the good. So, an approach to Deirdre Bloxham was the next thing on his agenda, and Ivy had made it plain that it was up to him to persuade her to cooperate.

He looked out of his dusty window and saw a fine sunlit evening. Right, no time like the present. He washed his hands, combed his hair over the patch where a small niece had told him his head was showing through, and set off in his car to find Mrs. Deirdre Bloxham, MBE.

TAWNY WINGS WAS a strange house, built by a patriotic builder for his own family in Barrington. He had made his millions putting up cheap little dwellings miles away on the outskirts of Thornwell, but for Tawny Wings he had chosen a picture village and had designed and built the house in the shape of a V sign. Deirdre often wondered whether he had been inspired by Churchill's famous gesture. Odd as the exterior appeared, it was a comfortable house. Even the bath in the master bathroom was extra large. The builder had meant to have nothing but the best, and Deirdre felt thoroughly at home.

As she gazed out of her drawing room window her eye was caught by a battered-looking car approaching slowly up her driveway. Who on earth could that be? She looked at her watch. Seven o'clock, and her supper browning nicely in the oven. Ah well, she would soon send him packing, whoever he was.

She answered the doorbell, and saw to her surprise that her visitor was Augustus Halfhide, friend of Ivy and something of an enigma.

"Good evening, Mrs. Bloxham!" Gus at his best could be very persuasive. "I apologise for calling at such an hour without making an appointment first, but I wondered whether you would have ten spare minutes to talk to me?"

"What are you selling?" said Deirdre bluntly. She had not spent years in her husband's motor car business without knowing all the tricks of the salesman's trade.

Gus lifted his eyebrows, and gave her a quizzical smile. "Goodness me, Mrs. Bloxham! I am not a commercial traveller, you know. No, I have been talking to Miss Beasley—a cousin of yours, I believe?—about a rather interesting project, and she encouraged me to think you might be willing to participate. She has been telling me about all your numerous good works, and the MBE, of course, and I cannot help but think you would be enormously helpful to our little scheme."

"Cut the cackle," said Deirdre, standing back and opening the door wider. "You'd better come in and explain in plain words what you're on about. I can't spare many minutes."

This was not going to be easy. Gus was thinking rapidly. There could be no disguising the fact that he wanted financial backing for a very small detective agency with a decidedly unconvincing combination of partners. One elderly spinster, one retired investigator of dubious reputation, and, if Deirdre agreed, a rather less elderly widow with time on her hands and a good deal of common sense regarding money in the bank.

"You may not have heard," he began, "that Barrington has witnessed a very unpleasant murder. Very unpleasant for me, since she was my next-door neighbour, an old lady looked after by her unmarried daughter. The old dear was found dead on the floor with a bread knife point down in her chest."

Deirdre shrugged. "Of course I've heard. Very nasty. But I can't see what that has to do with me?"

"Nor, in the beginning, could I see that I would be involved in any way. I suppose," he added, as if he had just thought of it, "I could be a suspect! But I think not, and anyway, the general feeling is that the daughter had every reason for wanting her pest of an old mother out of her way."

Deirdre looked once more at her watch. "Could you get to the point, Mr. Halfhide?" she said wearily.

Gus drew himself up to his full height and said firmly and rapidly, "Miss Beasley and myself intend to investigate privately this murder case. And since both of us have a taste for research, perhaps better described as a lively curiosity, we intend to set up a small, at first amateur, agency. *All Problems Solved*—that sort of thing."

"I see. Or, more simply, you and Ivy are soul mate nosey parkers, have no money, and think I might be useful in setting up a business? Office space in my house, perhaps? Advertising in the local paper my dear old Bert bought many years ago? That sort of thing? Oh, and by the way, *All Problems Solved* is a terrible name. How about *Enquire Within*?"

Gus looked at her with a tentative smile. "Um, does that mean . . . ?"

"When do we start?" said Deirdre.

"IS MISS BEASLEY available?" Gus said. "It is rather late to visit her, I know. But if she is still up and about, I just need a few minutes' chat."

"Mrs. Spurling doesn't like her ladies and gentlemen to be upset too close to bedtime," said the stout little woman who acted as her deputy.

"Oh, I wouldn't dream of upsetting her!" Gus said quickly.

"Upsetting who?" It was Ivy, coming into the hall clutching a hot water bottle. "If you mean upsetting me, I don't upset easy. You can safely leave him to me, Miss Pinkney. In there, Gus," she added, pointing to the sitting room. "We can find a corner away from the telly. None of them can hear, and one or two can't understand what they do hear, so we'll be fine."

Miss Pinkney looked annoyed, but stamped her way back into the office. Gus and Ivy found a quiet corner, and he filled her in with what had happened at Tawny Wings. "So it looks as if we're in business, Ivy!" he said excitedly.

"Calm down, young man," she said. But her eyes were bright, her back straight, and the old Ivy was back. "Be here at ten o'clock tomorrow morning, with your car," she said. "I'll warn Deirdre we're coming. Sooner we get down to it the better."

Eight

TUESDAY MORNING, TEN o'clock sharp, Deirdre had said, and on the dot Gus and Ivy rang the bell on the heavy, mock-Tudor front door of Tawny Wings. The three investigators of the Enquire Within detective agency, feeling rather nervous but determined not to show it, climbed the broad stairway to a large room overlooking the back garden.

"Guest room," explained Deirdre, "but since I don't have many guests, except on the rare occasions when my daughters arrive from far-flung lands, we can set ourselves up permanently in here. Plenty of other rooms for whoever. Now, who is going to be chair?"

"What on earth are you talking about, Deirdre," Ivy said, beginning to bristle at what was clearly Deirdre's attempt to take over.

Gus smiled charmingly at the ladies, and said that as he probably had the most experience in the field of detection, perhaps he should take the helm?

"Hear, hear," said Ivy quickly. "Anyway, it was all Augustus's idea, so I vote for him as—ahem—chair."

"Exactly what I was about to suggest," lied Deirdre. "Then, as I have a computer and some secretarial skills, I should probably take on the work of admin, records and all that?"

Gus nodded.

"What's left for me to do, then?" said Ivy crossly.

"Good heavens, Ivy!" Gus said. "Yours is the most important job of all. You will be the eyes and ears of Enquire Within, looking and listening and making mental notes. We shall meet regularly, and your input will be vital to our investigations. To put it shortly, Ivy, the agency couldn't operate without you."

Ivy knew perfectly well he was exaggerating, but was mollified nevertheless. "Right," she said. "Then it's just as well I'm still in possession of all my marbles."

Deirdre began to think her own role was diminishing to typist and filing clerk, and said, "Still, Ivy, you'll need transport, and I shall be very happy to take you wherever you want to go. We shall be a good team!"

Ivy gave her a look to quell the bravest upstart, and said wasn't it time they got down to business and opened the investigation into the murder of Mrs. Winifred Blake.

"Just one snag," Gus said apologetically. "Nobody's asked us to, so no client. No client, no fee."

"Ah," said Deirdre, "I think I may have a solution to that one."

"Excellent!" said Gus. "Solutions are our business!"

"Calm down, young man," Ivy said, and added that she would like to hear Deirdre's solution to this particular problem.

"The Hon. Theo, he's going to be our first client, though he doesn't know it yet," said Deirdre triumphantly. "A murder in a property lowers its value immediately. And nobody's going to pay a wicked rent to live in a glorified hovel haunted by an evil old woman."

"Spot on, Deirdre!" Gus laughed. "My little cottage is not far from a hovel with a few bodged improvements. You are right about the wicked rent, too. And how are you going to approach the village squire?"

Deirdre tapped the side of her nose with a manicured forefinger in time-honoured fashion, indicating conspiracy. "Leave it to me," she said. "Theo Roussel and I go back a long way. . . ."

"Steady on, Deirdre," Ivy said caustically. She looked at Gus and said, "And what do you say to that, Chair?"

Gus sat back and folded his arms. "First, I would like to stress that it will be vital that we trust each other. If one of us has a hunch and does not wish to talk about it until some following up has been done, fine. So, second, I would say good luck to Deirdre. But I propose we have weekly meetings, when we bring each other up to date on progress. Now, how do you feel about working on more than one case at once?"

"One's plenty," Ivy said, "and three brains are better than one. I propose to start by talking to that awful Beattie woman. There's nothing escapes her notice, and old Theo Whatsit lets her get on with it, so I hear. She's a member of the Women's Institute, and so, for my sins, am I. There's a WI meeting on Thursday afternoon, and no, I don't need a lift, Deirdre. I can manage to walk to the village hall, thanks."

Gus was delighted. All this getting going so soon! Nothing like a couple of bossy women to go straight to it.

Ivy wiped the smile off his face with practised skill. "And you, Augustus? What are you going to do? As far as I can see, the chair don't do much except make fancy speeches. Where are you going to start?"

Gus was used to quick thinking, and said at once that

he had already made a start. "Miriam Blake is already a friend," he said. "We have shared the cup that——"

"Yes, yes, we know all that," interrupted Ivy, "but how do you mean to tackle her?"

"Friendship. The poor woman is bereft and lonely," Gus said. "Now is the time to release all her past resentments and feelings of revenge," he added. "She is obviously suspect number one, but in my experience it is seldom number one who turns out to be the guilty party."

Deirdre gazed at him in disbelief. "Never mind the psychology," she said. "She's just a bitter old spinster, and from what I've heard hasn't turned a hair at drowning kittens and strangling cockerels in the past. With a bread knife handy, I wouldn't put it past her to . . . well, you know."

"Coffee time, I think," said Gus, feeling slightly queasy.

Ivy nodded. "I could do with a nice strong cup of tea, Deirdre," she said. "And none of your scented muck with bits of flowers floating in it. PG Tips will do nicely."

UNAWARE THAT SHE was being roundly insulted by Mrs. Deirdre Bloxham, MBE, Miriam Blake sat at her tiny kitchen table with her mother's last will and testament spread out before her. It was a simple document, leaving all Winifred Blake's goods and chattels to her beloved daughter, Miriam. The sting in the tail was that there was all of five hundred pounds in total to bequeath.

"Old devil!" Miriam said aloud. There had been a lot more money squirreled away somewhere, nothing surer. She knew perfectly well that her father had been a mean old bugger, scrimping and saving and hoarding all he could for some imagined emergency. She was sure there was cash somewhere. Her mother had been paranoid about locking doors, and always hung washing on the line to show it was not an empty house, when in fact they were away

on their annual one week's holiday in Southend-on-Sea.
On the face of it, there was nothing worth stealing. But
somewhere . . .

Miriam folded up the will and replaced it in its envelope.
What the old thing left in the bank would not even pay for
the funeral. She would have to hunt properly and systematically round the house. But not straightaway. It would look
bad, unseemly even, to be turning out cupboards and looking under floorboards before her mother was laid safely to
rest. Last night she had awoken to see the familiar lined old
face looking at her over the rail at the bottom of the bed.
Miriam had pulled the bedclothes over her head, yelling at
the apparition to go away and leave her alone.

Nine

IN THE SPOTLESS kitchens of Springfields Home for the Elderly, Miss Pinkney was giving the Polish girl a piece of her mind. Fortunately, the girl could understand little of what the red-faced woman was saying. She had quickly discovered that the best thing to do in the face of this kind of meaningless tirade was to say nothing, but have an expression of anxiety to please on her face.

As far as Katya could tell, the crime she had committed was leaving a pot of jam on the table without its top screwed on, a perfect target for the cloud of wasps that already buzzed around in ecstasy.

"Sorry, Miss Pinkney. I will not do again," she said humbly.

"Do *it* again, girl! We like all our staff to speak good Queen's English. Aren't you going to classes?"

Katya nodded obediently. She caught the word *classes*, and for once could answer, knowing what she was agreeing to. She and another Polish girl who cleaned in the village went to weekly English classes in Tresham. This friend,

Anya, had a greater aptitude for languages than she did, but she was trying hard. Katya liked working at Springfields, and though some of the old people were rude and unpleasant, most were kind and appreciative. She felt sorry for some of them, dumped by relatives who never came to see them. There was only one that she was really frightened of, and that was Miss Ivy Beasley. Although she did not understand all that the old dragon said to her, the expression on her face when she was cross was enough to frighten the Pope.

"Get on with your work, now," Miss Pinkney said, her voice softening. Although she had no children of her own, she regarded the staff at Springfields as her family. Some of them were wayward and had to be kept in check. But she prided herself on being fair, and on the whole was not unpopular with the rest.

"Will you put two coffees and a couple of extra biscuits on the tray for Miss Beasley, please," Miss Pinkney said. "She has a visitor this morning. It's that new chap in Hangman's Row. He's got a funny name. I noticed Miss Beasley referred to him as Augustus. Quick work on his part. She's not so fond of Christian names! Mrs. Spurling tried calling her Ivy, but got a flea in her ear. I do hope he's not a con man, working on the old thing to get her money."

Katya smiled. She had got the gist of that, and said, "Gus *is* nice man. Very nice to me, and Miss Beasley likes him."

"Hope you're right, girl," Miss Pinkney said. "Now hurry along, else we shall have you-know-who ringing for service.

GUS HAD MADE a plan. He had already said good morning to Miriam Blake over the garden wall. She had looked pale and distressed, but had said would he like to come to her house this afternoon for a return cup of tea? He had accepted with pleasure, and organised his day around this important visit. The better he got on with Miriam, the more likely he was to spot any slips in her account of what had happened on the fateful day.

Meanwhile, he looked forward to calling on Ivy. He hadn't much faith in Deirdre's ability to persuade Theo Roussel to pay out good money to Enquire Within to take on the case. For one thing, there was another side to it that Deirdre hadn't mentioned. With the old woman gone, and Miriam in healthy middle age, perfectly capable of getting a job, the squire would have no compunction in moving her on, with Miss Beatty ably abetting him. Contrary to what Deirdre had said, Gus considered Theo would not worry about possible tenants being put off by the murder. There are some ghouls who actually like such things, though Gus didn't fancy them as neighbours.

No, he put his money on Ivy being the more useful of the two women, and now considered, as he marched along the main street purposefully, how he intended to direct the conversation. He looked in the shop window and noticed that Will was clearing the notice board. He remembered his previous plan to be a general painter and decorator, and decided to forget that. If the agency took off as he intended, he would not have time for anything else. In any case, he liked the image of a private detective a whole lot better than that of a man in a white overall, carrying a paint pot up ladders.

"Morning, Mr. Halfhide!" Will said, as Gus passed by. The shopkeeper had noticed Gus's apparent friendship with Ivy. It was the talk of the village, and had taken first place in the gossip list, displacing the disgraceful behaviour of the local lads with that Polish girl working at Springfields, but not, of course, the murder.

"Morning, Will—and please call me Gus."

"Fine, and how are you settling in? Bit of a shock to find you're living next door to a murder, wasn't it?"

Gus paused. Village shops were clearinghouses for local news, so he turned back and followed Will inside. "A white sliced, please," he said.

"Need a bag? We're trying to cut down on bags—carbon footprint and all that stuff. We have to compete with supermarkets."

"No, no bag, thanks. That's all I want at the moment. And to answer your question, yes, it was a bit of a shock. Poor Miss Blake is in a bad state. Pale as a ghost and very shaky. I suppose she was fond of her mother, living together all those years. When did the father die?"

"Years ago," said Will. "And not much missed, as far as I can tell. As for being fond of her mother, our Miriam and the old woman scarcely spoke to one another. Miriam said Mrs. Blake was so sharp and unkind that she had given up talking to her. Everything she said, apparently, was found fault with, and the poor girl found keeping quiet was the best policy."

"Still, a mother is a mother," Gus said, picking up his bread. "Bound to be lonely, poor Miriam. I shall do my best to be a good neighbour."

He left the shop, and Will said under his breath, "Well, just watch it, mate. Miriam Blake eats unattached men for breakfast."

When Gus reached Springfields, he saw Ivy waiting for him at the garden gate. "You're late," she said. "Might as well be off straightaway."

"Off where?" he said. He'd been looking forward to coffee and biscuits.

"To the graveyard, of course. Follow me."

"But the old lady is not buried yet," objected Gus. "They'll keep the body for a while yet, while police investigations are going on."

"Not the old lady. We're going to see the old man. Poor old Blake. Had a terrible time with those two women, so I hear."

"Maybe," said Gus. "But what use is it going to look at a mouldering gravestone? The dead can't speak, Ivy."

"That's where you're wrong. And don't argue, even if you are the chair."

Gus sighed. "Right," he said, "just the morning for visiting a graveyard. Sun shining, birds singing, a warm breeze. Where else would you want to go on such a day?"

"We shall all be in there for good soon enough, so might as well get used to it," Ivy said, and walked on steadily.

The graveyard in Barrington was in fact a pleasant spot. Dutiful parishioners cut the grass and trimmed the roses that lined the path to the church door. The churchyard itself was full, but Ivy led Gus to an extension round the back, and stopped at an overgrown grave with moss covering the lettering.

"That's him," she said. "You can just make out his name. Now, before we uncover the inscription, what do you notice, Augustus? You're the gumshoe."

"The what?!" he said.

"Isn't that what private detectives are called in America?"

"For God's sake, Ivy, couldn't you just stick to Gus and leave it at that?"

"Right, Augustus," she said, with an unaccustomed smile on her face. "Well, what do you make of it?"

"Neglected, first of all. And why? Because nobody cares for it, and maybe nobody cared for its occupant. Who should have cared? Mrs. and Miss Blake, of course. Well, maybe in later life Mrs. B was too disabled, but Miriam could, or should, have tidied it up once in a while. And what about flowers at Easter and a holly wreath at Christmas? No trace of either. How am I doing, Ivy?"

Ivy had to admit that he had done very well, and said so. "Now you have to scrape off the moss," she said, and, brushing leaves from a nearby tomb, perched herself comfortably on it and prepared to watch Gus get down to some real work.

Ten

AFTER GUS HAD cleared the face of the gravestone of moss and algae, he sat down next to Ivy and said, "Well, what does it say?"

"You can read, can't you?" said Ivy.

"Not without my glasses," admitted Gus. "How about you?"

"'In Loving Memory,'" she read, and added that this obviously didn't mean much, judging by the state of the grave. "'John Frederick Blake, born 12 March 1908, died 3 February 1985.'" So that was quite a while ago, Gus, as I said."

"What's that in smaller letters at the bottom under the grass?"

Ivy peered at it, moving the long grass to one side. "'*He did the best he could.*' Well," she said, shocked, "talk about damning with faint praise! What a dreadful thing to say."

"Oh, I don't know," Gus replied with a shrug. "Seems about right for most people," he said. "Probably more like the truth than the usual eulogy."

"Huh?" said Ivy, straightening up and wincing silently. "Usual usogy, usual eulogy?" she grunted. "Better stick to plain English, Augustus," she said, and turned back along the grassy path to the graveyard gates.

They stood outside the church, looking down the village street, and Ivy said shouldn't they go back to Springfields now and have coffee and biscuits? "Still plenty of the morning left, and we can decide what to do next."

As Gus's only commitment that day was tea with Miriam, he agreed. He might see that pretty Polish girl again, and then there was Mrs. Spurling to keep sweet. It occurred to him suddenly that he was surrounded by women. He'd not met a single man so far to share a pint with him at the pub. Perhaps he would call in again at the shop on his way home, see if Will was the matey sort. He would certainly be in possession of a good deal of useful information. Who else? Theo Roussel was probably a snooty toff who would never set foot in the village pub, even if the Beattie woman would allow him to. Nobody else, as yet.

He would ask Will what else went on in the village. He knew there was a Women's Institute, but obviously not for him. Cricket club? Darts team? Reading group? Ivy had pointed out to him the old Reading Room, bequeathed by Theo's grandfather to the village, and lately restored. Logical place for a reading group, he thought, but did he want to read books chosen by other people? Depends who are the other members, he decided. Lots of questions, all of which could be answered by Will the shopkeeper.

By the time they reached Springfields, Gus realised he hadn't listened to a word Ivy had been saying. Still, he gathered early on in the conversation that it was mostly about the iniquities of the people of Round Ringford, Ivy's home for most of her life.

"Morning, Mr. Halfhide!" Mrs. Spurling was in the hall, looking as if she had been standing there waiting for them. "Ready for your coffee now, Miss Beasley? Katya took up your tray, with a cup for Mr. Halfhide, only to find you two had absconded!"

"Eloped, perhaps?" laughed Gus. Oh God, he thought, is this really me?

"No chance of that," said Ivy sharply. "And yes, send the coffee up to my room at once. And shortbread," she added.

"What's the magic word?" muttered Mrs. Spurling under her breath, but she smiled bravely and disappeared towards the kitchens.

When they reached Ivy's room, she turned on Gus. "I'll thank you to show a little more respect," she said. "Eloped, indeed! Do you know how old I am?"

"Age is of no importance where love is concerned," Gus said, "but no, Ivy, it was a small joke. Not meant to offend. You can be sure I have great respect for you and will watch my foolish tongue in the future."

"Right," said Ivy, sitting down in her chair by the window. "Now, what is next for us to do. I shall see Miss Beatty tomorrow, but we have no time to waste."

Gus reflected that he had planned to put his feet up and watch the racing with Whippy, who always watched fixedly as the sweating, snorting horses galloped by. Then it would be teatime with Miriam. He would have to be careful that Ivy did not take charge, else all three of them would be slaving eight hours a day following up red herrings. Fortunately, there was a knock at the door and the pretty Polish girl came in with a laden tray.

"Morning, Katya," Gus said quickly, before Ivy could find anything to criticise. "How are you settling down in England, my dear?" Ivy scowled at him, but he pretended not to notice.

"Very well, thank you, sir," Katya said, smiling broadly at him. He spoke so beautifully that she could understand every word. "You like something else?"

"Won't you stay and tell us about Poland for a while?" Gus said hopefully.

Katya raised her eyebrows. "Oh, no, sir. Not allowed! Thank you, sir," she said, and rushed from the room.

"Fool!" Ivy said. "D'you think old Spurling would let her fraternise with the guests? She allows them two sentences per inmate, and that's it."

Gus was quite sure that Ivy was making this up, but consoled himself that he was quite likely to meet Katya in the street some time, and then he could take things further. Poor girl was probably lonely, and would welcome a fatherly friend to take care of her.

"Down to business," Ivy said, seeing Gus lost in a daydream. "You can drive, can't you? Time to get a decent car for you, and then we'll be safely mobile without asking Deirdre for the loan of her Rolls Royce every time we want to go into town."

It was beginning to look like Ivy intended Gus and herself to be an investigating twosome, and he was not sure this was a good idea. She could cramp his style more than somewhat, and he said that yes, he could drive, but had no money for new cars at present. Maybe later. Meanwhile, he must drink up his coffee and get going. "Some important research to do," he said vaguely, and palmed a couple of shortbreads into his pocket for later.

Eleven

THE SHOP WAS full of people who had just got off the Tresham bus, bags full of purchases from the market. Will was trying hard to restock the shop with more interesting items than had the previous owner, hoping to lure customers who would eventually give up supermarket shopping. A forlorn hope, but worth a try, he thought. The post office was still a useful adjunct, but there was a constant threat to its continuation. Post offices were fast disappearing from rural areas, and elderly people were up in arms at the loss. Where would they get their pensions, their TV licence stamps, post their letters to home and abroad?

At present, the shop was flourishing. Will was popular, and already had been elected to the parish council. He was a bachelor, young and good-looking, and gaggles of teen-aged schoolgirls made straight for the shop's new selection of ice creams the moment they got off the afternoon bus. Will was only human, and appreciated long legs and flut-tering eyelashes along with the other youngbloods in the village. But he was very careful not to overstep the mark, and was regarded as trustworthy by all.

"Hi, Will," said Gus, adopting the jargon, he hoped.

"Good morning again, Gus," Will said with a smile. "Forgotten something? Milk, some of my delicious new cheeses?"

"No, sorry. Maybe later. No, I came in to see if you could fill me in on activities in the village. Something likely for me to join? I mean to be a useful part of the community, in time."

"Blimey! Better not say that too loud, else you'll find yourself dragged into everything, even the WI if you're not careful. They're talking about having men's evenings, if you can believe it! No, you know what they say about a willing horse. Well, it's certainly true in Barrington. But," he added, "to be serious, I am sure there's a couple of things to interest you. First the pub, and then the reading group . . . well, only possibly the reading group."

Gus laughed. Here was a man after his own heart, even though he was—um—several years younger. "Well done," he said. "Just what I wanted. Now, I suppose I could go down for a pint tonight, but . . ." He hesitated, and Will said obligingly that he would be glad to meet him there around nine o'clock and introduce him to some of the lads.

"And by lads," Will added, "I mean lads aged from eighteen to eighty! Some of the old locals are great. And just watch out if they challenge you to dominoes. They'll have all your loose change off you in no time!"

"Thanks a lot," Gus said. "Are you also a member of the reading group? What's that like?"

Will shook his head. "Don't have time to read the books. Running this place is more than a full-time job. They meet once a month, and I believe they're a nice lot. You can go just for one evening to try it out—doesn't even matter if you've not read the book, apparently!"

"Are they all highly educated, well read, and all that?"

"Shouldn't think so. The ones I know are just average readers. Anyway, you could give it a try."

Gus spotted the shelf of jams and chutneys, and took a selection. "These'll brighten my meagre diet," he said, and handed over a surprising amount of money. "Only the best, I assume?"

Will nodded. "Of course," he said. "Though her up at the Hall, our Miss Beatty, says they're rubbish, and expensive rubbish at that."

"Best recommendation you could have, I've been told," said Gus. Then several people came in at once, and he left, pleased with himself for having made an excellent start.

At exactly three thirty in the afternoon, he knocked at Miriam's door. He had spruced himself up, including cleaning his shoes. In his experience, women were very particular about shoes. His own mother had always said that if your shoes were clean, then the rest wasn't so important. Wrong, of course. Just like she was wrong about saying that if the corners were clean, the middles would take care of themselves. That was rooms, of course. She had cleaned a good many of them, and should have known better.

Miriam opened the door, smiled and beckoned him in. There was a strong smell of air freshener, which Gus loathed. But he smiled in return, and handed her a posy of flowers he had picked from his overgrown garden. She blushed to the roots of her hair, and buried her nose in them. As most of them were dandelions, there was very little scent, but that did not matter.

Settled safely on a well-worn sofa in the front room, Gus looked about him. Brown was the predominating colour. Brown carpet and curtains, cream paint and brown cushions on brown moquette chair covers.

As if reading his thoughts, Miriam apologised for the state of the house. "Mother would never spend any money on it," she said. "I hope to put that right in due course, but at the moment I can't think of anything but the poor old

lady who was my constant companion for so many years
after father died."

"Perhaps your mother, God rest her soul, hadn't any
money to spare for interior décor," he suggested.

"For what?—oh, I see, yes, well, that's what she said,
but Dad had never spent much either, so I reckon they
must have saved a bit. Mind you," she added hastily, "what
with rent and electricity and coal an' that, it was probably
difficult to make ends meet."

Gus was used to sifting the wheat from the chaff, and
noted in his mind that Miriam had hopes of finding a nest
egg somewhere. A motive? He complimented her on her
tea, and asked if she had made the gingerbread set out on
a plate before him.

"Oh yes, I'm a good cook," she answered. "Trouble
is, there's only me to cook for now. I expect you find the
same? It's not worth cooking for one, is it? Expensive, too,
with all the waste."

Watch out, Gus. He had seen these signs many times,
and was practised at sidestepping them.

"Oh, I can live on a sixpence," he said. "Food doesn't
interest me much, so long as there's something to fill up the
hollows. Mind you," he added politely, "I'd love a piece of
your excellent gingerbread!"

Miriam beamed, and said he should try her jam and
cream sponge. "I'll make you one for Sunday," she said.
"Maybe you'd like to come in and we could share it?"

Oops! Thinking quickly, Gus said he would probably
not be around on Sunday. He had to go to London to settle
a few things, he lied. "Maybe some other time, thank you,
Miriam," he said.

The conversation flowed easily, Miriam being quite
able to conduct a monologue for hours. Gus cunningly
steered her in directions that would be useful to him, and
noted several leads to be followed up. He gathered that her
mother was not as ill as she made out, that she was bad-

tempered and picky over food. She had told a good story to the doctor and the nurse, having been a leading light in the village's amateur dramatic group. In all, Miriam did not really have a good word to say about her mother, and this did not sit easily with her professed deep grief at the old woman's demise.

"So what work did you do, Miriam, before you had to stay at home and look after Mother? I am sure you have many talents."

Miriam blushed again. "Well, first of all I worked on the telephone exchange in a big company in town," she said. "It was quite difficult work, and they did say I was a natural. The voice was important, you see, and I handled people very well—so they said," she added modestly. "Now, of course, it's all automatic. Press this button, press that button. No friendly voices needed!"

"And after that?"

"Funnily enough," she said slowly, "I worked at the police station, doing typing an' filing an' that. That Frobisher man who's an inspector now, he was just a young sprog at that time. Pushy, he was, even then. Now he's investigating the murder of my dear mother. . . ." She covered her face with her hands, but Gus noticed that no tears squeezed out from between her fingers.

"How long were you an honorary policewoman?" Gus said, laughing reassuringly.

Miriam shrugged. "Didn't last," she said, looking embarrassed. "My face didn't fit. Happens sometimes, doesn't it? Anyway, enough about me. What have you done with your life up to now?"

Gus gave her one of the many versions of his career which he had handy for any eventuality. This one, as well as being an author and journalist, included setting up charities for worthy causes, running organisations concerned with animal welfare and wildlife preservation. Never mind that the only animal he cared about was his own beloved Whippy. He judged that Miriam would be suitably impressed and he was right.

"Oh, how good of you!" she gushed. "My dad was a great one for wildlife," she said. "He was in charge of the pheasants they reared for the shoots up at the Hall."

Gus swallowed an urge to laugh and looked at his watch. "Goodness," he said, "is that the time? How the time flies when you're enjoying yourself! Thank you so much, Miriam, for tea and delicious gingerbread. My turn next." He had no intention of returning her hospitality, but she saw him to the door with such pleasure on her face that he felt ashamed. Well, almost ashamed.

AS HE WALKED along to his own front door, Gus was startled by a shadow which passed the window inside his sitting room. What was that? He knew he had locked up securely before tea with Miriam, but he could have sworn someone was in there. He ran the rest of the way and approached his back door silently. Gus could move very quietly when necessary. The door was still locked, and he eased the key quietly, gently squeezing himself through the opening. Silence. Then he heard the unmistakable sound of his front door opening with a loud squeak.

Damn! He rushed through, hearing footsteps disappearing down the lane towards the woods. The front door had been slammed shut as the intruder ran, and by the time Gus had forced it open—it stuck with damp, as did every other door in the house—the lane was empty and quiet.

"Damn, damn!" Gus said out loud now. No point in trying to catch him—or her. Gus was well aware that he was out of condition, and would soon run out of breath. Better check if anything was missing. He reassured himself that there was nothing worth stealing. Except those papers upstairs . . . but who would know about those, or, for that matter, still be interested in them?

He walked around the house, and could find nothing amiss. The papers were safe in their red folder secured with white tape and labelled "Bills unpaid." That's all right, then, he said to himself, and decided a small whisky would be the best thing to stop his hands from shaking in this stupid way.

Twelve

DEIRDRE LOOKED AT herself in the long mirror in her bedroom, turning this way and that, and decided her reflection was not bad, considering. She saw a plumpish but trim figure, nicely dressed in a suitably flattering dress from her favourite designer. She had been to the hairdresser, who had freshened up her apricot curls.

She smiled at herself, and was pleased to see how her face lightened up. It had been some time since she had seen Theo Roussel, and she had taken a lot of trouble to look her best for this evening.

Thank goodness Theo had answered the phone! If she had got the dreaded Beattie, the old bag would probably have said he was out or in the bath. Poor Theo. He'd lived under that woman's tyranny for years. But she could remember before that, when Theo had been an attractive man about the county, hunting and shooting and squiring all the prettiest girls in the neighbourhood to balls and parties. The nicest thing about him was a total lack of interest in what was the done thing. He had loved an evening at the pub with the rest, sitting for hours listening to the old men's tales of his father's philandering. Perhaps he had inherited some of his tendencies?

Theo had spotted Deirdre at a Golf Club Ball in Thornwell and for several months had convinced her that she was the girl for him. She wasn't, of course. He was a few years older than her, and when they parted, it was with amiable goodwill. Bert had come along to offer her genuine love and good prospects, and she had made a rational choice.

She had seen Theo on and off over the years, however, and they always had a friendly wave, so that now, when she telephoned him and asked if they could have a word, he had at once invited her to the Hall for a gin and tonic. "Still your tipple, I hope?" he had said, and his voice was just as she remembered it.

WHEN MISS BEATTY brought in Theo's afternoon tea, he said, "Oh, by the way, Beattie, I shall be having a visitor this evening for a drink. Mrs. Bloxham from Tawny Wings. An old friend from the past. I knew she was living in the village, but never liked to intrude after the death of her husband. I am sure you remember Bert Bloxham?"

Beattie's face was puce. "Of course I remember Bert Bloxham," she said. "Had his head under the bonnet of a car mostly. Came from nothing, and went to nothing in the end, like we all do. I believe she was a back-street girl, too."

"Beattie!" Theo said, and roared with laughter. Somehow that call from Deirdre had, as his father used to say, put a bit of lead in his pencil, and he felt full of energy, quite enough to challenge his minder! "I don't want to hear you talking like that about my old friend. She was a lovely girl, one of the best. Please remember that. And be a nice Beattie and make us some of those lovely nibbly things to have with our drinks."

This was too much for Beattie, and she stamped out of the room without shutting the door behind her. Unheard of, thought Theo, and he grinned. Now, he would have a shave and change out of his carpet slippers. He must not slip into his dotage before it was necessary. There were signs! First the carpet slippers, then next the juicy jellies, and then the wooden box . . . He had seen it happen to his contemporaries and he did not intend to have it happen to him.

In the kitchen, Beattie held on to the Aga rail, breathing heavily. What did that common woman want? Surely she was not pursuing Theo after all these years? She must think quickly what had to be done. She had spun her web around Theo so successfully, and had found ways of keeping rescuers at bay. He did not even realise she had done it, so clever had she been. Well, she was more than a match for a garage mechanic's widow. All she needed was a plan. She looked at the clock over the Aga. "Plenty of time," she said to herself.

GUS WAS AT the pub on the dot of nine, pleased to see Will standing by the bar talking to the publican, a large, genial man with a big nose and capable hands. Will spotted Gus and beckoned him over.

"Let me introduce you to Fred," he said. "Fred, this is Gus, just moved into Hangman's Row. Next to Miriam and her mother."

"Her ex-mother, you mean," Fred said, and smiled. "Bit of a shock when you'd only just moved in, I should think, wasn't it? Now, Gus, what can I get for you? On the house, your first drink in the Peacock and Royal."

The evening progressed very happily for Gus. With an introduction from Will, all the regulars drew him into their circle and quizzed him skilfully about his life and times before he arrived in their village. Gus decided he should stick to the version he told Miriam. He was beginning to realise how quickly news spread around the village, and how discrepancies in his story would be picked up and chewed over for days.

"Sounds like a bit of a wimp," whispered one of the girls sitting in a corner. "All that saving the wildlife stuff. Don't know what he'd think of my dad and his rat poison."

The others began to giggle, and were shushed by boyfriends playing darts.

Fortunately Gus did not hear them, and when the lads had finished playing, he suggested to Will that they might have a game. Now the watching girls were quietly admiring, as Gus threw one accurate dart after another, finishing with a spectacular bull's-eye that drew a round of applause.

"Are you as good as that with dominoes?" said Fred, scratching his nose. "We've got the county champion here, if you want a try?"

Gus nodded, and sat down. Alfred Jones was bent with age, but a wily old bugger, whose watery blue eyes were everywhere, missing nothing. He played his usual game, guaranteed to win. Gus was aware that a silence had fallen in the pub, and thought quickly. He could win, he saw that well ahead, but it would not do him any good at all. So he deliberately made wrong moves, and lost.

"Too clever for me," he said. "Another pint, Alfred?" he offered, and walked to the bar. "Well done, Gus," the landlord said. "It wouldn't have done to beat the county champion first go."

After that, Alfred opened up, and to Gus's delight said that he had known old mother Blake when they were kids. "Went to school with her, didn't I," he said. "She was a moody kid. Sneaky, too. Not popular with the other gels. Don't know how she snared old Blake, but then, she were twice as bright as him. That Miriam were born six weeks early, and a bonny baby in spite of that. I reckon John Blake had orders from above." He winked at Gus. "Know what I mean?" he said.

Gus thought he did, but was more interested in Miriam's relationship with her mother. "Didn't Miriam stand up to her mother at all? She seems quite a strong character, from what little I have seen of her."

"Not strong enough!" The old man chuckled, looking up at Gus from under bushy eyebrows. "Mind you, she's had her moments. Ask her about those, next time you go to tea."

Gus was sure that he had never mentioned the tea party. Nothing secret in Barrington, that was clear. But he was very much a newcomer, and the difficulty would be in winkling out old scandals from the locals, Alfred and his like. By the time he and Will emerged into the clear, starry night, he felt pleasantly mellow and almost one of the boys.

Thirteen

THE PEARLY ROLLS cruised slowly up the long drive to the Hall, and came to a halt outside the front steps leading to an imposing baronial style front door. Deirdre adjusted her tight skirt—not too tight, she hoped—and walked carefully up the steps. She knew the old dragon would open it and give her a frosty reception, but Deirdre was ready for her.

"Good evening, Mrs. Bloxham, please come in. A lovely evening, isn't it?"

Deirdre could not believe her ears. All she had heard and witnessed of Miss Beatty! And now this charming welcome. What was the woman up to? Deirdre was no fool, and was already on her guard.

"Come this way, please," said Beattie, stepping out across the tiled hallway and into the large drawing room. The sun shone through the long windows, and every surface gleamed from regular polishing. She must remember to look at Theo's shoes. Probably see your face in them. But where was he?

"Mr. Theo will be down in a few minutes, madam," Beattie said. "Won't you take a seat? I'll tell him you are here."

"Thank you," Deirdre said, and perched on the edge of a flimsy gilt chair by the large marble fireplace. She looked at her watch, and saw that she was exactly on time. Theo must have changed. She remembered clearly from her youth that of all the lads around town, he was always punctual, if not early. Good manners, her grandmother had said approvingly.

After what seemed like hours, the door opened and Beattie appeared once more. "I'm so sorry, Mrs. Bloxham," she said sadly. "Mr. Theo sends his warmest regards, but regrets that he is not feeling up to coming downstairs this evening. He wants me to assure you that he will be in touch to arrange another date. He is really sorry."

STARTING UP HER car, Deirdre rammed it into gear and stalled the engine. "Damn and blast!" she said. As she went more circumspectly forward, she glanced up at the window where she imagined Theo's room would be. "Dear God, there he is!" She drove slowly away, sure that he had been waving, but not smiling. In fact, he had looked very angry indeed.

She did not want to go home to an empty house, and felt that she must talk to somebody about what had happened. She would call on Ivy, a perfectly natural friendly visit. Ivy, for all her faults, was a good listener, and though she tried hard to seem invincible, Deirdre was sure she was lonely, and would be glad to see her.

"Good evening, Mrs. Bloxham," Miss Pinkney said, coming into the hall to greet her. At least this old spin was reasonably normal, Deirdre thought gratefully, and explained that Ivy was not expecting her but she would like to have a few words with her if that was all right.

"Of course," Miss Pinkney said. "I'll ring through and tell her you are on your way. Lovely evening, isn't it?" she added, and Deirdre answered grimly that she supposed it was.

"Well," said Ivy, "this is a surprise visit. Something urgent to report? Or were you feeling lonely?"

Deirdre sighed. "Yes to both of those," she said. "Am I in the way? Would you like me to go?"

"Don't be silly, Deirdre. I can see you've got something to say, so get on and say it. For goodness sake sit down. You make the place untidy."

The old phrase calmed Deirdre, and she sat down thankfully. Starting with her extraordinary welcome at the Hall from Miss Beatty, she gave Ivy a detailed account of what had happened. "And I saw him at the window, fully dressed, and waving frantically as I left."

"Why didn't you go back? That Beatty woman couldn't stop you going up to his room, could she?"

I wouldn't put it past her to bar the way with a Kalashnikov," Deirdre answered glumly. "No, I hadn't time to think it all out, but I shall certainly go back and insist on seeing him another day. Maybe tomorrow."

"Take Gus with you," Ivy said. "He'd stand no nonsense from Miss Beatty. I reckon he can be pretty nasty when needed. Not that you'd know it from the way he has been so far. But mark my words, he can be a hard man when necessary."

Deirdre stifled a giggle. Ivy claimed not to watch television. All rubbish, she insisted. But "a hard man"? Where else would she have picked up that?

"You're right, Ivy," she said. "I'll ask him next Monday at our meeting. Probably best not to go back to the Hall straightaway. Miss Beatty will be expecting me to try again, but if I leave it for a few days she'll have dropped her guard. Poor Theo," she added. "He was a really nice man, you know. Wouldn't hurt a fly."

"Not on our list of suspects, then," Ivy said caustically. "Don't let your emotions get in the way of investigation, Deirdre. We've a long way to go yet."

"Do you reckon? I sort of thought we might clear it all up in a couple of weeks."

"Oh no, we're up against a wily bird. Now, if you don't mind, it's my bath night and if I don't have it early the water's stone-cold. Luxury accommodation, you told me! I'd not have agreed to come here if I'd known the bathwater would be cold."

Deirdre stood up and leaned over to kiss Ivy on her warm cheek. "You're quite a comfort to me, you know, Ivy," she said. "Good night, God bless."

After she had gone, Ivy touched her cheek and smiled. Luxury accommodation, indeed!

AS IT GREW dark, Theo Roussel decided to ring the police. His door was locked and he had shouted himself hoarse. But what would Beattie say to that? He slumped down in the chair by his desk and tried to think clearly. She was a clever, devious woman, and would certainly have a good story ready to explain his imprisonment.

He closed his eyes for a few minutes, concentrating on the best course of action, and until he woke with a start did not realise he had fallen into a doze. How long he had been asleep, he did not know. He had been awoken by heavy footsteps and a knock at his door.

"Mr. Theo, *please* open the door," Beattie shouted. "It is getting dark, and I am worried about you!"

Theo shook his head, as if his ears were deceiving him. He had been trying to open the door for hours, or rather, persuading her to open it. He walked across angrily and prepared to give her a very stern warning. Then he noticed the key. It was in the lock, his side of the door. He felt quite dizzy, and held on to the door handle.

"Mr. Theo, open up at once! Please don't alarm me like this!"

He turned the key and opened the door, staring at her with pure hatred. "You locked me in, you wicked woman," he said.

"Now, now," she said. "You've been dreaming. Look, here's the key, on your side of the door. You must have locked it without thinking, and then fallen asleep. Now, come along, let's get you some supper and a nice hot cup of tea."

"I don't want your bloody tea!" Theo said. "Leave me alone. We'll talk about this in the morning." He shut the door in her face, and so did not see her retreating quietly down the passage, smiling.

He walked across the room and looked out at the twilit park. Deirdre! What had happened to her? She would have come and gone, with Beattie making some excuse. He must telephone her straightaway and explain. He lifted the receiver, but there was no dialling tone. He groaned. He would call her tomorrow then, after he had summoned the strength to give Beattie her marching orders.

Fourteen

THE NEXT MORNING, Will was up early, checking
stock in the back room and making sure that everything
on display was still in date. He frequently cursed the "best
by" rule imposed on all shopkeepers. Half the stuff in the
shop would be perfectly wholesome a couple of weeks
after its sell-by date. After all, he ate most of it himself
when it was supposedly past its best, and he was still alive
and kicking.

It was his day for going to the wholesaler for new stock,
and as usual his neighbour, a retired businesswoman,
would come in and look after the shop until lunchtime.
Sadie Broomfield had run a small office service in town for
many years, and was still an extremely efficient substitute
when Will had to be away from the village. He knew how
lucky he was, and had grown fond of her. He looked at the
clock bequeathed him by the previous owners, and realised
that Sadie should have been in by now.

The telephone rang, and he heard her voice, choked
with what was clearly a heavy cold. "So sorry, Will. I woke

up with it, and can scarcely breathe! Can you manage? Is there anybody else?"

"O lor, you poor thing," he said, thinking frantically around possible helpers.

"What about Miriam Blake?" Sadie said. "She's fancy free at the moment. Might be glad of something to do. I know she used to do quite tricky jobs, and is fairly bright. Could you try her?"

No, not if she was the last person left on earth, Will said to himself. But then he realised he had no idea who else could help out.

"I could give her a ring, I suppose," he said reluctantly. "But don't you worry, Sadie. Curl up in bed with a hot whisky and water, and a spoonful of honey, and I'll be round this evening to see how you are."

"Don't come anywhere near me!" Sadie croaked. "Can't have our shopkeeper going off sick. You don't sound too sure about Miriam Blake. Might not want her as a permanent fixture? Bye now. I'm fine. Don't worry about me. Bye."

Will frowned. Was he really stuck with Miriam Blake? But then, what did he have against her? She had been a dutiful daughter and a good customer, and had once before filled in for him in the shop. And her mother had been found lifeless with a bread knife sticking into her chest. . . .

He opened the telephone directory and looked up her number, hoping not to find it. Perhaps with luck she would not have a phone, or be ex-directory, and then he would *have* to find somebody else. He could go to the wholesaler tomorrow. But Sadie wouldn't be better tomorrow, that was sure. And anyway, there she was: Blake—Barrington 870493. He dialled the number and heard the familiar voice answer in a bright, professional way. Oh yes, now he remembered she'd been a telephonist. Right, here goes, he muttered, and asked her. There was a pause, and then she said that she would be really pleased, and what time should she come? Straightaway? Yes, that would be fine. "See you," she said, now friendly and confiding.

Half an hour later, Will had explained again most of the necessary details to Miriam, and she seemed to grasp it all with ease. "Now, if you are at all worried or have a problem, ring me on my mobile," he said. "Anything at all, just ring me."

She nodded. "Of course," she said, "but I'm really sure I shall manage perfectly well. I feel quite at home already," she added, slipping into a flowery overall. Oh God, Will said to himself, please let Sadie get better quickly. Please.

IT WAS QUITE a shock for Gus when he walked into the shop around eleven o'clock and saw Miriam behind the counter. He had been meaning to thank Will for organising such a good evening for him, and suggest they might do it again some time. Not that he intended to force a friendship on the pleasant shopkeeper, but there was never any harm in saying thank you.

"Morning, Gus!" Miriam said brightly. "You didn't expect to see me here, did you? I'm the new assistant. Will has had to go out, and Mrs. Broomfield has a rotten cold. So here I am, launched on a new career!"

Gus gulped, and said he was sure she would be ideal for the job.

"What can I get you, then?"

"Just a *Daily Telegraph*, please," he said. "I like to come and get it from the shop. Gives me a bit of exercise walking up from the cottage."

Miriam nodded. "Very true," she said. "And anything else? Some nice biscuits to have with your morning coffee? I've been thinking," she added. "Maybe Will might like to think about a coffee machine and a table and chairs outside the shop. Encourages customers to stay a bit longer and buy a few more things they forgot on their list!"

Poor Will, thought Gus. Little does he know how unwise he is to employ this unstoppable woman. Still, it might get her off his own tail a little. But no. Now she was asking him if he would care to watch a good film with her on the telly this evening.

"Sorry, Miriam," he replied. "No can do. Got some urgent papers to sort out. Now, here's the money. Good luck!" And he escaped before she could think of a reason why the papers could be sorted out later. He remembered just in time to unhook Whippy from where she had been patiently waiting outside.

On his way home, he wondered how Deirdre had got on with Theo Roussel. She had hinted that there had been something between them in the past. That could be very useful. He could encourage her to confide in him. Or maybe not. He had once learnt a very hard lesson, and it was now number one on his list of don'ts. Never become emotionally involved on a case. Apart from one exception, this hadn't been too difficult, as a good ninety percent of his "clients" had never met him, nor were likely to, and his assignments were completed in silence and nobody the wiser.

Now nearly home, he saw Whippy's ears flatten and she stiffened. The next thing he saw was an enormous shaggy dog coming towards them. He had no idea of the breed, but sympathised with Whippy. It looked horribly dangerous, baring its teeth and growling. As far as he could see, it had no owner, no lead, and was clearly capable of eating both Whippy and himself for lunch.

It approached the now stationary Gus and his dog in that measured way that animals have when they are about to spring, and Gus stepped forward. Some distant playground instinct surfaced, and he faced the bully, shouting at it to bugger off.

To his surprise, it immediately turned and slunk away, its tail between its long, powerful legs. Then he heard a sound which was more like the cackle of a startled hen than laughter. The woman he now knew to be Miss Beatty came round the corner of the lane, still sniggering.

"You should keep that brute on a lead, preferably muzzled!" Gus said, his voice loud with fear.

"Why?" Miss Beatty said. "Look at him. Butter wouldn't melt. You did the right thing, Mr. Halfhide. Face up to him and he's the biggest coward in Barrington. Sorry about your little dog, though. She's a whippet, isn't she?"

Her obvious efforts to be nice mollified Gus, and thinking on his feet he realised it would be much better to be Miss Beatty's friend than her sworn enemy.

"Yes, she's called Whippy. Not very original, I'm afraid, but thinking up names is not my forte! I should introduce myself," he added, but she interrupted him.

"I know who you are. You've got the end cottage. Settled in now? Oh, and I'm Miss Beatty, housekeeper and general dogsbody."

More like minder, from what I hear, thought Gus, but he said only that he was pleased to meet her, and yes, he was settling in now, though the dreadful accident next door had been rather upsetting.

"Accident? It was murder, Mr. Halfhide. You don't get a bread knife stuck in your heart by accident. We've heard nothing from the police. Have you?"

Gus shook his head. "Only that they are questioning just about everyone in the village. Miss Blake is very anxious for the matter to be cleared up, as she is unable to mourn properly until the culprit is found. In a sort of limbo, I suppose, not being able to lay her mother to rest."

"Huh! Is that what she told you? Well, here's a piece of advice, Mr. Halfhide. Take everything that our Miriam says with a large pinch of salt. That's all I'm saying. Now, I must be on my way. Lucifer here needs a good run in the woods. Good morning," she said, and with what passed for a smile on her plain face, she disappeared through a gap in the hedge.

"So that's the dreaded Miss Beatty," he said aloud to Whippy, who whimpered, still recovering from shock. "Quite a person," he said. "Someone with a large estate to manage and quite confident in her ability to do it. What do you think?"

"Talking to yourself, Mr. Halfhide?" a new voice said, coming from the garden of the first cottage. It was a young woman, naturally blond and rosy-cheeked, with a toddling infant holding on to her jeans to keep its balance.

This was more like it, thought Gus, and stopped, smiling broadly. "Good morning!" he said. "Yes, a bad habit, I'm afraid. But I wasn't actually talking to myself, rather to Whippy here. Best thing about talking to a dog is that they never answer back. Hello," he added gently to the child. He prided himself on being good with small children, and picked up Whippy to show to him. At least, he thought it was a boy, though you couldn't always tell these days. This one was dressed in blue dungarees, so it was a safe bet it was a boy.

"What a sweet doggie," the blonde said. "This is my son, Simon," she added, "and I'm Rose Budd. Now we're introduced, and if you need any help or information about the village, you must come and knock at our door. My husband works on the estate, and he's always around."

"How kind," he said. "It seems a very friendly village. I've just met Miss Beatty and her . . . um . . . dog. She was pleasant, though I'm not so sure about the dog!"

Rose laughed. "I can assure you that Miss Beatty is much more dangerous than Lucifer," she said. "Stay well clear. She runs the place, you know, and nothing is secret from her."

"Seems to be the general opinion," he said. "I shall take the advice. Oh, and by the way, what is her Christian name?"

"Beattie," Rose said, smiling.

"No, her Christian name," Gus said.

"Beattie. She's Beatrice Beatty, but always known as Beattie," Rose assured him.

"My God, no wonder she looks like she's swallowed a fish bone!" he said. "Fancy being saddled with that!"

To Gus's embarrassment, she answered that her own name was odd, wasn't it. "But at least Rose Budd sounds pretty, and anyway I acquired it by marriage. Apparently Beattie likes hers. Likes being different, she says. Old bag! Oops, there's the phone—must go." She scooped up the child and disappeared with a cheery wave. "See you later!" she called as she went.

"Hope so," said Gus, and proceeded on his way.

Fifteen

THE WOMEN'S INSTITUTE in Barrington was one
of the oldest in the county. Theo Roussel's grandmother
had set it up and become its first president. Originally, the
meetings had taken place in the Reading Room, and the
membership had never amounted to more than ten or so
women, all with husbands working on the estate. It had
been the usual thing for the lady of the manor to be president, or failing that, the wife of the grandest farmer around.
The village women had been encouraged to join and it was
made clear they were there to be educated in the traditional
homemaking skills, plus the occasional speaker and, as in
Barrington's case, an enthusiastic folk-dancing team as a
healthy hobby and a useful entertainment at village fetes.

Of course, things had inevitably changed over the years.
Presidents were voted in, and there was now an influential
national organisation overseeing the branches, conducted
in a democratic and broad-minded way. Very few folk-
dance teams could now be found, but instead there were

Scrabble tournaments, rounders, drama competitions, and
for the more adventurous, a college of education where
courses spanning a wide range of interests could be taken.
At the AGM in the Royal Albert Hall in London, serious
matters were debated and voted on. Some older members
said regretfully that the Institute was now neither one thing
nor the other.

Ivy Beasley had been a stalwart member of Round
Ringford WI, and when she moved to Suffolk, she had
immediately joined the local branch. There were a number
of things she objected to, but sensibly kept them to herself
until she became established. Her old friends would not
have recognised her. She had been known to be dreaded
by many a speaker, her awkward questions leaving them
trembling and unsure as they hastily packed up their leaflets and samples and left, excusing themselves from tea
and cakes on obviously trumped-up excuses. Now she sat
mostly silently, applauding with reserve, and phrasing her
suggestions in a completely non-Ivy way.

This evening, she had a new mission. She knew from
long experience that the WI was a clearinghouse for village
gossip. After the speaker's talk, plastic cloths were spread
on card tables and plates of homemade cakes handed round
by whoever was on duty for refreshments that month. Ivy
already knew the women who would be the most reliable
informants on rumour and secrets in the village, and she
folded her arms, planning the questions she would ask.

The speaker, however, proved to be an unexpected challenge to the new Ivy. Esther Chantry was a tall, narrow-
faced woman with the confident air of an infant teacher.
She wasn't a teacher, but an author, and her special interest was historical novels about village life. Claiming she
had always lived in villages, she described life in the
"olden days" and how today differed from those treasured
times. Ivy simmered, but said nothing. In the end, after
the speaker had said that *then* everybody had plenty to eat,

kept warm in winter, lived longer and was supported by the neighbours when illness struck, it was too much for Ivy.

"Bunkum!" she said loudly, her face scarlet and her glasses steamed up with fury. "Have you ever read the tombstones in a village graveyard? All them little'uns that died in infancy?"

The president was immediately alert. She had long practice in keeping the meeting to order, including being forced to have a private word with a member who had chipped in to every speaker's talk with her own opinions and experiences.

"Thank you, Miss Beasley," she said. "There will be plenty of time for questions and comments at the end. Please carry on," she added, beaming at the speaker.

So Ivy sat more or less quietly, except for the occasional "Huh!" until the end.

"Any questions, members?" said the president, with a reproving look at Ivy. She did not yet know that Ivy Beasley had never been permanently squashed, and did not intend to change.

"Yes," Ivy said at once. "I would like to know where you got your stuff about old days in the villages? My family lived in a Midlands village for generations, and tales told by them speak of hardship, illness, early deaths in farm accidents and children wasting away in damp, cold cottages. They had food, yes, but what food? We wouldn't touch it now. So where were your ideal villages, missus?"

To give the speaker her due, and even Ivy said this later, she reacted with an energetic defence of her evidence. Some villages were as Ivy had described them, she agreed, but it all depended on the squire, and there were probably a good few who were oppressive and mean. There were also, she stressed, many kind and paternal squires and their families. Neighbours *were* helpful and often shared what they had. There were feuds and enmities, of course. Any group of people could produce those, even the most affluent.

Finally, after the president had looked at her watch several times in as obvious a way as she could manage, the speaker very sensibly said she would love to continue their chat over tea, and Ivy subsided.

Settled with a thick slice of fruitcake, Ivy looked around at the women. They were quiet, embarrassed by Ivy's intervention. Then one of them, younger than the rest and known for being stroppy, said that she had quite agreed with Ivy.

"These women who think they know everything about country life, and live in restored cottages with loads of cats and scribble all that rubbish about lovely simple, uneducated people, ought to go back where they belong." Fortunately, the speaker had excused herself and disappeared into the Ladies. "Half of 'em are weekenders," the woman continued, "and never take part in the real life of the village. Well done, Miss Beasley," she said. "I bet that woman steers clear of our table!"

The other half dozen sitting with Ivy burst into laughter and all talked at once about the evils of incomers. The president tactfully steered Esther Chantry to a table at the other end of the room. "Sorry about the interruption," she whispered before the writer sat down.

"Don't worry, my dear," said the writer, "it's all good copy, you know." She smiled confidingly, and the president wondered what on earth she was talking about.

Meanwhile, Ivy was having a splendid time. Now their embarrassment had vanished, her companions were only too pleased to talk to Ivy. They quickly assured her that as she had not bought up a village house, but had come to retire in Springfields, she was not considered an incomer. She steered the talk around to the murder without difficulty. One said she was glad Miriam Blake hadn't turned up tonight, else it was going to be very difficult. "I mean," she said, "we none of us know who did it yet, and, well, she has to be one of the suspects, doesn't she?"

"I can think of others," said a small, thin woman, dressed entirely in beige.

"Who?" they chorused.

"Well, that new man, for a start. Who is he? Where did he come from, and why Barrington?"

"He's been seen talking to Miriam and going into her house," contributed another.

Ivy thought it was time she said something in Gus's defence. "He's all right," she said. "Came to Springfields and offered to be a volunteer. Not many of those around," she said meaningly.

"After the old folks' money, I shouldn't wonder," said the stroppy woman. "There's always cases in the newspapers about con men getting life savings out of old women."

Ivy laughed. "He hasn't tried it on me yet, and he'd better not," she said. "Anyway," she added, turning to the woman in beige, "who else is on the list of suspects?"

For a moment, the woman did not answer, and the others looked at each other.

"Well," said the stroppy one, "not so long ago, our Miriam spread it about a bit. You know, for a while she was anybody's, including other people's husbands. Several wives I could name who were so humiliated they would gladly have knifed *anybody* called Blake."

"But not the old woman, surely," Ivy said.

"It was said," the woman in beige pronounced with emphasis, "that Miriam's mother encouraged her. Was desperate to get rid of her, shift her on to someone else. They hated each other, Miss Beasley. We all knew, and some of us sympathised with the old woman. But others said a mother should control her daughter, that *she* was the one at fault. It must be stopped, the Mothers Union decided. It could be that somebody thought that by stopping the mother, the daughter would be shocked enough to give up her tricks. And also, of course, Miriam would be bound to be suspect number one."

It had proved quite the opposite, a sober-faced woman
said. Ivy recognised her as one of the church workers who
visited Springfields now and then. "Miriam's as free as a
bird now," this woman said. "Very chirpy when she forgets
to be the grieving daughter. And got her claws into that
new man already, so I hear."

Ivy smiled. "I doubt it," she said. "Any other suspects?"

A quiet woman, the only one who had said nothing so
far, cleared her throat.

"How about our own beloved squire?" she said. Everybody turned to look at Miss Beatty sitting at the speaker's
table, but she was deep in conversation. Which doesn't
mean she's not listening, thought Ivy.

The quiet woman lowered her voice to a whisper, and
leaning forward said she remembered when he'd been seen
going into the Blake's cottage on a regular basis.

"I reckon you'd better not say any more about that,
Doris," the stroppy one said. "You don't want to be had up
for libel. Still, what you said is very interesting, eh, Miss
Beasley?"

WHEN IVY RETURNED to Springfields, she immediately rang Gus. "Listen," she said. "Apart from that notice
about Enquire Within in the village shop, which anyway
sounds as if we're mostly prepared to look for lost dogs and
cats, I reckon we should keep our heads down. No extra
publicity. I got some really good stuff at the WI tonight.
But only because they think I'm a crotchety old woman
who's waiting to die in an old folks' home. Let's keep it to
ourselves for a bit," she added, and said she was about to
phone Deirdre to tell her the same thing.

"Did you tackle Beattie?" Gus said.

"No, not yet," Ivy said. "Better than that. Tell you Monday, if not before. Good night, Augustus."

She told Deirdre the same thing, and to her relief her

cousin did not argue. "Same thing had occurred to me," she said. "Glad to hear the WI was a success. I'm working on a way to get to Theo without the dragon knowing."

"Speak to me first, before you see him," Ivy said. "Come round for coffee tomorrow morning. Katya has promised to bake me a special cookie—whatever that is. Not such a bad child, that one. I may make something of her yet. Night, Deirdre."

BEATTIE BEATTY HAD stayed on in the village hall to help with the washing up. She did not usually do this, and the others were curious. Why now? They soon found out. Beattie buttonholed the ones who had sat at Ivy's table and asked what all the hilarity had been about. "Share the joke," she said, punishing a soapy saucer with a drying-up cloth.

After they had given her an edited version, leaving out all mention of Theo Roussel, she had more questions, this time about Miss Ivy Beasley. Who was she? Some relation of Deirdre Bloxham, she understood. Spoke her mind, didn't she. She approved of that. What else could they tell her about Ivy?

But the others did not cooperate, and said they knew no more than she did. Miss Beasley had seemed nice enough, once you got to know her.

Finally, the hall was cleared, and Beattie walked slowly up the long drive to the Hall. She was convinced that Ivy's table had been talking about Theo. She had even heard his name, she was absolutely certain. She quickened her steps. He had been about to say something to her this morning, and she knew perfectly well what it was. He was going to sack her for the imprisonment. But she knew him of old, knew things about him he would rather not have spread around. Then she was so nice to him at breakfast time that when she asked him if there was anything else before she started baking, he had hesitated and said no, nothing else, and had thanked her for a delicious breakfast.

She checked that every lock in the house was secure and went upstairs to her room. There she undressed and climbed into her high bed, took her book and began to read. Tomorrow was another day, and she would tackle the problem of Miss Ivy Beasley and her cousin Deirdre in the morning.

Sixteen

DEIRDRE ALWAYS ARRIVED promptly, and this morning was no exception. The new, imitation old, grandfather clock in the hall struck eleven as she came into the door of Springfields.

"Lovely morning!" she said, as she went upstairs to Ivy's room. Mrs. Spurling smiled and called after her that Katya had been busy baking for them both, and coffee would be up shortly.

"I think I'll move in here with you, Ivy," Deirdre said, as she settled down in a comfortable chair. "Lovely room with a nice view of the village, pleasant staff and good food. Waited on hand and foot, and an interesting man calling on you most days. What more could you want?"

"To be twenty years younger," said Ivy tartly. "I'd like to be back in Ringford in my own house, with Doris and Ellen, and the three of us going blackberrying in the autumn. Roots is what I miss, Deirdre."

"What *do* you mean, Ivy?" Deirdre asked, wishing she'd not said anything except hello.

"Family roots. Generations of Beasleys behind you. That's what I mean."

"Well, you've got me. And this is a good second best, isn't it?"

Fortunately, before Ivy could expand further on the value of roots, there was a knock at the door and Katya came in with a tray of coffee and cookies. Ivy's smile was warm, Deirdre noticed with surprise, and after the girl had gone, the last of the Beasleys praised the still-warm biscuits, saying only that, in her opinion, biscuits was a good enough name, since that's what they were.

"Now, down to business." Ivy then gave Deirdre a succinct account of what she had gleaned at the WI. "If you ask me," she said firmly, "the most important point out of all this is that our Miriam most probably had an affair with Mr. Theo Roussel. He must've been hard up for a woman, but still, there's no accounting for taste."

Deirdre bridled. "Hardly hard up," she protested. "He was a very attractive man in his youth," she said. "All the girls were after him."

"Including you?"

Deirdre shook her head. "No, he was after me," she corrected. "We had a fling for a while, but it fizzled out, like these things do."

"I wouldn't know," said Ivy, but reflected that she knew only too well. It was some years ago now, but the pain of being abandoned at the altar by her lodger was still a vivid memory. "Anyway," she continued, "it's even more important that you get to see Theo as soon as possible. Blackmail is about the only really solid reason we've got for somebody knifing the old woman."

"Ivy! You're talking like a private eye already! And yes, I am determined to get to see Theo in spite of his minder.

Have you any idea how I can do it without making a scene? I could go blasting in there with all guns blazing, but that would hardly put Theo in the mood for confiding secrets, would it?"

Ivy was silent for a few minutes. "We need Augustus," she said. "He's the man we want. I bet he's solved more things of this sort than we've had hot dinners. He'll tell us how to do it. No, don't go. I'll ring him now, see if he's at home."

Gus was at home, still in his pyjamas, reading a long letter from his ex-wife. She had enclosed a fistful of bills to be paid, and said that if he did not come up with the cash immediately, she would have to go to the lawyers again, and she was sure he knew how much that would cost. He sighed as he answered Ivy's call, but when she summoned him to Springfields at once, he was glad of the diversion and showered, dressed and was on his way in a very short time. It was a lovely morning, he noticed with rising spirits as he strode down the High Street. Something would come up. Maybe he'd go to the greyhound stadium in town tonight and have a few flutters on the dogs. Yep, he'd go to the dogs! As if he wasn't there already, he told himself, and roared with laughter, alarming Whippy who was, as usual, by his side.

BEATTIE BEATTY HAD prepared a cold salad lunch for Theo, and suggested to him that he might like to eat it in the orangery. "There's plenty of shade under the trees," she said, "and you wouldn't be worried by wasps and things. Shall I set it up there for you?"

She always hoped that he would invite her to join him, be a companion and share their lives more than before. But he never did. She remembered that in his youth he had been a gregarious young man, with friends in all strata of society. But she had seen nothing of that in him for years. He kept her firmly in her place socially, reluctantly allowing her to take over the running of the estate. But he never made a personal move towards her, never a one.

"Thank you, Beattie," he said. "That would be very nice. And shall we be quite clear that no doors are to be locked in future unless I lock them? That will be all now. Give me a call when lunch is ready for me."

So that's that, thought Beattie, as she went back to the kitchen. Maybe it hadn't been such a good idea. Perhaps she should have let that Mrs. Bloxham have a short talk with him. She could have stayed in her usual listening place and monitored what they said. Well, she hadn't, and so now she had to think of another way of keeping both those old women, Mrs. Bloxham and her cousin, away from any revealing conversations with her master. Master! If he was her master, it followed that she was his mistress, didn't it? If only that were true, how different things would be.

After washing up lunch dishes—no dishwasher for her—she retreated to a seat in the garden with her book. It was riveting, and she could hardly wait for the next chapter. Set back in Victorian times, it was a story based on an actual case of poisoning, and one of such fascinating detail that she had read several passages over twice. A young Scottish woman had taken an unsuitable lover, and met him clandestinely for scenes of unbridled passion. When he threatened to expose their affair, she worked out a most ingenious way of doing away with him, luring him into unmentionable practices involving a slow poisoning through ingestion.

"Phew!" said Beattie, loosening her blouse. It was really very hot this afternoon. Maybe she should make sure that Theo had not gone to sleep in the sun. Well, a few more minutes wouldn't do any harm, she thought, and turned the page.

* * *

GUS'S VISIT TO join Ivy and Deirdre had, as expected
by Ivy, been extremely useful. "We have to be even more
devious than Beattie," he said. "Out-think the old dragon.
Now, lets make a plan."

They had put their heads together over fresh coffee
and another supply of cookies, and were pleased with the
result. Gus had wanted to know if they had heard of any
regular trips into town made by Beattie. Didn't she go to
market every week? And did she take the morning or afternoon bus? Did Theo ever go out on his own? If so, where,
and how did he manage? Did he visit any local friends or
tenants? That Rose Budd was an attractive woman. Deirdre
had blushed. "Really, Ivy!" she had said. "I'm surprised at
you. She is a married woman."

"Be your age, and don't be so ridiculous, Deirdre!"

Gus had decided to change the subject. "Now,"
he'd said, "the best source of answers to my questions
would probably be Will at the shop. I can call on my way
back."

Now he sat in the window seat of the pub, thinking over
what Will had said, and making notes.

Beattie went to market every Saturday afternoon without fail. She arranged for the wife of their one remaining farmworker to sit with Theo, who, since this was the
bubbly blond Rose Budd, never complained. It was said in
the pub that Rose played croquet on the lawn with him
in the summer, and Scrabble in the drawing room in the
winter. Other humorous suggestions were made, but not
taken seriously. Remembering what Ivy had said, Gus took
them seriously.

This was really good news, Gus thought, chewing the
end of his pen. Now, what else? Theo had few friends,
apparently. Old chums had tried, but met a stone wall in
Beattie. Not that she antagonised them, but in a subtle

way led them to think that Theo had become very much a recluse, not wanting friends interrupting his mammoth task of writing his memoirs. Some persisted for a while, but in the end accepted what Beattie said, and gave up. She had exaggerated the memoir writing, of course, although he occasionally set down memories of the past.

Gus left the pub, and returned home to telephone Deirdre. Tomorrow was Saturday, market day, and while Beattie was in town they would have two and a half hours to allow Deirdre to renew her friendship with Theo. The key player would be Rose Budd, and Gus was confident that he could draw her into a plot to foil the old dragon. But first, Deirdre, then Ivy, to keep the old thing informed. Then Rose. She had said to ask her if there was anything he needed to know, so he had the perfect excuse for knocking on her door.

"Hello? Deirdre, is that you? Gus here. Now, good news, but listen carefully." He explained that they had to time the visit so that Beattie would have no suspicions. Ivy would be lookout, sitting on the seat outside the shop, when the afternoon bus picked up passengers. Then she would return later with Gus's mobile phone in her handbag, and would ring the Hall to alert them to Beattie's return.

"What about Rose Whatsit?" Deirdre said. "Will she let me in? You bet old Beattie has given her strict instructions to admit nobody!"

Gus smiled modestly. "I think you can leave Rose to me," he said. "I've met her already, and she was extremely friendly and helpful. I'm sure she would have every sympathy with an attempt to brighten the life of the old boy. Will at the shop says that her husband works like a slave on the estate, and is certainly not overpaid for his labours. Beattie holds the purse strings, it seems. Any attempt to get one back on the old dragon will be enthusiastically received, I reckon. Anyway," he continued, "if Rose won't play ball, I'll think of something else and let you know. So, best bib and tucker tomorrow afternoon, and best of luck."

"Bearing in mind what Ivy suspects about Theo and Miriam Blake," Deirdre said slowly, "my most important task is to find out what went on, what he knows and thinks about the whole murder mystery, isn't it? Persuading him to be our client seems to have taken a backseat, especially since Ivy decided we should keep our heads down for a bit?"

"Absolutely," said Gus. "Quite right. Get him talking, not too much reminiscing about your own steamy affair with him, and gently point him in the right direction. I'm sure you'll be fine." He wasn't that sure, but knew that this was a chance not to be missed. It was Deirdre on trial, really.

IVY NEXT. SHE grasped the whole plan in minutes. No, she didn't need a tutorial on how to use a mobile. Young Katya had one, and would be a willing teacher. "The young are so much better at it than we are, Gus," she said, well aware that he would object to being bracketed with an old lady in her seventies.

He grinned to himself. Ivy Beasley was one of the best, he decided. Meeting Ivy had made his settling in Barrington worthwhile. Then he thought of his ex-wife's letter and enclosures, and wondered if Ivy would be up for loaning him a small amount to help him out. Of course not! No point in asking, and in any case, it would scupper the whole project if he was in debt to her. At the moment he was precariously at the helm of Enquire Within, but at any time his position could be challenged by the cousins.

Gus looked at himself in the cracked kitchen mirror,

and smoothed down his thinning hair to disguise the fact
that his head was beginning to show through. He straightened his shoulders, persuaded himself that he was still an
attractive proposition, and set out to tackle Rose Budd.

Seventeen

THEO ROUSSEL WOKE up with the pleasant feeling he had every Saturday. Today, Beattie was going to market, and, even more pleasant, Rosebud would be coming to make his tea and keep him company. He couldn't believe his luck when Beattie had set up this arrangement. The only thing he could think was that she considered, mistakenly, that a young and lovely blonde would never in a million years fancy such a sedentary old man.

He got out of bed and tiptoed to the door, opened it and peered up and down the corridor. No sign of Beattie. It was early, and she would not bring his cup of tea for at least half an hour. He crept quietly along to his study and taking a key from its hiding place, he moved the portrait of his grandfather to one side and carefully opened the safe door.

He took out a small box, opened it and extracted an exquisite sapphire and diamond ring. It was like a small regal crown, released into the light, sparkling as if it was brand-new. He smiled, muttered that the sapphire would match her eyes, and slipped it into his pyjama jacket pocket. Then he shut the safe door, straightened the portrait, and silently retraced his steps to his bedroom.

When Beattie knocked at his door before bringing in his early morning tea, he was able to give a convincing performance of a man waking up for the first time, yawning and rubbing his eyes.

"Market day, Mr. Theo," she said. "Up we get as soon as we've finished our tea. I need to get breakfast out of the way, then a basketful of ironing, quick lunch and then off on the bus. Anything you particularly fancy from the market? They had some lovely ripe peaches last week."

Then why didn't you buy them last week, Theo said to himself, but he answered that peaches would be just the thing. Perhaps she could look for strawberries, too, and then he could have a fruity pudding tonight.

The morning went as always for Theo. He enjoyed his breakfast of bacon and fresh mushrooms gathered by Rose's husband David, then settled in his study with the *Times* crossword. Bouyed up by the thought of Rose coming after lunch, he hummed to himself as he consulted a pile of dictionaries and *Roget's Thesaurus* at his elbow. He prided himself on being able to complete the crossword before dinner, and as Rose was unfortunately no help at all with the clues, he would have only this morning and an hour or so after tea to finish it today.

GUS WALKED BRISKLY along the terrace and stopped at the Budd's house. He had tried to find Rose several times yesterday, but there had been no one at home. It would be bad luck if they had gone away on holiday! But no, someone was coming to the door. It was David Budd, and he smiled in a friendly way at Gus.

"Mr. Halfhide? Rose told me you'd met. Is there anything we can help you with? Come on in. We're in our usual squalid muddle, but that's children for you. Rose!" he shouted. "Here's Mr. Halfhide!"

David was a good-looking thirty-year-old, his face tanned by an outdoor life, and with not an ounce of spare flesh on him. He had done well at school and set out to be an architect. But the years of study needed to qualify were too daunting for him, and in any case, he had always wanted to be a farmer like his maternal grandfather. Agricultural college had proved ideal, and he had enjoyed his time there. In fact, it was there he met Rose. It had been love at first sight for both of them, and in due course they were married.

There was no money for David to buy a farm, and so he had ended up in Barrington, working on the Roussel estate. It suited him well, apart from having to deal with Miss Beatty. But he kept well away from her, and apart from paying lip service to some of her more bizarre instructions, like keeping a piglet in an old rabbit hutch in the empty stable, he had the management of the land more or less to himself.

Even the piglet project was dropped when, as David had tried to warn her, the piglet grew too big for the hutch.

"What can we do for you, Mr. Halfhide?" Rose said, clattering down the stairs in lilac-coloured plastic clogs.

"Please, do call me Gus."

"Okay—and I'm Rose and he's David. And little snot-nose there is Simon."

"I won't take up much of your time," promised Gus, as they insisted they should all sit down and have a coffee.

David nodded. "I do have to get going very soon," he said. "Otherwise old gimlet-eyes at the Hall will be giving me a lecture on punctuality."

"It's about Miss Beatty that I've come," Gus explained. "Beattie and Theo, that is. My good friend Deirdre Bloxham is an old flame of Theo, and would very much like to chat about old times with him. Try to bring a bit of outside interest into his life, she says. She arranged to call on him, but Miss Beatty made several excuses and Deirdre had to go away without seeing him. Since then, she has been unable to get through to the Hall. The phone rings, but as soon as someone answers it their end, it goes dead."

"We could certainly get the telephone engineer to look at it," David said sympathetically. He felt permanently sorry for his boss, though privately thought the man was not that old, and should stand up to the Beattie woman.

Gus shook his head. "Nothing wrong with the phone, I'm sure of that," he said. "It's being monitored by Beattie Beatty. You can hear her breathing."

"So how can we help?" Rose said, lifting Simon onto her lap and feeding him with a soggy biscuit dipped into her coffee.

Gus explained the plan. Deirdre would arrive at the Hall immediately after Beattie had been seen by Ivy boarding the bus to town. Rose would admit Deirdre directly to the drawing room where Theo would be sitting waiting for his first game of Scrabble.

Then Rose would make herself scarce, leaving the two old friends alone together.

Rose went very pink and clapped her hands like a little girl. "What a lovely surprise!" she said. "He'll be so excited to see her. They'll have a good two hours. I can keep an eye out for other visitors, or raise the drawbridge if, heaven forefend, Miss Beatty returns on the early bus. Which, to my knowledge, she never has."

Gus was alarmed. "I didn't know there was an earlier bus," he said.

"Just runs in the summer," said David. "It comes back an hour after they've got there, so there's hardly anybody on it."

They talked a bit more about how they could make the arrangements foolproof, and then Gus got up to go. "It is so kind of you both," he said.

"Theo's a sweetie," Rose said. "We'd do anything to brighten his life. I'm always hoping that one day he'll get so angry with Miss Beatty that he'll send her packing and live a more normal life. There's nothing wrong with him, you know. Fit as a fiddle, and all his marbles in place."

"I hear he was quite a ladies' man in his youth?" Gus said, as he stepped outside into the sunshine.

"Still is!" said David. "Rose has to keep him at bay sometimes, don't you, duckie?"

Rose didn't answer, but laughed so much that Simon bounced off her lap and began to yell. She followed the men into the garden, and assured Gus that all would go smoothly. "If it works," she said, "we can make it a regular assignation. One in the eye for old Beattie. I reckon she has hopes of a Roussel ring on her finger one of these days."

"No!" said Gus. "That must be prevented at all costs."

"And she's not the only one," said David, grinning. "Somone approaching down the lane has had similar ideas."

Gus turned his head. It was Miriam Blake, still in her shop overalls and smiling broadly at the sight of her new neighbour. The three stood in the Budds' garden and said hello as she passed.

"She's a new woman," whispered Rose, and David nodded. "Must've found the nest egg," he said.

"Sshh!" Rose waved a hand to Gus and disappeared into the house, and David said he was going Gus's way and would accompany him the few yards to his end of the terrace to save him from marauding spinsters who were more than likely lying in wait for him.

Eighteen

IVY WALKED STEADILY along the street from Springfields down to the shop, where she purchased a packet of
Polo mints and said she was quite puffed out, and would
sit for a while on the Hon. John Roussel memorial seat
outside.

After about ten minutes, she was delighted to see a
familiar figure approaching briskly from Hangman's Row
into the High Street, and then along to the bus stop outside
the shop.

Beattie Beatty recognised Ivy, and managed a gruff
"Good morning," then turned and looked along the street
in the direction of the oncoming bus. She was cutting
it a bit fine, thought Ivy, as the bus stopped and Beattie
climbed aboard. Thank goodness she made it, else all our
plans . . .

At this point, to her horror, Miss Beatty reappeared
at the bus door and came rapidly down the steps into the
street! She rushed across the pavement, into the shop,
and disappeared. Ivy thought fast. Should she phone Gus

straightaway? She prayed to God that she had mastered the mobile phone in her handbag.

But no, after only a few seconds, Beattie rushed out of the shop and clambered clumsily back into the bus, to be greeted by cheers from the passengers already seated. As Ivy stared, she saw Beattie find a seat next to the window and, scarlet-faced, mop her brow with a tissue wrestled from a new packet.

So, she forgot to put a hankie in her pocket, Ivy guessed as the bus moved away. Just like her to keep everybody waiting. Now, her next job was to ring Gus and give him the all clear. She took the frighteningly small mobile phone from her bag, and switched it on. So far so good! She had memorised his number and carefully pressed the buttons. With each button, the thing beeped at her. She supposed that was to tell her she'd pressed it hard enough. What next? She put it to her ear, but there was no ringing tone. She stared at it again.

"You have to press the green telephone, Miss Beasley," a girl's voice said. Ivy looked up in surprise and saw Katya beaming at her.

"Good heavens, girl!" Ivy said. "Just in time to rescue me!" She pressed, and listened again. Now it was ringing, and then Gus's familiar tones. "All clear," she said, as arranged. Nothing more. He said nothing in reply, and then there was the dialling tone. "Oh my," she said, breathing fast and patting her chest to quieten her thudding heart, "I feel just like Mata Hari."

"Are you all right?" Katya said, looking worried. "Can I get you glass of water?"

"No, no. I'm fine, my dear," Ivy said, and indeed, she was beginning to feel quite chirpy at the idea of having completed this part in the plot successfully. She stood up, and Katya said she would come back to Springfields with her. It was her afternoon off, but she had nothing planned.

"Well, in that case," said Ivy, "we don't want to go back

to the tender loving care of Miss Pinkney, do we? I shall take you for a walk, not too far, and show you something really interesting and historic. Come along now." She refused to hold Katya's arm, and they set off in the opposite direction from Springfields, past the school and on towards the church.

GUS IMMEDIATELY DIALLED Deirdre, and with a loud whoop of delight she said she would set off at once. He replaced the phone and went to the window, where he intended to keep vigil for the next two hours. After no more than five minutes, he saw Deirdre's swish car go by, and saw her gaily waving as she passed his house. He hoped she would be discreet. In his long experience of working undercover, he knew they must be alert to the unexpected. If it *could* happen, then it very likely *would* happen. Maybe not this time, but if they repeated the exercise, it would be important not to get careless.

Deirdre thought how lovely the Hall looked, as she drove up to the grand front and then round to the stable yard at the back. Gus had thought it a good idea not to park so obviously outside the front door, but Deirdre had argued that if there was a risk of Beattie returning early she could make a quicker getaway from the front. Gus had insisted, and so she agreed.

As she turned off the engine and began to open the door, she stopped. She was doing nothing wrong! All this skulduggery was quite ridiculous. There was absolutely no reason why she should not visit her old friend. If Miss Beatty had gone to market, so what? Either she would be admitted by Theo, or by Rose Budd in the house with him as usual. It was a perfectly normal course of events.

No it wasn't. Her commonsense reasserted itself. There was a primary reason for her visiting Theo. It was to find

out as much as she could from him about the Blakes, and
Miriam in particular. A reunion with an old lover was a
bonus. It would be important, she knew Gus and Ivy would
both argue this, to make it possible to visit Theo more than
once, and if the old dragon so much as suspected, let alone
found Deirdre ensconced with Theo, Beattie would find a
way of putting a final stop to it.

Why did she shiver at this thought? Deirdre shook herself and made for the kitchen door, which was now standing open with a smiling Rose welcoming her in.

KATYA WALKED BESIDE Ivy, feeling somehow relaxed
for the first time since she had been working at Springfields. She was not unhappy there, and was well aware how
lucky she had been to find work so soon after arriving in
England. Her parents back in Poland were pleased and
proud, and she received a stream of letters and cards from
her large family back home. But still she had not relaxed.
She could not understand much of what was said to her,
and she still found her English classes hard going.

But now, strolling along with this funny, sharp old
woman, she began to look about her, see how lovely the
trees and flowers were, breathe in the air which, compared
to the industrial town she had come from, was like champagne. At least, she supposed it was. She had never drunk
champagne, though that nice Mr. Halfhide had promised
her a glass very soon.

"Now, in we go," Ivy said, turning through the lych-gate
and into the churchyard. Either side of the path, pink flo-
ribunda roses and bushy lavender scented their way up to
the church door. "Hope it's unlocked," Ivy said. "So many
vandals these days, most churches are locked unless there's
a service or people doing the flowers and brasses."

"*Brasses*?" said Katya.

"Candlesticks and crosses—oh, you'll see, my dear. I'll explain."

"And *vandals*?"

"Criminals," said Ivy. "Like the Communists," she said firmly.

Katya had still not understood, but meekly followed Ivy into the dark interior of the eleventh-century church.

"We could do with some light," Ivy said loudly, and, as she had hoped, the vestry door opened and the vicar came towards them, smiling broadly. He had met Ivy when she first arrived at Springfields, and at first his heart sank. But then on better acquaintance he realised that she was a lonely old woman, far from everything familiar in her life, determined to survive and make a place for herself in Barrington. "I think she's being very brave," he had said to his wife. "We shall be kind to her."

Now he went into the bell tower and switched on lights in the body of the church.

"Thank you, Vicar," Ivy said, and marched up to the chancel, beckoning Katya to follow her. To Ivy's dismay, she saw Katya genuflect and cross herself in front of the altar. Oh dear, she was one of those, was she. Well, Ivy reassured herself, she could soon persuade her out of all that nonsense. To Ivy, God was a solid being, always there to be consulted, one she respected but was not averse to criticising if she thought He had made a wrong decision. When no one was listening, she talked to Him as if to a benign but certainly not omnipotent friend. She could imagine His chuckle as the Polish girl bobbed up and down and muttered something incomprehensible. Poor God. Ivy was quite sure English was His chosen language.

"Now then, Katya," she said, "come and look at this."

Katya followed Ivy towards the left of the altar, where a large and impressive seventeenth-century memorial plaque was fixed to the wall. A family crest framed in stone curlicues headed an inscription in Latin, which Ivy asked the vicar to translate. It was the usual lord of the manor stuff, but underneath was something quite chilling. Katya drew in her breath sharply.

"What happened?" she said.

Two kneeling figures, sculpted in high relief, with their hands together in prayer, and their long draped clothes beautifully moulded, faced the altar. The sculptor had been skilled, and the hands were delicate, one with a ring quite visible. But they had no heads. Where their heads should have been were two empty spaces.

"How terrible!" said Katya, turning quite pale.

Then Ivy asked the vicar to tell the story of how in the English Civil War, when Noncomformists and Catholics were at each other's throats, a band of soldiers had entered the church on horseback, clattered up the aisle, and with cheers of triumph had knocked off the idolatrous heads of the Catholic squire and his lady. Their stone victims had crashed to the floor, but remained unbroken. So the soldiers had thrown them from one to another, until finally they used the stone pillars as targets and the heads broke into a hundred pieces.

"But that was so long ago!" said the vicar, seeing a tear rolling down the girl's face. "Now we are a pleasant, peace-loving community, each one of us doing our best to be good Christians with our fellows."

"Speak for yourself," muttered Ivy, and walked back down the aisle. To her surprise she heard a few tentative notes on the organ. She looked back, and saw Katya had stopped and was gently fingering the keys.

"Please!" said the vicar. "Do play if you would like to. The organ has just been restored, and needs to be played. Come, Miss Beasley," he said, beckoning her to the front pew. "We can have a private recital. Please," he repeated, "do play for us."

He could see that Katya did not need much persuading,

and as they sat listening to the magic notes of a Bach prelude, he smiled at Ivy, closed his eyes, and companionably rested his hand on hers. She removed it immediately.

ALL WAS GOING well at the Hall. Rose had a quick chat with Deirdre, explaining that Theo did not know she was coming as she'd not wanted to disappoint him if things went wrong.

"You look much younger than Mr. Theo," she said cheerfully to Deirdre. "A real cradle-snatcher he must have been!"

Deirdre saw through this flattery, but felt pleased and reassured, as Rose had intended. The years had put weight on Deirdre, and crow's-feet wrinkles around her eyes were at odds with her carefully coloured hair.

They went through the hallway and stopped outside the tall double doors of the drawing room. As Rose put a finger to her lips for silence, Deirdre felt a quiver of nervousness. Supposing he didn't remember her? Or did, and had no desire to see her again?

Rose opened the door quietly, and said, "Mr. Theo, you have a visitor."

"But how about our Scrabble, my dear?" Deirdre heard the voice, and marvelled that she would have known it anywhere.

"Later, Mr. Theo. I promise. Now, let me introduce . . ."

She drew Deirdre into the room, and Theo Roussel leapt to his feet like a young man.

"No need to introduce us!" he said. "Deirdre, my dear," he said, and hurried over to take her hand. They looked at each other without speaking, and did not notice Rose Budd quietly leaving the room.

* * *

LATER THAT EVENING, when David came home from work and demanded from Rose to be told all about it, every detail, she willingly settled him down with his supper and said, "It was like a film. Honestly, David, if the drawing room had dissolved into a beach scene with those two skipping into the sunset, I'd not have been surprised. Couldn't have been better."

"And the rest?" he'd said, laughing. "Did Beattie Beatty come creeping in later and discover them in flagrante delicto?"

"Of course not, you idiot! It all went like clockwork. She came back on time, in a bad mood as usual from trudging round the market and not getting the bargains she expected. Usual questions about phone calls and visitors. I dealt with that! I reckon I should've been an actress. Theo was brilliant, too. I could see he'd had a marvellous afternoon, but he pretended it had been boring, playing the same old Scrabble and snakes and ladders. He even said he was glad to see her home again!"

"Blimey!" said David. "Who'd've thought it? Good old Theo. I might even get a raise if he's feeling so happy."

"No chance," said Rose. "Not while Beattie holds the purse strings. Still," she added, "if we play our cards right, we might be able to do something about that. Us and Deirdre Bloxham . . ."

DEIRDRE HAD LEFT the Hall with plenty of time before Beattie returned, and waved a prearranged signal to Ivy as she passed the shop. In due course, Ivy returned to Springfields and found Deirdre waiting for her.

"Ah, there you are," she said, opening the door of her room. "I'll order tea. Sit down, girl, you look all of a do-dah."

She walked to the door and peered along the corridor. "Katya!" she called. "We need tea here, and some of your biscuits. Quick as you can, dear," she added, looking at Deirdre's expression.

"Was it as bad as that?" Ivy said.

Deirdre frowned. "What do you mean, Ivy?" she said. "It wasn't bad at all. Everything went without a hitch. It was just such an extraordinary meeting after all these years. I knew he lived at the Hall, of course, and often wondered why I didn't bump into him round the village. Now I know. That dreadful Beatty woman has forced him into being a recluse, more or less. If he wants to go anywhere, she takes him in the car and sticks to him like glue. Treats him like an invalid, though when I asked him outright what was wrong with him, he said nothing at all. He seemed quite surprised himself when he said he was hundred percent fit, as if it had not really occurred to him."

"Probably happened gradually. I wouldn't put anything past that Beatty woman. She's after his money, I reckon, though quite how she plans to get it, I'm not sure."

"Not just his money," Deirdre said, leaning forward confidingly. "He's sure she's after him, and I believe him. She never gives up, he says, trying to get more familiar with him. That's part of the reason he stays in his room out of her way as much as possible. He says it's easiest to agree to anything she says, so long as it's not an engagement ring! Do you know, Ivy," she continued, "I'd forgotten what a really nice man he is, and he has a really good sense of humour."

Ivy scowled. "GSOH," she said mysteriously.

"What?"

"You're not there to be keeping a date from the lonely hearts column," Ivy said sharply. "You know, GSOH, Good Sense Of Humour. Let's get on to the Blakes. What did you discover about his affair with our Miriam? And did you talk about the old woman's murder?"

Deirdre bridled. "Well, Ivy," she said, "I didn't actually walk into the room, shake his hand and ask him to tell me about his sexual relations with Miriam Blake. It needed a bit more subtlety than that!"

"You were there two hours," answered Ivy. "So stop messing about and tell me what you learned."

"It's true," Deirdre said baldly. "Just like today, when Beattie was at market, Theo used to nip down to Blakes' cottage, and with the old lady's connivance, would go upstairs hand in hand with Miriam for a spot of rumpy-pumpy. Do you know what he said, Ivy?"

Ivy shook her head.

"You won't believe it," Deirdre began.

"Try me," said Ivy.

"He said Miriam was good at it. Experienced, he said. Just what a virtual prisoner needed on a Saturday afternoon. He was quite honest about it, Ivy. We had a good laugh, I can tell you!"

"And why did it stop? Did Beattie find out?"

"No, it was the old woman. She blackmailed him. Said she'd tell Miss Beatty what was going on, unless he promised to marry Miriam. He said he seriously thought of topping himself. There seemed no way out. Disaster, whatever he did."

"So what *did* he do?"

"It was a brilliant piece of luck," Deirdre said, helping herself to another of Katya's biscuits. "He had an anonymous letter, delivered by hand on a Saturday afternoon, and he happened to see it on the mat. When he opened it, it had a message in it that saved his life."

"Oh, don't spin it out, girl!" Ivy said.

"It said that the writer had absolute proof that Miriam Blake was Theo's half sister."

Nineteen

THERE WAS SOMETHING different about Theo. Beattie had noticed it straightaway, and made a mental note to find out what had happened while she was at market. Outwardly, he was just the same, if a little more pleasant than usual. He'd been lavish in his praise of the strawberry and peach meringue pudding she made for him. "So good of you to remember," he had said.

But when she thought she might try a small advance and suggest they watched the *Antiques Roadshow* on television together, he retreated fast, saying he had some important reading to catch up on. "You watch it, Beattie," he had said with a quick smile. "Let me know if I've got anything worth millions!" He had almost run upstairs to his study. She had not seen him so quick on his feet for years.

Now he sat in his comfortable leather armchair, a small lamp illuminating a book which he had no intention of reading. He was daydreaming, remembering Deirdre's flowery perfume, fancying he could smell it on his cheek where she had kissed him good-bye. He replayed their reminiscences realising that he found her just as attractive as when they first met. What had she thought of him? The signs were good, he decided. She had been firm about her intention of seeing him again. Next Saturday, she said, and he knew then that Rosebud was in on the scheme to deceive Beattie. Hooray! At last, maybe the end was in sight!

He had put the ring in his jacket pocket, ready to replace in the safe. He wouldn't give it to Rosebud for her birthday after all. A happy grin spread across his face. He might have another use for it.

He began to doze, but was awakened by a sudden thought. He had told Deirdre about his affair with Miriam Blake and the old woman blackmailing him, and his final lucky escape. Had that been wise? It had sounded sordid as he described the episode, and he remembered vividly his own feelings of disgust.

But Deirdre had laughed, hadn't she? No doubt in her marriage to that garage mechanic she had seen all sides of life. And when he'd told her about the anonymous letter and Miriam being his half sister, she had looked really excited, and wanted to know all the details. All he knew from the anonymous letter, he had said, was that his father, the Hon. John, had employed Miriam's mother as a cleaner, and required a few extras on the side. Miriam had been the result, and a husband—poor old John, employed on the estate—had been found for her mother in time for the birth certificate, and although he was lazy and a bad influence on the other workers, his job was safe so long as he kept his mouth shut.

With this ammunition, Theo had been able to counter-threaten both Miriam and her mother. He would ruin their reputations with spreading the story of illegitimacy far and wide. As for his own reputation, he knew from experience that the entire village probably already knew about his visits to Miriam. Squire's privilege, the old blokes in the pub would say with a nudge and a wink. But the letter implied that the secret of Miriam's biological father *had* been successfully kept. The old woman had seen at once that they had more to lose than he had, and a truce had been reached. He had, of course, not visited Miriam since.

His eyes closed slowly, and he smiled. Deirdre . . . Little Deirdre with the red hair and a charming Suffolk accent . . . Roll on next Saturday, he thought, and in seconds was asleep.

GUS HAD ALREADY been round to Tawny Wings for a report from Deirdre, but had found nobody at home. Deirdre's car was not in the garage, and he was reluctant to conclude that she had not yet returned. So where had she gone? He had seen her car going past his window away from the Hall, and then he had checked off Beattie, as she lumbered home with her shopping. He wondered why the silly woman did not drive herself to market and not have to carry home heavy bags. Probably the parking problem, he decided. By the afternoon on market day, parking was impossible, with jams of cars trying to get away in all directions. The bus was a better option.

He looked briefly in the garden, but was left with nothing to do but to go back home. Just as he was emerging from the baronial gates, Deirdre drove back in, tooting as she passed him. He turned around and joined her as she unlocked her front door.

"Come on in, Gus," she said cheerfully. "It's little drinkies time, isn't it?"

Oh God, thought Gus, remembering his father's strictures never to work with women.

But he smiled and said that would be terrific, and followed behind as she led the way into her sparkling kitchen.

"Sit down, boy," she said, as she opened the fridge door and took out a frosted bottle of white Frascati. She poured him a generous glass, and taking another for herself, perched on the high stool next to him.

"Bottoms up!" she said, raising her glass.

Why not, thought Gus, and said he hoped she had had a pleasant afternoon.

That was all the opening Deirdre needed, and for the next half hour she gave Gus a highly entertaining account of the success of their plan. "Couldn't have gone better," she said, and looking sly, added that she meant from all points of view.

"Did he drag you off to bed, then?" Gus said. Ivy wouldn't like that, he thought. "Call a spade a spade" was her motto, but she drew a definite line at vulgarity.

"Of course not!" Deirdre grinned, and said maybe next time.

"But to be serious for a moment," Gus said. "Did you talk about the murder at all?"

"Hardly at all," Deirdre replied. "It somehow did not seem necessary. As I've told you, we chewed over his affair with La Blake very thoroughly, and the revelation that she was his half sister was quite a shock, I can tell you. I mean, fancy tupping your half sister without knowing it!"

"Marginally better than if you *had* known it," said Gus drily.

"Well, anyway, the murder plot certainly thickened with that revelation! Now we have three possible suspects: Miriam, who hated her mother; Theo, who also hated the old woman and had still regarded her as a loose cannon; and Beattie Beatty, who hates everybody but Theo, and loves either him or his money, or both."

Gus laughed. "Very good summing up, Deirdre," he said. "Full marks! So on Monday, we shall have plenty to talk about at our meeting. We must fill Ivy in with what has happened."

"Oh goodness, she was the first person I told!" Deirdre said. "It's more than my life's worth to keep her in the dark for longer than necessary. She'll have mulled it all over by Monday and come up with some good ideas. You'll see. She didn't rule Round Ringford with a rod of iron for all those years for nothing! Cousin Ivy coming to Springfields is the best thing that's happened to me since Bert died, now I've got to know her."

"Better than renewing your friendship with Theo Roussel?"

Deirdre laughed like a girl. "Now, Gus," she said, "naughty, naughty! Ready for a fill-up?"

Twenty

SUNDAY BEGAN PLEASANTLY for Ivy. Katya had asked if she could accompany her to church, and although Ivy was pleased, she hoped there wouldn't be too much bobbing and crossing. They were early. Ivy was a firm believer in arriving in good time, and she led Katya up the aisle to the front pew. In Ringford, the front pew had always been Ivy's, and she was not intending to change her habit of a lifetime. "We can keep an eye on the vicar and all those brats in the choir," she whispered to Katya.

The church was fuller than usual, and when the people were invited to the altar to take Communion, a snaking queue formed to receive the bread and wine. Katya went ahead of Ivy, and when they reached the organ, the girl became so absorbed in friendly Fanny Neston's plump hands moving over the keyboard that Ivy had to nudge her to keep going.

After the service, a special benefice one, coffee and biscuits were served, and Ivy introduced Katya to the few people she knew. After a few minutes, Miss Neston had come down from the organ and asked for a glass of water.

"Thirsty work?" Ivy said, greeting her. "This is Katya, my Polish friend from Springfields. She also plays the organ, don't you, dear?" After seeing that the two became instant friends, Ivy eased herself away and made for the vicar's wife in order to give her a few suggestions, including how to avoid such long queues for communion. She glanced over at Katya from time to time, and saw that she and Fanny were still getting along famously. Then she saw the pair of them going back to the organ and soon there were floating runs of notes that certainly would be beyond the skill of Fanny Neston.

Ivy felt a glow of pride. Her good deed for today, then. Now, she thought, as she noticed that the vicar's wife had melted away, I must go back to Sunday lunch to see whether Mrs Spurling has taken note of my complaint about last week's leathery chicken.

She walked up to the organ and whispered to Katya, who was in full flow, that she would see her back at Springfields. Then she walked briskly out of the church and through the sunny churchyard into the street. To her surprise, she heard a voice calling her name. She turned around and was not delighted to see Miss Beatty hurrying to catch her up.

"Good morning!" said Beattie, now in quite a different mood from the grumpy woman who had boarded the bus and scarcely acknowledged Ivy.

"Morning," said Ivy. "I must get back, I'm afraid . . ." she began, and then remembered that befriending Beattie Beatty was one of her Enquire Within tasks. There had been no opportunity at the WI, she told herself, not entirely accurately. Well, now here was another chance.

Gus Halfhide, strolling happily along to the pub with Whippy, saw the unlikely pair and grinned. Blimey, talk about body language! Not exactly bosom pals, he reckoned,

seeing the distance between them. Now why are they stepping out together, if only reluctantly? He could take a good
guess at Ivy's motive. Pumping Theo's housekeeper for
information was her assignment. But Beattie's reason for
this unlikely duo?

Whippy whimpered, and Gus looked at the emptying
church. There was Katya, deep in conversation with funny
little Miss Neston. He could see that Fanny was doing most
of the talking, but then he knew that Katya's English was
still minimal, though she seemed to understand more than
she could speak.

Katya caught sight of Gus and Whippy and waved. She
had met them several times around the village, and Gus
had always been most kind. She said good-bye to Miss
Neston and came over to make a fuss of Whippy.

"She's so pleased to see you!" Gus said. "It's a compliment, you know. Whippy chooses her friends carefully."

"What is *compliment*?"

Gus pondered. What *was* a compliment? "It's something nice that somebody says to you. Meant to make you
feel good." Well, that wasn't quite it, but it would do.

"So I must thank Whippy!" Katya said, and smoothed
the little dog's head.

"May I walk you home?" Gus said, in his best gentle-
manly manner.

"Of course," Katya said. "You are a nice person to walk
with. Is that compliment?"

MEANWHILE, IVY AND Beattie were walking slowly.
Each had decided to spin out this opportunity for probing,
and when they came to the seat outside the shop, Ivy suggested they rest in the sun for a few minutes.

"Dedicated to a Roussel, I see," Ivy said, as they
sat down.

Beattie nodded. "Mr. Theo's father," she said.

"Nice idea," Ivy said, looking closely at her companion.

"I can think of more accurate ways of remembering him," Beattie said, a touch of acid in her voice.

Ivy attempted an innocent expression. "Oh, really?" she said. "How would you remember him?"

"I'd rather not," said Beattie. "He was a rotten husband and a rotten father. Responsible for a lot of trouble in the village and on the estate." Then she clamped her lips together, making it quite clear that she had no more to say on *that* subject. But Ivy was not so easily foiled.

"His son is a lot different, so I've heard? A real gentleman, so they say up at Springfields." This was a lie, as Ivy had never heard anything of the sort. Theo Roussel was hardly ever mentioned.

Beattie visibly relaxed. "Oh, yes," she answered. "Mr. Theo is a lovely man. He is quite a private person though. Likes to sit in his study writing his memoirs and doing the *Times* crossword. Friendly, too," she embroidered. "He always asks me to help if he's stuck with a difficult clue."

What a whopper! thought Ivy. This stupid woman couldn't do the crossword in the *Women's Friend*. "He must rely on you a lot, Miss Beatty," she said.

"Oh, you can forget the 'Miss,'" Beattie said, spotting the loaded question and sidestepping it. "It is so nice to talk to somebody who is fresh to the village," she said. "What brought you here, Miss Beasley?"

Ivy did not return the invitation to use her Christian name, but said that her cousin Deirdre had organised it. "Most of my old friends are either in Heaven—or the other place—or in the local old folks home in Ringford. I wasn't happy about moving, but now I'm here I intend to make the best of it."

"Ah, yes. Your cousin Deirdre lives at Tawny Wings,

doesn't she? Such a nice person, though I don't know her well. A widow, I believe?"

"And a merry one," chuckled Ivy. She knew exactly where this was leading, and decided to give Beattie Beatty her money's worth. "When our Deirdre was young, she was a real goer, as they say. I secretly envied her, but with my mother there was no chance I could have a good time with a different lad every night, like our Deirdre."

"I am sure she settled down," Beattie said sourly. "I believe her husband owned the big garage in town?"

"Bert? Oh, yes, he was one of many. Deirdre always aimed high, mind you. Money was her goal, and if possible a title to go with it!" She chuckled again, but this time at the look on Beattie's face. "How come Mr. Theo never married?" she asked.

"It was his choice," Miss Beatty said sniffily. "As you and I know, there is a lot to be said for the unmarried state."

"Not so sure about that," Ivy said. "I had the one chance, but nothing came of it."

"Well, Mr. Theo was very popular with the girls, come to that," Beattie said defensively. "He could have married any of the eligible girls around."

"Ah, yes, of course!" Ivy said, as if she had just remembered something. "I *knew* I'd heard his name somewhere before. Must have been when we came over from Ringford to see Deirdre's family, when she was unattached and fancy-free. It was Deirdre who mentioned him. Always off out somewhere, she was! Mind you, she was a very pretty girl. Still is, in her way, don't you think?"

Miss Beatty stood up, her face thunderous. "Must be getting back," she said, and strode off without attempting a pleasant farewell.

Ivy got more slowly to her feet. She saw that Gus and Katya were approaching, and waited until they reached her. Gus immediately offered her his arm, and she took it.

"Are you all right, Ivy?" he said, feeling her arm trembling as they set off.

"Fine," she replied, and Gus realised that the old thing was shaking with laughter.

Twenty-one

DEIRDRE POTTERED ABOUT the garden, cutting roses for the drawing room and snipping off dead heads as she went. The sun was warm on her back, and she relived for the umpteenth time the couple of hours spent with Theo up at the Hall. How easy she had felt with him! That relaxed charm had not been erased by the years, and the warmth of his personality had made her feel as she had not felt since Bert died. No matter how much money she had—and she had a lot—nor how many luxuries she surrounded herself with, there was no substitute for another compatible person living alongside her, always there in good days and bad, worrying and rejoicing in turns at news from their daughters and grandchildren.

"I hate it!" she said violently, snipping off a perfectly formed rose without noticing. A blackbird sitting on the edge of the marble birdbath flew off, squawking in alarm. "I hate being alone! Why did you have to go and die, Bert? Just like you to be so selfish!"

She sat down on a beautifully carved bench, presented

to them by a grateful county council when Bert retired. Tears came to her eyes, and she let them flow. The roses fell from her hands and she cried until her handkerchief was a sodden ball.

"Now then, our Deirdre!" It was Ivy, walking with her stick across the velvety lawn towards her. "Whatever makes you give way like that, it can't be so bad that you've forgotten our meeting, surely?"

Deirdre hastily pulled herself together, and looked at her watch. "Not time yet, is it? I make it a quarter past. The meeting is not until half past, I'm sure."

"Quite right," Ivy said. "I just thought I'd walk up and collect you. Springfields can be airless on a day like this."

"Oh, well, all right then. I'll just change my shoes and be with you. Have a seat on the council bench."

Ivy laughed. Deirdre improved on better acquaintance, she thought. Some of the old family bloody-mindedness had been handed down, Ivy was pleased to note.

They walked companionably back to Springfields, and saw Gus hurrying up the street towards them, Whippy trotting along beside him.

"Morning, ladies!" he said. "How are we?"

"I don't know how *we* are," Ivy said, "but I'm very well, thanks."

"Glad to hear it," said Gus blithely.

"And I'm very well, too," Deirdre said, with a sharp look at Ivy to remind her not to say anything about earlier tears.

"Shall we convene, then?" Gus ploughed on.

"Yeah," Ivy said. "An' we can start our meeting, too."

Gus gave up. "Come on then. Can we get a cup of coffee from Mrs. S., d'you think?"

Ivy said that with the money she was paying them, Springfields should be able to come up with champagne if required.

"We'll settle for coffee," Deirdre said, rescuing Gus. He

risked a contribution. "And your nice little Katya might have been baking again, Ivy," he said. "I suppose the cleaners will have finished in your room?"

Ivy said that she had given instructions that her room must be cleaned and ready for an important meeting well before eleven o'clock. "I think you'll find all is in order," she said, mounting the stairs like a woman half her age.

The others followed, and in due course coffee and cookies were produced. "Right," said Gus, "perhaps we should start by each of us giving a report of how things stand, up to the present time. You first, maybe, Deirdre?"

He had smuggled Whippy up to Ivy's room, as it had been made very clear to him that dogs were not allowed. Now he heard Mrs. Spurling's dulcet tones along the landing, and eased Whippy under the bed. "Stay!" he said, and the little dog put back her ears, but did as she was told.

Deirdre had, of course, already told both of them about her successful visit to the Hall, but added a few details that she had remembered since. "I reckon that given time, Theo could live a perfectly active life without all that nannying he's got used to from Beattie," she said.

"She keeps him under her thumb, does she?" Gus said.

"Completely," Deirdre said. "I nipped down to the kitchen to see if the phone there was connected to the one in Theo's study. It was, of course. The kitchen one is the master phone, and Theo's is an extension. So Beattie can listen in at any time. Theo and me practised to see if he could tell I'd lifted the kitchen phone. He said he didn't hear any clicks, but the silence changed. Then I said "testing only," and he heard that all right. We had a good laugh then! I honestly don't know why he didn't sack the woman years ago."

Gus dutifully laughed, too, but Ivy said she couldn't see anything to laugh about. Listening in to other people's conversations was a serious matter, if not a criminal activity.

"Well, thank you, Deirdre," Gus said. "Now I have little

to report, except that in conversation with nice Rose Budd, I gathered that Beattie has total control of the Hall expenditure, and is as tight as a—"

"Quite enough of that, Augustus," Ivy interrupted. She looked down at Whippy, and added, "Does that dog need to go somewhere? If you ask me, cats are the best house pets. They take themselves in and out, and know when they're not wanted. I used to have one myself, until . . ." Her voice tailed off, and Deirdre was reminded that Ivy's beloved puss had gone on its final journey before she moved to Springfields.

Gus ignored Ivy's question, and said he'd left the best until last, and it was Ivy's turn to report. "You obviously had an interesting conversation with Miss Beatty yesterday after church," he said.

Ivy settled in her chair, preparing to make a good story of it, when a knock at the door interrupted her. "Come in," she said in a sharp voice.

It was Mrs. Spurling, and she apologised for disturbing them. "I have a message for you from young Mrs. Budd," she said. "Her husband came in, and I told him you were at an important meeting, but I could give you a message."

Ivy was well aware that this was revenge for her requiring her room to be ready in time. Mrs. Spurling would normally have ushered the man up to Ivy's room at once. "How understanding of you," Ivy said. "Well, go on, then. What is the message? I have no secrets from my friends here."

Mrs. Spurling hesitated. "Well, apparently Miriam Blake is ill. She won't have the doctor, and has asked that Miss Ivy Beasley should call on her as soon as possible. On no account should Mr. Halfhide try to accompany her. I think that was it," Mrs. Spurling concluded.

"Me?" said Ivy. "I scarcely know the woman. She can't just send for me like that. Don't she realise I'm a disabled old woman? Please give me her phone number, Mrs. Spurling, and I shall put her straight. What nonsense! The woman's unhinged after the death of her mother, I expect."

Mrs. Spurling backed out of the room, saying she would find Miss Blake's number and give it to Ivy at lunchtime.

"Now," Ivy said, "where was I before I was so rudely interrupted?"

"Your friendly chat with Beattie," Gus reminded her. He was puzzled. He doubted if Miriam was really ill, but her instruction that he should not go with Ivy denied the possibility that it was a ruse to get him into her clutches. Unless it was a double bluff? He would not put anything past devious Miriam.

Ivy then seemed to put the episode out of her mind, and told the other two about Beattie's obvious fury at the suggestion that Deirdre was an attractive woman, still interested in Theo, and a very determined person once she had set her sights on something.

"Ivy!" Deirdre said. "Is that entirely true?"

"Yes," Ivy replied firmly. "And old Beatrice Beatty stormed off as if an ole bull was behind her." She chuckled again at the memory. "But that wasn't all," she continued. "Before she went, we had a talk about Theo's father, and Beattie hasn't got a good word to say for him. I reckon she knows all about old Mrs. Blake an' her bun in the oven that turned out to be Miriam. *And* who the father was no doubt, Deirdre, that's why he hasn't sacked the woman years ago."

There was a silence between them, and then Gus said slowly, "Do we know exactly when Beatrice Beatty took up her job at the Hall? We need to know how old she is, where she was before she came to the Hall, and as much about her family background as possible."

"Does that have anything to do with the murder of Mrs. Blake?" Deirdre said. "And if it does, wouldn't I be the best person to find out what we need to know? From Theo, I mean. He should know all the answers."

"You don't fool me, Deirdre Bloxham," Ivy said with a laugh. She turned to Gus. "That Beattie doesn't know what she's up against," she said. "If you ask me, our Deirdre has set her sights on being the present Mrs. Hon. Roussel! Go to it, gel," she added, and patted Deirdre's arm.

Gus was out of his depth, but bravely swam on, saying he thought it was a very good idea, and as they seemed to have worked out a successful way of getting Deirdre into the Hall, they should set up another meeting as soon as possible.

"That'll be next Saturday market day, then," said Deirdre. Gus thought how very attractive she looked, her face glowing and excited. He almost felt envious of Theo Roussel, but reminded himself that he had younger fish to fry.

"So what next for me?" Ivy asked. "When I agreed to this business of ours, I expected something to occupy most of my time. So what next, Augustus?"

Gus felt that things were moving so fast he could scarcely keep up. It was a new experience for him, and he hadn't had a single sleepless night worrying about debt collectors, nor any violent urges to find the nearest racecourse and lose his shirt on a limping nag.

"Eyes and ears open, Ivy," he said. "I suggest you make yourself indispensable to one or two of the residents who have local families. Probably some of them have lived in this area all their lives. Should be mines of information. Unlike some, you're in the prime of life, Ivy," he said, hoping to flatter, "so how about offering to read romances, or play cards with those not as fortunate as you?"

"Cards?!" exploded Ivy. "Mother would turn in her grave! Cards were the work of the Devil, according to her." She frowned, and then her face cleared. "Still, she's not around, is she," she said cheerfully, for the first time ever, feeling the shadow of her mother lifting away from her. "I could even tell fortunes, at a pinch. Good idea, Augustus. I shall make a start tomorrow."

"What's wrong with this afternoon?" Deirdre said smugly. She looked at Gus. "And what about you, Gus? How are you planning to move the investigation forward?"

"Ah," said Gus. "Well, I'd rather not say until our meeting next week. I hope to have revelations for you then." A born liar, his father used to say, thought Gus sadly. But he was soon buoyant again. "Now Ivy," he said, "let's send for little Katya and see if she has any more of those delicious biscuits. You'd like a biscuit, wouldn't you, Whippy-dog?"

Ivy looked at the curled up little whippet, wrinkled her nose and pointedly opened a window. "Not biscuits, cookies," she said, and rang the bell.

Twenty-two

MIRIAM BLAKE HEARD the telephone ring, and sprang nimbly out of bed. She was fully dressed, and just remembered in time to affect an invalid voice as she picked up the receiver.

"Hello?" she quavered.

"Miss Blake?"

"Yes, who's that?"

"Miss Beasley. What's all this about a message from Mr. Budd? I am sure it must be a mistake. Well?"

"No . . . not a mistake, Miss Beasley. I do have something of a confidential nature to tell you. I can't confide in any of the old gossips, and I know you are something of a stranger here. I need some advice, Miss Beasley, and I wondered if . . ."

Her voice trailed off. Ivy frowned. What was the woman up to? With all that they now knew of her and her mother, she was deeply suspicious.

"And what's all this about being ill? Sounds like it's a doctor you need, Miss Blake. On no account do I intend to make my way down to your cottage. I suggest you—" She broke off, clearing her throat where a piece of cookie had lodged, and in that small pause she realised that information of any kind, and especially coming from the daughter of the murder victim, could well be important for Enquire Within.

"I suggest you first of all get better," she continued, "and then come up to Springfields. My room is completely private and we shall not be disturbed. When do you think that might be?" Her suspicion that the illness was faked was instantly confirmed when Miriam said she could be with Ivy by about three o'clock in the afternoon.

Ivy looked at her watch. It was nearly lunchtime, and Gus and Deirdre would be back home by now. She dialled Gus's number. Just when she was about to give up, thinking he must have called in to the pub, the receiver was lifted and she heard a voice.

"Augustus?" she said.

"Um, no," answered the voice. It was clearly a man, and Ivy felt a momentary stab of alarm.

"Who are you, then?" she asked bluntly.

"Um, just a friend. He will be back shortly."

Before Ivy could continue, there was a click and the dialling tone. She put down the receiver, and felt a shiver down her back. Why? It could have been anybody—some old friend of Gus's come to stay. Or a . . . a what? How had he got into the cottage? Gus hadn't mentioned having a guest, or even a caller. In fact, as he and Deirdre left, Ivy had heard him say he had to go up by Tawny Wings and would walk Deirdre home.

Two strange calls in one morning. Ivy shook herself. Just a coincidence, she was sure. She left her room and walked downstairs to the dining room. Remembering her new instructions, she smiled kindly at the shy old man who always sat in the corner. "Lovely day," she said, and took a seat next to him. He looked up, and she attempted a gentle tone of voice. "Do you play cards, Mr. Goodman?" His reply startled her.

"Rather!" he said. "Cribbage, Miss Beasley? I have a board in my room. Would you care for a game this afternoon?"

Ivy bristled. This was a bit sudden, wasn't it? Still, in for a penny. "Yes indeed," she said. "My father taught me long ago, but Mother disapproved of any form of gambling so we had to play when she was out."

To her horror, the supposedly shy old man reached out and patted her hand. "In this place, we have all the time in the world, my dear," he said. "Shall we say four o'clock?"

Ivy blinked. "Well," she said, "I have someone coming to see me at three. But she'll be gone by then," she added, quickly adjusting herself to this new situation. Goodness, how was she to have known that Mr. Goodman had a roving eye!?

Katya hovered, announcing lunch, and, smiling at the two elderly residents, offered to take them into the dining room.

Mr. Goodman stood up without help, offered his arm to Ivy, and refused Katya's offer of help, but in the nicest possible way.

Swept off my feet! thought Ivy in surprise, and positively glided in to lunch.

WHEN GUS RETURNED home, he opened the door and knew immediately that someone else was in the house. His long experience of undercover work had given him a sixth sense. He could feel the presence of an intruder in his private space in seconds. This had served him well in tricky situations, and now he moved forward as silently as a ghost. There was not much daylight in the cottage at the best of times, owing to tall, overhanging yew trees on the opposite side of the lane. But now it seemed extra dark.

He saw then that the curtains had been drawn across the small front window. His heart began to pound.

Nobody in the sitting room. He breathed more easily. Perhaps the intruder had beat a hasty retreat. Gus silently tiptoed up the stairs and as he put a hand out to open his bedroom door he heard the tiniest footfall behind him. He swung round, but too late. A crack on the head felled Gus to the ground. Satisfying himself that his target was unconscious, the intruder stepped over him and fled.

IN MIRIAM'S COTTAGE next door, she had left her sickbed and was watching television, at the same time eating a hearty brunch from a tray on her lap. She had hatched her plan, and now looked forward to putting it into operation. Miss Beasley was a cousin of that woman at Tawny Wings, she knew, and Miriam had decided she'd have more luck with the lonely old woman at Springfields than the rich, well-established widow.

The noise of Gus's garden gate clicking shut reached her, and she turned down the television sound. By the time she had put down her tray and got to the window, there was nobody to be seen. But wait a minute, by craning her head round the lace curtain she spotted a figure moving very fast along the footpath that edged the wood a hundred yards up the lane. Man or woman? Too far away to tell, she decided, and went back to the television. It was not Gus, she was sure of that. Ah, well, her neighbour was still a bit of a puzzle, but he reckoned without Miriam's cunning! All those years living with her mother had sharpened her wits, and she grinned to herself. Miss Beasley was the one. Sitting up at Springfields like an old spider, she would be the one.

Twenty-three

GUS STIRRED, AND shrieked with pain. His head felt the size of a beach ball, and even a tiny movement stabbed him with sharp knives. Waves of nausea overcame him, and he blacked out. When he briefly became aware again, it was dark, and he had no idea where he was, nor did he much care. He drifted back into a blessed state of unknowing.

When he surfaced again, he was aware of a distant knocking sound. With huge difficulty he struggled to his feet, felt overwhelmingly faint and put out a hand to save himself from falling. The banister at the top of the stairs supported him, and he felt his way slowly along the landing, and stopped. Now he had his bearings, and knew that his next step would send him hurtling downwards. He tried out his voice, and that seemed to be working.

"Who is it?" He tried desperately to control his nausea, and sat down on the top stair.

"Me! Deirdre! Gus, are you there? Are you all right?"

He shook his head, and then wished he hadn't. Another step. Very carefully, he made his way down and managed to reach the front door before collapsing on the *Welcome* doormat.

Deirdre pushed the door open until she could just squeeze inside. At the sight of Gus, prostrate in front of her, she gasped, but being first and foremost a practical woman, she pulled her mobile from her pocket and dialled 999. "Gus! Speak to me," she begged.

He opened one eye and said hoarsely, "Has he gone?" Then he passed out again, and Deirdre cradled his poor head in her arms, praying for the ambulance to turn up.

IVY HAD HAD a busy day, but was still up and about, not feeling at all like sleep. First the Blake woman, who had called as promised and sat, looking the picture of health, in Ivy's best chair, nattering on about nothing very much, until Ivy had pointedly asked what exactly *was* the advice she needed. Miriam Blake had then said people were being horrible to her, not exactly accusing her of killing her mother, but dropping such heavy hints that she had begun to avoid conversations in the village. What should she do? It was making her so miserable. Ivy had said she was sure that once the real murderer had been found, all would be well. Miriam would just have to put up with it. Then the questions began. Why had Ivy come to Barrington? Was she close to her cousin at Tawny Wings? Had they grown up together, and been teenaged friends? And on and on, until Ivy became thoroughly annoyed and had more or less shown her the door.

Then on to her game of crib with Mr. Goodman, and while waiting for him to decide which card to play, she had pondered on Miriam Blake's motives. It was Deirdre, of course, who had been the subject of most of the questions. Deirdre Bloxham, attractive and rich, a merry widow and old flame of Theo Roussel.

"Penny for them?" Mr. Goodman had said, playfully

wagging his finger at her. She had gritted her teeth and concentrated on the game. She had won, of course, and left his room promising to have the return match with him very soon. He had said a few interesting things already, and she needed to follow them up.

Finally, settling between her cool sheets, she had said her prayers and reported to the Almighty that life at Springfields was looking up.

IT SEEMED ONLY a couple of hours later that she was awoken by her telephone ringing. She looked at her bedside clock and saw that it was already eight o'clock.

"Ivy? It's Deirdre. Can you be ready by half past nine? We have to go into the General Hospital in Tresham. Gus has had an accident. I found him, and the ambulance men were brilliant. We need to see him. I'll pick you up half nine. Bye."

Ivy had not moved so fast for a long time, and by nine fifteen she had washed, dressed, breakfasted and was waiting in the reception hall for Deirdre to collect her.

The grand car cruised to a halt, and Deirdre came swiftly up the path. "Ivy?" she shouted as she opened the door.

"I'm ready," said Ivy. She called to Mrs. Spurling that she did not know when she would be back, but not to worry about lunch, and then the pair were moving off at speed towards Tresham.

Mrs. Spurling frowned. This could not go on. Springfields was supposed to be for the elderly and infirm. Miss Beasley was certainly elderly, but not at all infirm! She treated the place like a hotel, issuing orders right, left and centre, and obeying none of the rules that made the home run like clockwork.

She turned to go back into her office, and saw Katya waiting for her. The girl was not looking happy, and

Mrs. Spurling wondered if Miss Beasley had been sharp with her. But on asking her outright if this was so, Katya had said, "No, of course not! Miss Beasley is very kind to me and makes me feel homely. She is an interesting person, do you not think, Mrs. Spurling?"

"Then is something else bothering you?"

Katya hesitated. "Nice Mr. Goodman. He asks for Lands' End catalogue? Is this clothes? I did not understand all he say, but he points to his coat and says it is 'boring.' Is this right? I am not sure. . . ."

"Nor am I, Katya! Still, some of our residents do make odd requests from time to time. Just tell him you have ordered a catalogue, but don't do it. He'll have forgotten about it by tomorrow. We really cannot add to the mountain of junk mail we receive every morning. A genuine, hand-written letter for a resident is quite a rarity, unfortunately."

"Thank you, Mrs. Spurling. Was that Mrs. Bloxham collecting Miss Beasley? It is great *compliment*—is that right?—to Springfields that Miss Beasley is so happy and, er, busy, is it not?"

Mrs. Spurling suggested that Katya might have some work to get on with, and sat down again at her desk. A compliment, was it? Something she might add to the Springfields prospectus? "All our residents are happy, busy people, etc., etc." Yes, it sounded very positive. Perhaps Miss Ivy Beasley might be regarded as an asset after all. She picked up the pile of charity demands and catalogues delivered this morning, and without looking at any of them, tipped them straight into the wastepaper basket.

THE CAR PARK spaces were not really wide enough for the Rolls, so Deirdre parked across two, saying they were lucky to find any spaces at all. They had hardly exchanged a word on the journey, too shocked and concerned with their own thoughts. Finally Deirdre said, "Usually the whole wretched car park is full, with weeping drivers going round and round knowing they are missing their appointments."

"And then you have to pay if you do find a space," said Ivy, noticing the machine for tickets. "Daylight robbery," she said. "If you ask me, it's exploiting the sick and disabled."

Deirdre locked the car and they headed for the main entrance. There were queues everywhere: for the reception desk, the public telephones, the snack bar with its coffee machine and sad array of buns and biscuits, and, when Deirdre and Ivy finally found out where they should go, there was a long impatient queue for the lifts.

"He is sleeping at the moment," said the nurse, as they found Burton ward. "You can sit by him for a bit, but don't try to wake him. He needs rest and quiet."

As Ivy looked around and heard the cacophony of sounds that exists in most hospital wards, she doubted if Gus would be very peaceful in here. As soon as he was able, she would arrange for him to have a week or so in Springfields. He would mend quickly then, she was sure.

Both women were shaken as they looked at Gus, his face twitching as he mumbled in his sleep.

"My God," said Deirdre quietly, "he made a proper job of it, silly fool."

Ivy shook her head. "Did you call the police?" Deirdre said no, she had just got the ambulance as quickly as possible.

"I had this feeling that Gus might not want the police involved," she said.

"Sshh!" Ivy said, and then added in a stage whisper, "He's coming round!"

Gus, now sedated and relatively pain free, opened his eyes, and then quickly shut them again. It couldn't be, could it? He must be hallucinating. Then he heard Ivy's voice, and knew they were really there beside his bed.

"Augustus, it is only Deirdre and me. You've been getting up to mischief, I see."

Mischief! Gus tried a caustic reply, but the effort was too much, so he just sighed. After all, it was early in the morning, and the two must have set out very promptly to come and see him.

"You just lie quiet," continued Ivy, "and we'll do the talking."

"But Ivy," Deirdre interrupted. "We were supposed not to disturb him."

"I don't intend to disturb him," Ivy said, straightening her skirt as she sat down on a chair brought by a young nurse. "There are only two things I want to say, Augustus. First, I shall make sure you are looked after properly when you come out of here. And second, our nice little Katya sent you her . . ." She hesitated, and then said firmly, "Well, she said her love, but I'm sure she meant her kind regards."

Twenty-four

"BUT THERE ARE no vacancies at Springfields at the moment," Mrs. Spurling said that evening.

She faced Ivy, who had asked for a couple of weeks' tender loving care for Gus when he was discharged from the hospital. "We are not a convalescent home, you know," she added. "I do have rules to obey, Miss Beasley."

"Rules are made to be broken," said Ivy firmly, "but if you insist, I'll stay with Mrs. Bloxham at Tawny Wings. Then Mr. Halfhide can have my room. I don't have to tell you that you disappoint me. I thought you'd be more sympathetic. I wouldn't like to have to take myself elsewhere for good. . . ."

Katya had been sorting a pile of magazines on a small table nearby, and had overheard the conversation. She turned with a red face and said, "Excuse me, Mrs. Spurling, but Mr. Halfhide must have my room. I can kip down—is that right?—with Anya for two weeks. She is my friend, Miss Beasley," she explained. "We came together for working at Springfields. My things I put in cupboards for some days."

Ivy was seldom surprised, but this was a real turnup. Then she remembered Gus's way with the girls, and understood. She would have to keep an eye on this. The girl was young and far from home. Ivy felt some sense of responsibility for her, and made a note to warn off the predatory Augustus.

"Very well, Katya," said Mrs. Spurling, secretly relieved to have a sensible solution presented to her. She just hoped there wasn't a union for these foreign workers who would cause trouble. Health and safety rules were bad enough. Still, it would be for only a short time. "You may tell Mr. Halfhide we shall expect him when he is well enough not to need nursing. This is not a nursing home, as you know, Miss Beasley."

"Some residential homes," Ivy said grandly, "have a guest room. I've been told the Beeches in Collsthorpe has a lovely guest room for friends of residents who come from a long way away."

Mrs. Spurling was tempted to suggest Miss Beasley take herself off to the Beeches as soon as possible, and good riddance. But it was more than her job was worth, so she turned on her heel and headed for the kitchens, calling for Miss Pinkney as she went.

NEXT MORNING, GUS was feeling very much better. "Poor old Spurling," he said, as he sat up in bed listening to Deirdre, who had been talking to Ivy before she popped in to see Gus for a few minutes. She was a practised hospital visitor, having spent hours with Bert on many occasions before he died. But with Gus, half an hour was quite long enough to keep conversation going in the artificial atmosphere of a hospital ward. In any case, although he was obviously much improved, he still looked tired and wan.

"Anyway," continued Deirdre, "Ivy said she had thanked Katya for her kind offer. She also said she reckoned the girl had a crush on you, and she expected you to be very careful to discourage her."

Deirdre was pleased to see colour come into Gus's cheeks, and she laughed. "I told her you didn't need to cradle-snatch. Plenty more mature fish in the sea."

"Lead me to them," Gus said. "A bouncing blonde would be just the thing to restore me to health and vigour . . . *and* to save me from the clutches of Miriam Blake."

"How about the very lovely Beatrice Beatty?" Deirdre said. "That would leave Theo for me. What could be more romantic?" She paused for a moment, and then said that she had to ask him a serious question. Gus's face fell. "Fire away," he said.

"Have you any idea who was in your cottage waiting to attack you? You said three words when I found you on the mat: 'Has he gone?' Then you passed out again."

"Ah," he said calmly, "yes, I have an idea, but I don't think he was expecting me to return so soon. He'd have been after my papers, notes I made a couple of years ago. I'm sure he clonked me one so's he could get away fast."

Deirdre raised her eyebrows. "Must have been very important papers?" she said. "Important enough for you not to tell the local police about an intruder?"

"Got it in one, clever Deirdre. Although the case was closed, there were some questions left unanswered, and those who were caught and duly punished were after evidence to get them off the hook. And I'm afraid that's all I can say. Perhaps we could leave it there, all three of us? Confidentiality, you know. All people need to know is that I fell downstairs and knocked myself out."

"Pooh! You mean you like having a glamorous past! Well, I shall say no more, and I'll keep what you told me to myself. But I can't help being curious, especially as I can't believe a word you say."

"Time's up, Mrs. Bloxham," said an approaching nurse.

"Gus is much better, but we don't want to prejudice his chances of going home, do we?"

"Not going home," said Gus, grateful for the interruption. "My friend has arranged for two weeks' luxury care at Springfields residential home. But when I do go home I mean to be careful not to trip myself up again, especially going downstairs."

The nurse knew that his notes told a different story, but she tactfully did not contradict him. Deirdre, too, remembered her promise, and reluctantly nodded her head.

"You'll die of boredom in Springfields!" the nurse said. She quite fancied Gus. Charming man, all the girls had agreed.

"Best possible thing to get him going again," said Deirdre, rising to her feet. "He'll not be able to get away from the demon whist players and juicy jellies fast enough."

MIRIAM BLAKE HAD cadged a lift from Rose Budd, who was going supermarket shopping in Tresham. The four-by-four smelt of sheep, and Rose's little son was doing his best to fight his way out of the safety harness, but Miriam steeled herself. There was no other means of transport. No buses today, and it was too far to even think of cycling.

She had been horrified when she heard about Gus's accident. The stairs in her own cottage were lethal. Her mother had never stopped complaining about them. Miriam dreamed of a modern bungalow, one of those for elderly people up in the village. She knew that the rules could be bent to allow younger, needy people to rent the bungalows, and once the murder thing had settled down she intended to put herself on the list. She would feel safe there.

Now she had put on her best dress and shoes, and meant to visit Gus in the hospital. She would be her sweetest self and be sure to capture his affection while he was vulnerable and lonely. She hummed a little tune, and looked out at the passing landscape.

"You sound happy, Miriam," Rose said. She didn't like her, but felt sorry for the woman who was now alone and thought by too many of the villagers to have done in her old mother. There was some sympathy for Miriam Blake, however, as Rose had discovered whilst waiting to be served in the village shop. Three old tabs had been gossiping and reckoned that Miriam's mother had been a nasty old woman, selfish and stingy, and had made her daughter's life a misery.

"It's nice to get out of the village," replied Miriam. "Shame we haven't got more buses. Still, when everything's sorted out, I'm hoping to get myself a little car, then I'll be more mobile."

"You'd have to take a test, of course," said Rose.

"Oh no, dear," Miriam answered. "When I was working as a telephonist, I had a nice little Ford. Passed my test first time, and buzzed about very happily. It was after Mother fell ill, when I had to give up work and could hardly ever leave her, that I decided to sell it. Not worth the licence an' insurance an' all that. I was a bit sad," she said, and then added that the car had been a present from an admirer.

Rose decided this was a joke, and then was distracted by seeing her son nearly upside down in the backseat, still anchored to his harness. "Can you straighten him out, Miriam? Thank goodness we're nearly there."

Miriam gave Simon a surreptitious push, harder than was necessary, and got him upright. "Perhaps he'd like a sweet?" she asked. She had very little experience of small children, but remembered that sweeties were always popular. She pulled out a packet of fiercely spiced Fisherman's Friend cough sweets, and Rose was only just quick enough to prevent her giving one of them to her precious toddler. "Here we are!" she said brightly, and came to a halt with relief in the supermarket car park.

"See you at half past four, then," Miriam said. "I can get a bus up to the hospital. Only takes five minutes, and they're really frequent. Bye, have a nice shop!" She marched off cheerfully, and Rose lifted out Simon and set him down. "There we are, my love," she said. "You can't help feeling sorry for Mr. Halfhide, can you!"

"Sweeties," said Simon distinctly.

Twenty-five

"ANOTHER VISITOR, GUS!" the nurse said. "Have you got a fan club, or what?"

Gus's heart sank when he saw his greatest fan walking humbly towards his bed, clutching a large bunch of red roses. Must have cost her a fortune, he thought. He did not miss the significance of red roses, and was not sure that he felt strong enough to resist her advances.

"Nurse," he whispered urgently.

"Need the loo?" she said, bending down to listen.

"No. Get rid of this one as soon as poss, if you don't want a relapse on your hands."

The nurse straightened up. "Good afternoon," she said sternly. "I am afraid Mr. Halfhide is feeling rather tired at the moment. We have to be careful with this sort of injury, so please limit your visit to not more than ten minutes. Thank you, dear," she added kindly, smitten with conscience at the way Miriam's face fell.

"Miriam," said Gus weakly. "How nice of you to come and see me. Sit down on that chair. As nurse says, I am not so good at the moment, but just tired. You do the talking. Tell me what's new in Barrington."

Miriam was reassured. She smiled lovingly at him and launched on a long account of the iniquities of Beattie Beatty, who had summoned her to the Hall and more or less told her she would either have to pay more rent, or find another place to live.

"And what's more," she added, "the increase in my rent is ridiculous. I can't possibly afford that much, and the old devil knows it. I shall be looking for a job, of course, but it's not that easy when you've been out of circulation for so long."

Gus realised that this could lead somewhere interesting, and called to a passing nurse. "Would you be able to find us a cup of tea?" he said, with his winning smile. "I'm feeling a bit better now, and I'm sure Miss Blake would like one."

Miriam flushed and said that it must be her presence that had bucked him up so quickly. "I shall come again soon," she said.

"Stay for your tea," Gus said. "I'm so sorry about the rent increase. Couldn't you see Mr. Roussel about it? He must be able to override Beattie's decisions, surely?" After all, he remembered, Miriam had been Theo's bran tub for quite a while. And, of course, she was a blood relation. He wondered again if Beattie knew this.

"Not likely!" Miriam accepted her tea, and smiled at the nurse. "Got any more patients who need reviving?" she said confidently. "Look at Mr. Halfhide here! A new man, don't you think?"

The nurse—the original warning one—blenched. God, who was this woman? Still, Gus did look more alert. She would have a word with him later.

"You were saying that Theo wouldn't reverse old Beattie's decision?"

"No, she rules the roost. I've watched it happen, Gus. When she first came, she was all meek and mild like an old cow. Well, she is an old cow!" She laughed at her own wit, and continued. "Then gradually she began to tighten her hold on him. Made him rely on her for everything. She took over more and more of the estate jobs, until finally he turned the management over to her and claimed to be spending all his time writing."

"Writing what?"

"His memoirs, *she* says."

"Should make interesting reading, Miriam," he said, with a suggestive look.

She narrowed her eyes. "None of my business," she said shortly. "Now, I'd better be going, else that nurse dragon will be after me."

"One more question," Gus said, and she looked hopeful. Was it going to be THE question? No, it wasn't. Gus just asked her if she would check that Will at the shop was still happy to look after Whippy. Deirdre had taken her home, but gratefully handed her over to Will when he had offered, saying that Whippy would be useful keeping the mice out of his storeroom.

Disappointed, Miriam said that she was sure the dog was fine. "Would you like me to come again?" she asked, feeling that she had not really had her money's worth.

"Oh, I hope to be out very shortly, but thanks for coming today," he said firmly.

"Good-bye, then," she answered, and walked slowly out of the ward. That was a bit ungrateful, wasn't it? Those roses had cost a fortune. Just as well she had finally found the nest egg. Mother had thought she was so clever, tucking the brown envelope down the back of the wardrobe. But I am cleverer, she congratulated herself. Clever enough not to tell anybody about it. Especially Beattie Beatty, who thought she could outwit a Blake as easy as pie.

But Miriam already had a plan, and as she went down the stone steps of the hospital to catch the bus back to the supermarket, she began to hum again. Gus had been really nice to her! He was part of her plan, and now she felt much happier about him.

HALFWAY BACK TO Barrington, with Simon asleep in his seat, Rose remembered what Miriam had said. She had owned a car, and it had been a present from an admirer. Blimey! Some admirer!

"You know you said about your little car that you sold," Rose said. Miriam was once more humming and looking out of the window.

"Yes, I really miss it now," she said, turning back to Rose. "Should have kept it, I suppose, but I thought the money would come in useful."

"That admirer of yours must have been very keen," Rose said. "What happened?"

"Mother happened," Miriam said. "It was a real drama, an' I never really got to the bottom of it. She was all for this man of mine, and then suddenly she turned against him. Put a stop to him visiting, and said I was to have no more to do with him."

"But surely in this day and age . . ."

"Oh, I know. I should've stood up to her. But you never knew how she could be. On and on she'd go, in that whiny voice of hers, until I'd have agreed to anything. I suppose you'd call it emotional blackmail. Dad was dead by then, and she claimed he was turning in his grave. I know! It was all rubbish. But I took the easy way out."

"Was he a local man? Did you have to go on seeing him around?"

Miriam nodded. "It was painful," she said. "I'd rather not talk about it, if you don't mind, Rose. Look, we're nearly home and there's your David waiting for us. Shall I tickle young Simon and wake him up?"

* * *

BEATTIE SET THE dining table for one, and banged the gong in the hall on her way back to the kitchen. Mr. Theo liked the old customs to be kept going, though she often thought he would be much happier having supper in the warm kitchen with her. She could put a nice armchair in there, next to the Aga, and he could spend the evening reading the *Times* and doing the crossword. Ah well, a girl could dream, couldn't she?

She took in the first course, steak and kidney pie with tinned mushy peas—his favourite—and paused.

"Yes, Beattie? Was there something?"

"I have been wondering about your new tenant, Mr. Halfhide. Did I tell you he had had an accident in the cottage, and hurt himself badly enough to be in the hospital?"

"Good heavens, no! You did not tell me, Beattie. When was this?"

She told him and said she was wondering whether he would like her to visit Mr. Halfhide in the hospital. Representing him, of course, she stressed.

"I am perfectly capable of visiting him myself," said the new Theo. "Ask Budd to check the car. I shall go in tomorrow. Rather a nice chap, Augustus Halfhide. Sorry about the accident. Have to get somebody to look at the stairs. Don't want to lose him, you know. A good tenant, and pays a realistic rent."

Beattie could not resist the opening. "Unlike Miss Blake," she said. "I have had a word with her, as discussed, and she was not helpful, I'm afraid. Says she means to find a job, but it'll be difficult. She threatened lawyers and so on, but I doubt if she has a leg to stand on."

"This delicious pie will be getting cold," Theo said, dismissing her. "By the way," he added, "are these peas tinned?"

"Yes, as always, Mr. Theo."

"I should think you have plenty enough time to prepare

mushy peas yourself. See what you can do next time," he said, and began to eat.

Beattie fumed. He always had them tinned! Ages ago, he had said nobody could do mushy peas like the tinned ones, which he much preferred. She turned on her heel and stamped her way back to the kitchen. As she sat at the big wooden table, gobbling the pie and peas in angry haste, she decided he'd been strange for the last few days. Stubborn, where he used to be so malleable. What could have happened? She thought back, and reckoned she had first noticed the difference when she came back from market last Saturday. Had Rose Budd, or Rosebud, as he called her, pushed her luck too far with him?

"A word with Mrs. Rose Budd, I think," she said aloud, and the old green parrot in his cage in the corner echoed her. "Rosebud, Rosebud, who's a pretty Rosebud?" he cackled.

UPSTAIRS, THEO FELT rebellion stirring. Beattie really was getting too uppity! It was his own fault, of course. He had let her take over everything, including himself, but now he felt like a man recovering from a long and serious illness. Time to sack the nurse? God, how marvellous it would be if he could get rid of her altogether! He would have to get used to running the estate himself, of course, but that shouldn't be too difficult. He was absolutely sure her files and records would be in good order.

He looked around his room, at family photographs and portraits, and sadly came to his senses. Beattie was family. She had made herself so, and more than once had hinted at tales she could tell. And then again, she could be very sweet to him on good days. What would the poor woman do, if he sacked her? Where would she go?

Not yet, he told himself. Maybe later. Definitely later, when he could work out some kind way of doing it. Meantime, he was quite enjoying the subterfuge!

Twenty-six

NORMALLY A METHODICAL girl, Katya found herself muddling up her personal possessions, putting books in with boots and makeup in her wash bag. Her mind was not on the job, she told herself. She could think of little else but the exciting prospect of having Gus Halfhide sleeping in her room for two whole weeks. She would be able to pop in to see him, and help him down the stairs when he was ready. She would bake cookies for him from the recipe book her mother had insisted on giving her, sure that in England her daughter would find nothing nice to eat and consequently starve.

Finally her room was empty of all belongings, sparkling clean and cool, with fresh curtains billowing in the breeze from the open window. Mrs. Spurling had said that Mrs. Bloxham would be bringing Mr. Halfhide from the hospital to Springfields around eleven o'clock. "It is kind of you, Katya," she had said, "to give up your room. I will make sure he is gone after the two weeks. Miss Beasley is insisting on paying for the room while he is here, so I have decided to give this extra fee to you. It will be a nest egg for you."

Never mind about nest eggs! thought Katya. She had seen some really lovely clothes in Tresham's finest shop. How nice of Mrs. Spurling! She would work extra hard to please her.

"Oh, just one more thing," Mrs. Spurling said. "I shall be glad if you will keep the matter of the extra money to yourself, Katya. Have you understood? Do . . . not . . . tell . . . anybody . . . about . . . the . . . extra . . . money . . . I . . . shall . . . be . . . giving . . . you," she added with emphasis. "The others might be jealous."

Katya nodded and said she understood. She did understand the words, but had no idea why she had to keep it secret. Still, that was no problem for her. She shut the door on the immaculate room and went downstairs and into the garden. A few roses would cheer him up, she was sure.

DEIRDRE HELPED GUS into the passenger seat of her car, and covered his legs with a soft tartan rug.

"For God's sake, Deirdre!" he said. "I only had a bash on the head! And it's not as if we're in the middle of winter. Here, fold it up and keep it for the next deserving case."

Deirdre laughed. "Make the most of it, Gus," she said. "The charitable impulse is soon exhausted. Now, back to Barrington," she said. She looked at her watch. "Just time for a quick gin at Tawny Wings before I surrender you to the care of Mrs. Spurling."

"Better not," he answered. "I don't want to arrive smelling of gin. Ivy's bound to notice, if nobody else does. No, we'll have a celebration drink this evening. Is alcohol allowed?"

"Not sure," said Deirdre, "but if it's not, our Ivy will

change the rules. She's developed a taste for a small sweet sherry before supper."

They talked idly on the way back to Barrington, speculating on who Gus's intruder might be. "You haven't told us much about your past," Deirdre said bluntly. "What exactly did you do?"

"I told Miriam, and I thought I had told you. No mystery about it. I was an investigative journalist, among other things."

Deirdre laughed. "Yeah, and what else?" she said.

Gus looked at her. "I'm telling the truth, Deirdre," he said. "I was working undercover. Sworn to secrecy of course. Solemn oath, and all that. But I made a few enemies on the way."

"So you think one of them might be after you?" Deirdre could still not be sure she believed him.

"Possible," said Gus. "It's happened before."

"Is that why you came to Barrington? Hiding away from trouble?"

"There's never a real hideaway," he said, "but yes, I did think our village would be remote enough, especially if I kept my head down. Ho hum!"

"You reckoned without the gossips network. It was all round the village a couple of days after you arrived. Anybody in the shop or the pub could have picked up all the details of the new tenant in Hangman's Row. The one with the funny name. Is it your real name, by the way?"

"Don't ask," replied Gus. "I've had so many, I've forgotten which is the real one."

They drew up outside Springfields, and Deirdre helped Gus out of the car. "Just look a bit feeble," she whispered in his ear, "else old Spurling will have you out on your ear, Ivy or no Ivy."

A small reception committee awaited Gus. Mrs. Spurling stood with a fixed smile, while on her left was Katya, with a dazzling smile, and on her right, Ivy looked on impassively as Deirdre manoeuvred Gus through the swing doors.

"Welcome, Mr. Halfhide," greeted Mrs. Spurling, as Katya rushed forward to help a wobbly-looking Gus. Ivy's voice was sharp as she said that she was sure that Gus would prefer not to be fussed. "After all," she added, echoing his own words, "he only had a bang on the head."

"There is always a danger of concussion," Mrs. Spurling reprimanded Ivy. "We can't be too careful, can we, Mr. Halfhide?" She thought privately that the man was making the most of his opportunity, but Miss Beasley was paying well, so her protégé would get the best that Springfields could offer.

Gus himself was thinking that Ivy was quite wrong. He was looking forward to being fussed as much as possible, especially by young Katya. How pretty she looked, with her pink cheeks and hair neatly brushed into a ponytail! He took a couple of steps forward, and was surprised to find he genuinely felt weak. He accepted Katya's arm gratefully, and Mrs. Spurling said he should go straight to his room. She would send up coffee and biscuits, and the two ladies could join him there, if they wished.

Deirdre took his other arm, and he winked at her. "So kind," he murmured, and she squeezed his arm until it hurt. "Don't overdo it," she whispered, and they continued on their slow way up the stairs.

Katya vanished once Gus was settled, but reappeared ten minutes later with a tray of coffee. "Specially baked for you, Mr. Halfhide," she said, handing round a plate of golden cookies.

"Does that mean *we* can't have one?" Deirdre said, smiling.

"No, it means that Katya is following the aims of

Springfields Residential Home, to make *all* its guests welcome and comfortable," Ivy said severely.

The three investigators of Enquire Within chatted desultorily for a short while, and then Gus said, "Right. So where are we, ladies? Shall we have a summing up of the situation so far? Start with what we do know, and then we'll make a plan for finding out what we don't know. Would you like to begin, Ivy?"

"Augustus," Ivy said gently, "you ain't quite right yet, my dear. Since you went in to the hospital, Deirdre and me have spent time visiting you, arranging for you to come here for a bit, an' I for one haven't given much thought to Enquire Within."

Deirdre nodded. "Most important thing is to get you better. I haven't got anything new to report."

Gus looked smug. "Well, I have," he said. "A small thing like a bash on the head doesn't bother Augustus Halfhide. Duty first, I was told when I first got into this investigating business." Well, that was not far from the truth, he excused himself.

"So what secrets did the nursing staff of the hospital reveal to you?"

"It wasn't a nurse. It was Miriam Blake," he said with a smirk. "My delightful next-door neighbour. She came to see me, bearing red roses."

"Coo-er!" said Deirdre.

"And as we talked of this and that, she mentioned that Beatrice Beatty is trying to get rid of her."

"What!?" chorused Deirdre and Ivy.

"Oh, not that," Gus said. "No, of course not, you sillies. No, she wants Miriam out of her cottage. The rent is small, from when her mother was alive. Now Beattie has first of all put up the rent to an astronomical amount—"

"So Miriam Blake said to me," interrupted Ivy.

"—and Miriam can't and won't pay it. She has told

Beattie she will see a lawyer if necessary. I think she is quite enjoying facing the Beatty woman."

"What about Theo?" Deirdre asked. "Can't he intervene?"

"Not according to Miriam. She says what we all know already, that Theo is putty in Beattie's hands. He leaves everything to her."

"Except his money, we hope," said Deirdre. "Anyway, I'll see what I can do next Saturday when I go to see him. I reckon the worm will just about have started to turn."

"There's more," said Gus, helping himself to another cookie. "Miriam said she remembered Beattie in the early days. When she first came to the Hall she was mouse-like. Did exactly what she was told, and never ventured an opinion. There were rumours went round the village that there was something bad in her past. But gradually things changed, according to Miriam. Finally, Theo had more or less handed over everything to Beattie to manage, and it's been like that ever since."

Ivy sat up like a ramrod in her chair. "Did you say something *bad* in her past? Did Miriam say what it was?"

"I asked, but she said the rumour died down, and in the end got forgotten."

"But not by Miriam," Ivy said. "Write that down, Deirdre. Question for Miss Blake."

"This is not a meeting, Ivy," Deirdre said, checking on Gus, who was looking really tired now.

"Just a memo," Ivy said blandly. "We might forget. Then we must leave him to get some rest. He's beginning to look a bit peaky."

Gus protested that he was fine, but Ivy was firm. "Come along, Deirdre," she said. "I've had a letter from our cousin in Thailand I want to show you. See you later, Gus. You might feel like coming downstairs to meet Mr. Goodman. He's eighty-six and has lived in Barrington all his life."

Oh, how lovely, groaned Gus to himself, but then he remembered that Ivy was paying for all this, and he felt obliged to sing for his supper. "That would be very nice," he said.

"WE HAVEN'T GOT a cousin in Thailand," Deirdre said, as they went along to Ivy's room.

"I know we haven't," Ivy said. "I just wanted to get you away. Poor Augustus was wilting."

"Yes, well, he's quite a tough flower," Deirdre said huffily. "What do you really want?"

"I want to know if you are really visiting Theo Roussel this Saturday, because if you are, the weather forecast is not good and I am certainly not sitting on the seat outside the shop in the pouring rain so that you can cuddle up to the squire on the sofa."

"Ivy!" Deirdre stared angrily at her, then suddenly burst out laughing. "You are a tonic, Ivy," she said. "Thank goodness you decided to come and live in Barrington. You'd be wasted mouldering away in Ringford."

"I don't moulder," said Ivy. "But I'll give you this, Deirdre Bloxham, life at Springfields is very far from what I expected! And this is mostly due to Augustus. We two would have mouldered away, as you put it, in this village like any other village. WI, church, market day in town, whist and cribbage. Nothing more exciting than what I've been doing all my life. But now, well, you know . . ."

This was a long speech for Ivy, and Deirdre was amazed to see that she was actually blushing. Ivy blushing! What was it about Gus? she thought. He was not really conventionally attractive. Skinny body, thin gingery hair all over the place, oddly uncoordinated in his movement. But his smile was warm, and made you feel good.

"So," said Ivy, back to her sharp self, "we must keep going. On second thoughts, I shall be able to shelter from the rain in the shop, and can see Beattie safely on the bus. And you must remember you're at the Hall to find out as much as you can about Beattie before she came to work there. Theo must know a bit about it. He wasn't always a recluse."

"He certainly wasn't," said Deirdre. "Not by a long chalk. Leave him to me, Ivy. Enquire Within is on the warpath."

Twenty-seven

GUS, WITH HIS shoes off and stretched out on the counterpane of his comfortable bed, slept more soundly than he had for weeks. He did not wake up until a light tapping at his door caused him to look at the clock beside him. It was six o'clock, and the sun was in the west, shining low through his drawn curtains.

"Who is it?" he called sleepily.

"Katya. May I come in, Mr. Halfhide?"

Gus hastily ran his hands through his scrappy hair and rubbed his eyes. "Of course," he replied, and Katya poked her head round the door. "Supper in fifteen minutes," she said. "You like supper here? Or to come down the stairs and be happy with the others?"

Gus laughed delightedly. "Oh, I must come down and be happy with the others," he said, and swung his legs off the bed. "Oh, steady on, Gus," he said. "Still a bit dizzy, I'm afraid, Katya," he added, and stretched out his hand. She immediately came forward and took his arm. "Let me help you," she said. "Perhaps you sit in the chair? I will put on your shoes."

She was kneeling down tying his shoelaces when Mrs. Spurling entered.

"I'll do that," she said abruptly. Katya stood up, red in the face, and rushed out of the room. Mrs. Spurling looked Gus straight in the eye.

"It will be good for you to tie your own shoelaces, Mr. Halfhide," she said. "Or if you can't manage— genuinely—we can find you a pair of slippers to wear while you are here. Katya is a vulnerable young girl. I believe I do not have to say any more. Now, will you be all right to come down for supper? Take it steadily. The exercise is necessary for your recovery." She marched out of the room without further comment.

Suitably chastened, Gus arrived in the dining room and saw Ivy beckoning to him. She was sitting at a table by the window, with a neatly groomed little man next to her. Gus sat down carefully, and Ivy said she was glad to see he was looking rested.

"This is Mr. Goodman," she continued, and turned to the old man. "And this is Mr. Halfhide. He is a friend of mine, recuperating from a nasty accident."

Gus thought a spot of informality would warm the atmosphere, and said he would much rather be Gus than Mr. Halfhide. He looked enquiringly at Mr. Goodman.

"Good idea," the old man said, "I'm Roy. They ask you in here if you'd like to be known by your Christian name and I said yes. But it made no difference. They all call me Mr. Goodman. Because of my great age." He chuckled, and added that he was a boy at heart. "Always a boy at heart," he repeated, and smiled warmly at Ivy.

She ignored him, and said she understood that cod was on the menu for this evening. She could recommend it, she told Gus. "Fried in batter," she said.

"With chips?" said Gus.

"Of course," said Roy delightedly. Here was a man after his own heart. "Do you play cards, Gus?" he said. "We usually have a game of whist after supper."

Gus frowned. "Pontoon's my game," he said, looking warily at Ivy.

"*Vingt-et-un*," she said, with a decidedly English accent. "Dad was an excellent player. And we always played for matches," she added firmly.

"Fine," said Roy, producing a box of Swan Vestas from his pocket. He was a pipe smoker, but it was not allowed at Springfields. He kept the matches in his pocket as a comforter and would hold them in the palm of his hand when feeling down.

Now he said that a game of pontoon would be marvellous. He felt brighter than he had for ages, and hoped the Lands' End catalogue would arrive soon. He noticed that Gus had a most attractive jacket. Perhaps he would get one like that. Maybe Ivy would help him choose, though he suspected she had very conservative tastes.

The cod arrived, and Gus was pleased to see a full bottle of tomato ketchup on the table. "Great!" he said. "Let's get stuck in."

THE GAMBLING THREESOME was the object of great interest in the lounge after supper. Four ladies, all somberly dressed as befitted their widow status, had their usual game of whist, but could not concentrate. The frequent bursts of laughter and whoops of triumph from Gus and Mr. Goodman disturbed them. One of them put her finger to her lips as she caught Ivy's eye. "Ssshh!" she said. Her message fell on deaf ears. Ivy was enjoying herself, taken right back to the rare occasions when her mother was out for the day, and she and her father settled down to a hand or two of pontoon. They had played for matches, as they were doing now, but she remembered that her father had a bar of chocolate at the ready for the winner. And Ivy was always the winner.

This time, Gus won, and Ivy miraculously produced a bar of Fruit & Nut from her capacious handbag. "Well done, Gus," she said, and suggested another game tomorrow evening.

"Ra-ther!" enthused Roy. Really, things were definitely brightening up at Springfields.

With coffee all round, they settled back comfortably, and began to talk. As Ivy had hoped, Roy did most of the talking. With very little encouragement, he told them the story of his life. His family had been farmers in Barrington for generations, and when he, the last of the line, failed to get married and produce an heir for the old farmhouse and acres, he had decided to sell and use the proceeds to pay for luxury care in his old age. Naturally, he had chosen Springfields. He soon knew that he had made a mistake. Although he was physically infirm now, he still had all his faculties intact. He had been bored to tears, in spite of his best efforts to make friends and get something lively and interesting going amongst the other residents.

A reading group had ground to a halt when members pleaded they could no longer read well enough to keep it going. Failing eyesight and lack of concentration were blamed. Then, remembering his love of amateur drama in his youth, he had rounded up enough residents to attempt a Christmas revue to entertain the others. All the old songs, he had assured them, and a few jokes from old time music hall. He would be master of ceremonies, and Miss Pinkney had unexpectedly agreed to play the piano for them. They had made a start, but one by one the volunteers had backed out, mostly with feeble excuses, but nothing he could do would persuade them to return. The revue had been cancelled.

But now here were Gus and Ivy, playing pontoon with

him and listening with interest to his reminiscences. He had reached the point where he had told his father he had no wish to continue at school, but wanted to be a full-time farmer and keep the family tradition going. He had been fifteen, and his father was delighted.

"Were you an only child?" asked Ivy. Gus's eyelids were drooping, but at Ivy's intervention he snapped awake.

Roy laughed. "The only boy!" he said. "I had three sisters, much to Dad's disgust. Girls are no use to man nor beast, he used to say. Then mother would list all the things she did around the farm, and he would disappear fast to the pub."

"Three girls, eh?" said Ivy. "I expect the village boys approved, even if your father didn't." Gus saw where this was leading, and looked on admiringly as Ivy steered Roy to the subject of the Roussels up at the Hall.

"Oh, lord, yes!" he said, as she asked if there was a wicked squire in those days. She had made a joke of it, but Roy revealed that one of his sisters had had to go off to stay with a distant aunt for a few months. She finally returned in a depressed state, and had been seen often walking round the village peering longingly into friends' prams.

"So the Roussels had a reputation, did they?" Ivy suggested.

"They certainly did," Roy said, "and made sure they kept it going. I remember when Mr. Theo was a lad—" He broke off and smiled, wagging his head at the memories.

Gus and Ivy held their breath.

"He was worst of all, I reckon. Mind you," he added, "he was also the most handsome and charming. All the village lads wanted to be like Mr. Theo. We all tried!"

"But he never married?" Gus asked. He began to think this investigation was getting a bit one-sided and he should at least put in a question or two.

Roy turned to him. "D'you know, Gus, that puzzled us all. He could have had any of the girls in the county. Rich,

beautiful, clever—they were all after him. But none suc-
ceeded. I still wonder about it."

"So Beatrice Beatty came to look after him," Ivy
prompted.

Roy was silent. He looked at his watch. "My goodness!"
he said. "It is long past my bedtime! Such an enjoyable
evening. Thank you both for keeping me company."

Katya appeared and took the old man's arm. "Come
along, Mr. Goodman," she said. "Lots of time tomorrow
for more games. You say good night to your friends?"

Roy thought of protesting that he was not in his second
childhood yet, but he knew the girl meant well. She tried
very hard with her English, and in any case, she was charming and pretty and they needed girls like her in dreary old
Springfields. He obediently allowed her to escort him out
of the lounge and up the stairs to bed.

"Bugger," said Gus softly.

"Pardon?" said Ivy.

"Bugger," repeated Gus.

"Indeed," said Ivy.

READY FOR BED, Ivy drew back her curtains and looked
out along the main street of Barrington. It was a beautiful
moonlit night, and an owl hooted to his mate in the wood
outside the village. She could see the lights outside the pub,
and a shadowy couple, closely entwined, walked along the
path in the distance. She thought of love, and the damage
it could do.

"Beatrice Beatty, what bad thing did *you* do?" she said
aloud.

As if in answer, there was a tap at her door. Who on
earth . . . ?

"Who is it?" she said.

"Me," said a hoarse voice, and the door opened a crack.
Roy's white face peered round and he said, "Can I come

in for a minute? Something on my mind, and I shan't sleep until I've told you."

For one moment Ivy was tempted to ring her bell and have him forcibly removed. Then she remembered he was eighty-six and feeble.

"Just for a moment, then, Mr. Goodman," she said. "It's probably strictly against the stupid rules, so you'd better come in."

Twenty-eight

"I THINK I'LL give the market a miss tomorrow," said Beattie. She was standing by the window in the kitchen, looking out over the stable yard. Theo had come down in order to tell her that for once he would not have Friday sausages for lunch. He had intended to say he would be going to the pub in the village for a change, but she had interrupted him with her announcement.

"But you love going to market," he said, suddenly anxious that Deirdre might well keep her promise to see him again soon. Tomorrow was soon, too soon perhaps. She might well leave it a week or two. But it *could* be tomorrow, and he had no intention of letting Beattie spoil it all.

"It was terrible last week," she said. "Too many people, not enough stalls. Not like it used to be in the old days, when you'd meet people you knew. And then everything much cheaper than in the shops. Not so nowadays. More and more difficult to find a bargain."

"Well, that is a nuisance," Theo said, thinking rapidly. "I wanted you to get some special aftershave balm from the chemist. My face has been a little sore lately, and I read about this stuff in the *Oldie* magazine. Works wonders, so it said."

Beattie's head was throbbing. She had woken with a headache, and in spite of taking painkillers, it was still there. She had planned a quiet day at home tomorrow to give herself a chance to recover. Her mother—God rot her soul—had been a migraine sufferer, and she had inherited it from her, along with a number of other tendencies.

But Mr. Theo had been different again these last few days, quite sharp with her on occasion. His good mood seemed to have evaporated. Perhaps it would be best not to irritate him further.

"Of course I'll go to market, then," she said. "Can't have you with a sore face! What will Mrs. Budd think?"

Theo realised with horror that she was implying that Rosebud might think that Beattie and he had been having a close encounter, and he shivered.

"Right, I expect they'll have it at Boots," he said. "Oh, and I shan't be in for lunch," he added. "I have arranged to meet a friend in the village."

Beattie could not remember when he had last met a friend in the village. Her head thumped even harder, and she swayed on her feet. But Theo turned around and went out through the kitchen door into the stable yard, saying over his shoulder that he needed a word with David Budd. Beattie sat down quickly and waited for the giddy spell to pass. He had not needed a word with David Budd for at least five years, and she suddenly had a strong urge to burst into tears.

DEIRDRE WAS IN the shower, when she heard the telephone. "Damn!" she said, and hoped that it would soon stop. Whoever it was could ring later. Her answerphone came on, and the ringing stopped. Then it started again.

"Damn, damn!" she said, and stepped out of the shower, pulling on her towelling robe.

"Hello!" she said crossly.

"It's Ivy. Where were you? I've been trying to get hold of you."

"I realise that," said Deirdre. "I was in the shower. Anyway, I'm here now, so what can I do for you?"

"You can be here at eleven o'clock for coffee with me and Augustus," she said. "Something's come up, and we need to discuss it. And make sure you're on time."

"I'm always on time!" said Deirdre. But Ivy had rung off.

At eleven o'clock sharp, Gus knocked at Ivy's door. Deirdre had already arrived, and was sitting with Ivy, showing her the latest photographs of her daughter's children.

Coffee and biscuits were on the little table by Ivy's armchair, and Gus sat down. "Morning, colleagues," he said cheerfully. Deirdre gave him an answering smile and said she hoped he was feeling much better. She knew perfectly well that he was taking advantage of Ivy, but judged that it was none of her business, and if the old thing was feeling charitable then Gus was in luck.

"This is a business meeting," said Ivy sternly. "Last night, after our game of pontoon, I was getting ready for bed when Mr. Goodman knocked at my door."

"Who?" said Deirdre, who had forgotten Ivy's intended research with the oldest inhabitant.

Gus explained that Ivy had an admirer, and the three of them had sat up all night gambling in the lounge.

"That's quite enough of that, Augustus," Ivy said. She told Deirdre the correct version of events, and Deirdre said, "You didn't let him in, I hope?"

Ivy glared at the pair of them. "The poor man could not sleep, and said he had something to tell me. Couldn't rest until he'd got it off his chest."

Gus smothered his desire to laugh. He dare not look at

Deirdre, who was snuffling into her handkerchief. "Ah, yes," he said taking a deep breath. "Now I remember. We had just asked the old boy about the time Beattie arrived in the village, and he clammed up and went to bed. Was it about that?"

Ivy nodded. "He came in, sat down, and it all came tumbling out. He said Beattie had come from nowhere. Nobody knew anything about her. She just turned up one day at the Hall."

"Somebody must have known about her," Deirdre said. "They wouldn't have employed a girl without knowing at least where she came from. And they'd have wanted references, surely?"

"How old is she?" Gus said. "You girls would know better than I. I am easily deceived!"

Ivy ignored this. "I would put her at about fifty. What d'you say, Deirdre?"

Deirdre nodded. "Yeah, fifty to fifty-five, I'd say."

"Mr. Goodman said she was in her late teens when she came," Ivy continued. He remembered, because his nephew in the village was always on the lookout for new girls. But he didn't fancy Beattie, apparently."

Ivy said she supposed Theo Roussel was about the same age as Deirdre. "He was older than me," Deirdre said, "but not much. It seemed a lot at the time, but it was probably no more than five years' difference."

"What else did he say, Ivy?" Gus was sure there was something more important than this.

"Now, this is where it gets interesting," Ivy answered, enjoying spinning it out. "Mr. Goodman was a committee member of the local farmers' union, and used to get about quite a lot. Around that time, he was over the other side of the county attending a meeting, and a young farmer came up to him and asked if he lived in Barrington. Then he asked about a girl called Beattie. Had she come to work in the village? And did Mr. Goodman know where she was working?"

"So did he tell?" said Deirdre, now eagerly listening.

Ivy shook her head. "He said he had this funny feeling that it would cause trouble if he told. He said he didn't know anyone of that name, but asked the young farmer why he wanted to know, and the lad had just laughed. It wasn't just him who'd like to find her, he'd said. Several others would be glad to have the information."

"And what else?" Gus asked.

"A while later, quite by chance," Ivy replied, "Mr. Goodman's cleaning lady at the farm was turning out old newspapers from the attic, and the one on top of the pile, dated way back, had a big photo. This and the story beneath it had been ringed with a red pen, faded, but still clearly there. Underneath was the news story of a woman who had disappeared, leaving two children alone in a tenement flat. It was several days before a neighbour heard them crying, and managed to get in to release them. They had been taken into care, and the police were hunting for the missing woman."

"And the photo? Oh, come on Ivy, don't keep us in suspense." Deirdre was sitting on the edge of her chair now.

"He said it was the image of Beatrice Beatty as she is now. The missing woman was in her forties, the paper said."

"And her name?" said Gus impatiently.

"He couldn't remember exactly. Something like Katherine, or Caroline Bentall, he said." Ivy helped herself to another biscuit.

"Did it give the children's names and ages?" Deirdre asked.

"No, it didn't. They usually don't," Ivy said.

"And he said somebody had ringed it round with a red pen?"

"That's right. So Roy's family were interested, maybe even involved, with this mystery disappearance?"

"Looks like it," said Ivy. "But he couldn't remember anything else. I said it was good that he remembered so much, an' he said we oldies can remember the past but not what happened yesterday. Can't say that applies to me . . . yet."

"Over to you, Deirdre," Gus said. "We need to know urgently now what Theo remembers of Beattie's arrival at the Hall. Tomorrow will be a busy day for you. I'd like to help, but I am a little feeble still." He was actually feeling fine, but determined to make the most of this unexpected break.

"Oh, we can manage without you," Ivy said. "I can ring Deirdre and give her the all clear when I see Beatty safely on the bus tomorrow. So," she added, "off you go Deirdre, and Gus, you can go and chat up Mr. Goodman. See what else he's remembered. I need to do some thinking."

Twenty-nine

THE NEXT AFTERNOON was after all sunny and bright.
Ivy sat on the seat beside the bus stop and this second time
felt more confident. She chatted to people going in and out
of the shop, and kept her eye on Hangman's Row, waiting
for the dumpy figure of Beatty to appear.

Once more, all went well. Beattie saw Ivy sitting there,
and asked if she was coming on the bus. "We could go to
market together," she said, in spite of a reluctance to have
anything to do with Miss Beasley. She realised a bus journey would be the ideal opportunity to pump the old woman
for more details of Deirdre Bloxham and her easy come,
easy go ways with the opposite sex. She was sure this ex-
girlfriend of Theo had something to do with the strange
way he had been behaving lately. But how? She had kept a
close ear to telephone calls, and a close eye on correspon-
dence and visitors. There had been no opportunity for a
return visit from Deirdre Bloxham.

"Perhaps next week," said Ivy. "Young Katya is taking

me for a walk later. But yes, Miss Beatty, next week I might like to come with you."

Even as Ivy said this, a horrid possibility occurred to Beattie. Today! And last Saturday! While she was at market, had Theo somehow managed to get in touch with the Bloxham woman? And was Rose Budd to be trusted?

Ivy could not believe her eyes when Beattie came hurrying down the steps of the bus, just as it was about to depart, exactly as she had last week. But today was different. Beatty reached the bottom step, stopped and shook her head, turned and went back into the bus.

Ivy heard the driver shout, "Make up yer mind, missus!" and the bus departed.

Ivy had been practising with her mobile phone, and in seconds was talking to Deirdre. "She's gone," she said. "But it was touch and go again. This time, she didn't get right off the bus. Just came to the bottom step, then went back in again. Goodness knows what that was about, but she had a face like thunder."

Deirdre, looking her very best, felt a sudden shiver. She was not cold. It was a beautiful day. It was like someone had walked over her grave, her mother would have said. She gave herself a shake, and said she was on her way.

All the way to market, Beattie boiled with fury. That must be it. While the cat's away the mice will play. Never a truer saying than that. Perhaps she should have got off the bus and returned to confront Theo and that wretched girl Rose. But it would be too soon. They'd wait until she was well on the way to town. "You can't trust nobody," she muttered to herself. She had learnt that at an early age, but years of living in security at the Hall had softened her. Well, now she was hard again. She would get a lift back early with that helpful Broomfield woman next to the shop. She knew she always went into town on a Saturday and came back in the early afternoon. She would find her car in the car park, and wait by it, no matter how long it took. Then they would see how clever they were!

ROSE STOOD BY the kitchen door in the stable yard, grinning from ear to ear as the big car glided to a halt.

"You're looking very smart," she said, greeting Deirdre. "Do you know," she confided, "Mr. Theo has taken his best tweed jacket out of mothballs for your visit! Smells a bit, but it shows how much he's looking forward to seeing you again, bless him."

"You like him, then?" Deirdre said.

"Oh, he's fine," Rose said. "It's you-know-who that's the real nuisance. She rules the roost. Decides everything on the farm, though David says she knows damn all about farming. Anyway, come on in. He'll be so pleased to see you." She winked. "And I'll keep out of the way," she said. "Just don't forget that the old dragon will be back at the same time as last week."

Theo was waiting for her in the drawing room. This time he advanced on nimble feet and embraced her warmly. "Mmmm!" he said. "Same lovely scent as last week!"

He did not immediately let go of her, and Deirdre's blood quickened. "Same old Theo," she said. "You haven't forgotten how to get a girl going!"

They walked over to the sofa, and sat down, still holding hands. "Would you like coffee?" he said, "Or shall we go straight to bed?"

Deirdre laughed. Did he really mean it? She decided to call his bluff, and said straight to bed would be great. But he hadn't been bluffing, and still holding her hand, he led her up the wide staircase and along to his room, where a large bed with clean sheets put on that morning by an unsuspecting Beatty, awaited them.

He put his arms around her, and she did not mind the

whiff of mothballs. "It's been too long, Deirdre Bloxham," he said. "But we've all afternoon to make up for lost time."

All Ivy's strictures about remembering why she was there flew out of the window. Useful conversation later, she said to herself, plenty of time later.

Thirty

SADIE BROOMFIELD WAS very surprised to see a figure standing by her car as she returned from the supermarket. She was shortsighted, and could not see exactly who it was. Surely not a policewoman! She had definitely put money in the machine and the ticket was on her car's dashboard, visible to anyone.

As she got nearer, she saw that it was Miss Beatty from the Hall. What on earth was she doing there? Not my favourite person, she said to herself. Nobody's favourite person. Still, if the woman was in trouble, it was her neighbourly duty to help.

"Miss Beatty!" she said. "Can I help you?"

Beattie explained that she needed to get back early to the village. "Something's come up, I'm afraid, and I must be back as soon as possible. I knew you were in town most Saturdays, and hoped to find you. I recognised your car, of course," she added, as pleasantly as she could. "Such a sensible little vehicle," she added.

Sadie's car was a bright red Smart Sport, and she was

very proud of it. "Delighted to give you a lift," she said. "Jump in, while I stow my shopping. There's room for all," she said. This was an exaggeration, but in due course she, Beattie and the shopping were shoehorned in, and they set off.

Conversation was difficult. Sadie had never spent more than two minutes in Beattie's company, and now had nothing to say to her. She had tried asking what the emergency was, but got no answer. Miss Beatty was silent for at least half of the return journey, until she said suddenly, "Do you know Mrs. Bloxham?"

"Only by sight," Sadie said. "Seems a nice enough woman. She always smiles."

"Huh!" said Beattie. "She won't be smiling when I get home."

Sadie was about to ask her more about this odd remark, when a loud bang followed by a series of bumps caused her to stop the car and pull into the side. She got out, and her heart sank. It *would* happen this afternoon, when she had that unpleasant passenger! A flat tyre, and the first one since she had bought the car. She had no idea how to change it, nor did she intend to try.

Beattie had clambered out and came round to see what had happened. She saw the flat tyre, and said, "Now what do you intend to do? I must get home as quickly as possible."

Sod you, thought Sadie, and considered telling her to walk. Instead, she dialled the AA rescue service, and explained to Beattie that they would have to wait until an engineer arrived. "Or you could thumb a lift from this lorry coming along," she said nastily.

Beattie said nothing would persuade her to ride in a lorry with a strange man, and stood with her arms folded, watching while Sadie delved into the car pockets and slots to find the technical instructions for the car.

Time passed, and the AA still did not arrive. Sadie

wondered if Beattie needed the loo. It had been a long day, and she had stood vigil by the car, waiting for Sadie to finish her shopping.

As if reading her thoughts, Beattie said that she had noticed a cottage a hundred yards back, and thought she would take a walk to see if she could use their toilet. "Don't go without me!" she said, and set off at a fast pace. On the way, the bus from town passed her, and the driver waved merrily. She signalled violently, but he did not stop. Probably against the rules, she thought sourly, and trudged on.

Meanwhile, Sadie had had a call from the AA, apologising for the delay, but saying the engineer was now on his way. From where? Sadie had asked. Birmingham, said the girl.

Sadie looked in her driving mirror. No sign of Beattie returning, so she must have been lucky. The bus passed by, but Sadie could see that they had not stopped for her. She supposed she had better telephone the Hall and let them know what had happened. Mr. Roussel would be wondering where his housekeeper had got to. She had the number in her head from times when she was working in the shop and had to consult Beattie on their order.

"Hello? Who is that?" Rose Budd answered, sounding worried. Sadie explained, and Rose said she had to get home to the family, but was sure Mr. Theo would be fine by himself until Beattie returned. He was in a very good mood, she said, and giggled. Sadie was puzzled, but much more worried about her car, and so thanked Rose and ended the call.

The AA man arrived an hour later. Once there, he fixed the tyre swiftly, and they were once more on their way. Beattie had relapsed into a sullen silence, and Sadie was heartily relieved when she drove round into the stable yard and helped Beattie out of the car.

As she drove back down the long drive, Sadie reflected on her passenger's failure to say thank you for the lift.

After all, Sadie had been hijacked. Ah well, she thought, that'll teach her to cadge lifts in future. She smiled to herself. It was obvious the poor woman had not been missed. She remembered the giggle. Had Rose Budd and Mr. Roussel been up to no good? Well, good luck to them, Sadie thought, and as she unpacked her shopping she looked forward to a restoring cup of tea.

BEATTIE ENTERED THE Hall and went straight to her kitchen. Everything in order. She lifted the kettle and filled it, wondering how she was going to explain the delay to Mr. Theo. He would want to know what made her come back with Sadie Broomfield instead of catching the usual bus. It would have to be a sudden illness, she decided. After all, she had nearly fainted this morning, but she was not sure he had even noticed. She heard his footsteps on the tiled hallway, and looked apprehensively at the door.

"Ah, there you are!" he said. "Did you have a good time? Met a friend, did you?" He was beaming, and she was so surprised that for once she could think of nothing to say.

"Well, you're home now, and needing a cup of tea, I'm sure. No, no," he added, as she asked if he would like tea, though it was a little late. "No, I have been well looked after," he said, and chuckled. "I thought I'd have a stroll in the park. Should have a dog again. We must get a dog, Beattie," he said, and disappeared.

A stroll in the park? A dog? A nasty, snappy little terrier, no doubt. Beattie sat down at the kitchen table and put her head in her hands. What was going on? The wonderful security she had made for herself at the Hall was falling apart. A tear fell on the scrubbed surface, and she rubbed it away quickly. This would not do. It would take more than a young woman with no conscience to defeat Beatrice Beatty. For a start, she thought, the Budd family were entirely reliant on her for their cushy cottage in Hangman's Row, and Rose's husband took his orders from her.

Then she remembered Theo's sudden decision to have a word with David Budd this morning. Was this start of a new regime?

No matter, she said to herself. I'll fight them all. I've fought my way out of tricky situations before, and I'll do it again. There are one or two things I could mention to Mr. Theo that might make him think twice about undermining my position.

Feeling more cheerful, she went upstairs to draw curtains in the rooms he would be using later this evening. As she entered his bedroom, she paused. She sniffed, and walked over to the bed. It was rumpled. Not significantly, just the counterpane not quite straight, not as smooth as she had left it this morning. She sniffed again. She had smelled that perfume before, but could not remember where. She perched on the edge of the bed, overcome with dizziness once more.

Thirty-one

DEIRDRE SAT AT her dressing table, looking at her reflection. She saw a round face, almost free of aging lines, with cheeks suffused with a healthy colour, and a mouth that had always turned up at the corners, whether she was smiling or not. Her careful coiffure was not as perfect as when she set out that afternoon, but still the curls caught the light and shone a reddish gold, just as her hairdresser had promised.

"Not bad," she said aloud, and then burst out laughing all alone in her luxury bedroom. She looked back to the time before Ivy had come to Springfields. Her life had been exemplary, duty bound and boring as hell. Not that she had any idea if hell was boring or not. Perhaps she would go to hell, after this afternoon! This sent her off into further peals of laughter. Who would have thought Theo would still be so good at it?

Her telephone rang. She knew it would be Ivy, wanting to know how she had got on with gleaning information about Beattie from Theo. She sobered up. The fact was that their fun and games had been so sustained—and they both in middle age!—that only half an hour or so had been left for serious conversation. She had tried, but Theo was not listening. He was much more interested in arranging their next meeting, and in telling her how she had changed everything and he could only thank God that she had come back into his life in time.

"Deirdre? Are you there?" Ivy's voice was sharp, and Deirdre quaked.

"Hello, Ivy. How are you?"

"What d'you mean, how am I? I'm exactly the same as I was not many hours ago. I'm ringing to see if you got anything interesting out of Mr. Theo. Did he remember Beattie in the early days? How she got the job? References? Where she came from, an' all that?"

Deirdre sighed. "Ivy dear," she said. "I have just had a call from an old lady in town who I visit from time to time. I'm a social services volunteer, you know. She wants me to help her straightaway. I must be off now. We'll meet on Monday as usual, I hope? Gus will still be in Springfields, I expect. I'll tell all then," she added.

Uncrossing her fingers, she prayed for forgiveness and humming cheerfully went downstairs. She looked at the clock in the hall, and saw that it was little drinkies time. "It's not that I've forgotten you, Bert," she said aloud. She knew what he would say fondly. A leopardess cannot change her spots.

KATYA HAD ENJOYED her walk with Miss Beasley this afternoon. They had gone in the opposite direction from the church, and come out of the village into a tunnel of trees. Katya had asked Ivy if she would like to turn around now, but Ivy said she was quite capable of going farther and so they had strolled through the tunnel and out into a sunny lane leading to a farm. A tractor and trailer were parked in the nearby field, and as they watched, a young man heaved sacks of feed out of the trailer and tipped it out for the flock of sheep gathered around him.

This pastoral scene had made Katya nostalgic for holidays she had spent with her grandparents in rural Poland. Ivy, seeing her expression, had greeted the young farmer with a cheerful good afternoon, hoping he would come over for a word.

He had introduced himself as David Budd, and asked Katya pleasantly where she had come from and how long she would be staying. While they stood talking, his mobile had rung, and answering it, he had said that yes, he could be home by the time the baby-minder had to go.

He apologised to them, and said his wife Rose was up at the Hall, and had been kept later than usual. "She keeps the old man company while the housekeeper is at market, you know," he said. "Seems the old duck has been delayed, and Rose has to stay on a bit longer." He had excused himself, saying he must get on his way, but invited Katya to drop in anytime and meet Rose and the best toddler in the world, in other words, his son Simon.

This encounter had, as Ivy hoped, cheered up Katya, and they returned to Springfields in good spirits. After her abortive call to Deirdre, Ivy remembered Rose's call to her husband, and wondered what had happened to delay Beattie. Then she decided that so long as it was delay, and the housekeeper had not returned early, all would have been well. In any case, Deirdre had sounded happy. Odd, but happy.

Now she made her way downstairs to supper. Mr. Goodman was waiting at his table, and beckoned her over with a ready smile. She sighed. She would rather have had a quiet meal on her own, but knew that the old boy might well have remembered more about those early days, and the case of the disappearing mother.

"Good evening, Mr. Goodman," she said.

"Good evening, Miss Beasley," he said, and wondered when it would be safe to call her Ivy.

Ivy looked round for Gus, but he had not yet come down. "We must keep a seat for Mr. Halfhide," she said, and felt uncomfortable when she saw the old man's face fall.

"Had hoped to have you to myself," he whispered.

Ivy was in unfamiliar territory here, and said clumsily that Mr. Halfhide was convalescing and good company was part of his recovery programme. She saw Gus approaching, and with relief waved him to their table. When Gus saw that she was sitting with little Roy Goodman his heart sank. He thought that Ivy should at least have been prepared to defend him from the oldest inhabitant.

After they had made short work of roast chicken and apple crumble, the three sat on over coffee, chatting idly. Then Roy Goodman said something that made Ivy sit up. "When I was a lad," he began, "this was a private house, you know. Belonged to one of the Roussel family. They'd got a tenant in. A real recluse, she was. Never went anywhere, and had a woman looking after her. It was after she died that it was sold, and became an old folks' home."

"When was that?" Ivy said, and her tone made Gus look at her enquiringly.

"Oh, I'm not sure," Roy said. "I'm so old, I sometimes think I remember Queen Victoria!"

"Rubbish!" said Ivy, and added that she was not so far behind Mr. Goodman, and she could barely remember her mother telling her about Queen Mary. She looked around the dining room, and said that it must have been a lovely house when it was in private hands. "Did you ever come here, Roy?" she said, apparently casually.

Roy beamed. "Well, Ivy," he said, reaching out and touching her hand lightly, "I do vaguely remember that my mother sent me to Springfields to deliver a parcel that had been mistakenly sent to the farm. But the recluse didn't answer the door. It was the companion. Yes, that's right, she was called the companion. A quiet woman, she was. Not much seen about the village herself. Just came to the village shop for supplies, and that was about it."

"Not to church?" said Ivy.

Roy shook his head. "Never to my knowledge. And I was in the church choir at that time. Sixpence a time, we got. That's why we went, I'm afraid, not for the love of the Lord!"

Gus smiled. He had been thinking about the companion. "I don't suppose you could possibly remember who the parcel was addressed to?" he said. It was a forlorn hope, but worth asking.

"Good heavens, no!" Roy said. "I was in a hurry to hand it in and get away. There was something creepy about the place in those days." He paused, and then said politely, "Um, I wonder if you'd mind telling me why you're so interested in those old long-gone days?"

Gus looked at Ivy, and after a second or two she nodded almost imperceptibly. Gus got the message and cleared his throat.

"We should probably have told you before, Roy," he said, "those old days may be very important to us." Then he explained about being more or less thrust into matters surrounding the death of Mrs. Blake, and his decision to use his considerable experience in the field of investigation. "Being a stranger to the village, I needed a well-placed local assistant. That's Ivy here," he added, patting her hand, which she withdrew instantly. "And then she enlisted her cousin Deirdre at Tawny Wings, who has all the advantages of modern technology at her fingertips. And," he added, "though it is probably too premature to say so, we are a pretty good team."

Roy looked at them in astonishment. "Now I see it," he said. "But you forgot the person who could be most useful to you."

"Well, don't beat about the bush," said Ivy. "Who?"

"Me," said Roy. "Meet your new team member." He held out his hand, and neither Ivy nor Gus had the heart to refuse him.

Thirty-two

DEIRDRE WANDERED ABOUT the house, smoking a cigarette and being careful not to inhale. She had smoked only in stressful circumstances since Bert died, and was now suffering terrible morning-after pangs of conscience. The euphoria of yesterday had dispersed, and she had taken a hard look at herself. A trollop, her mother would have said. That's what you are, a trollop. A woman without pride or moral sense. Led astray in middle age by a former lover, who had never been a reliable character, even in his youth.

But had they done anybody any harm? Deirdre stopped her perambulating and stubbed out her cigarette. She frowned, and walked over to the grand piano, shining pristinely in the drawing room. It was never played. Tuned regularly, but never played. She had fallen for the sales talk: "The ultimate fashion statement for your home," the advertisement had promised. At one time she'd hoped her girls would learn to play, but they had preferred the guitar. Much easier, they had said.

Now it was a suitable surface for expensively framed

photographs of the family. She picked up the one of Bert
and herself outside the Palace. He'd been so proud of her
MBE. He had really deserved to have an award himself.
His work with misguided youth in the town was well-
known, but only she knew how much it had cost him. All
those evenings spent in draughty community halls, when
he would much rather have been at home watching the telly
with her.

"Bert," she said seriously. "I don't suppose you could
possibly let me know somehow whether I'm going astray,
could you? Please?" Her eyes filled with tears, and she
stared hopefully at the photograph. What! She rubbed her
eyes fiercely. Oh, my God, there it was again. Bert winked.
He definitely winked!

She rushed to the window with the photograph and
looked again. No, it must have been a mistake. He looked
proudly out of the photograph, as before. She sighed.
Wishful thinking, she supposed. She replaced Bert, and
opened the garden door. The sky was overcast, and a damp
mist filled the garden. Almost autumnal, Deirdre thought.
That's what we are, she thought miserably. In the autumn
of our lives.

"Deirdre!" A sharp voice interrupted her thoughts.
"Have you been smoking?"

It was Ivy of course. Who else would Bert send along
to accuse her of being sorry for herself? Deirdre laughed
aloud, and did a couple of skips back into the house.

"You could do with a doormat outside there," Ivy said.
"Just look at those wet footprints all over your carpet! Still,
if you will have white carpets, what do you expect?"

"Nice to see you, too, Ivy," Deirdre said, quite restored.
"Tea or coffee? I heard on the radio this morning that coffee is really bad for you. Shall we have tea?"

Ivy said she was too old to worry about whether things
were bad for her or not, but she preferred tea in any case,
hot and strong with two sugars, please.

"Now," she continued, when they were perched on uncomfortable stools in the kitchen, "I reckon you have something to tell me. No, don't interrupt. *I* think you said nothing to Theo Roussel about Beatrice Beatty's past. I think you spent a happy and fruitless two hours exchanging tweetie words and getting up to no good. Am I right?"

Deirdre thought of lying through her teeth, and then realised that Ivy already knew the truth and it would be easier to own up. "Right," she said apologetically. "Well, not *all* right. I wouldn't say it was completely fruitless."

"I have no wish to hear anything about that," Ivy said stiffly. "I've come along this morning to see how you can face Gus tomorrow morning. And," she added, "to see if you'd come to church with me. It's Holy Communion this morning."

"And confess my sins?" Deirdre said. Then she realised her sharp old cousin was really trying to help her out of a fix, and said that if Ivy would tell her when to stand up and sit down, she would come. "But first, can we make a plan for tomorrow?" She looked at the clock. "We've got an hour or so before church."

THEY WERE AN odd trio, Ivy, Deirdre and young Katya, walking through the lych gate and up the narrow path to the church. Ivy ignored the sidesman who tried to direct her to a pew towards the back. She marched straight up to the front, where she ushered the two others in, and then knelt herself to say a few words of greeting to her personal God.

Just as the service was about to start, and the vicar half-way from the vestry to his seat in the chancel, the door opened and a flustered-looking Beattie came in. Behind her, dignified and aloof, came the Honourable Theodore Roussel. He looked to neither right nor left, but walked with measured step to the front pew on the opposite side of the aisle from the three women. Beattie retired to a seat at the rear of the church, and the service began.

"Does he always come?" whispered Deirdre to Ivy.

"Sshh!"

"No, but does he?" Deirdre persisted.

Ivy shook her head. "Never," she whispered back.

Deirdre looked surreptitiously across the aisle, and saw that Theo must have attended regularly at some time. He knew exactly when to sit down and stand up. And, she heard with a kind of proprietary pleasure, he had a fine tenor voice and seemed to know all the hymn tunes.

When it came to the invitation to take Communion, Theo stood up and waited politely while Ivy eased herself from her seat and stood at the head of the queue. Deirdre had no alternative but to follow her, and realised with dismay that Theo had stepped out to take his place behind her. "Oh!" she gasped, with an intake of breath. Was that his hand?

The vicar prepared to dispense the bread and wine, and they knelt humbly with hands resting on the altar rail to await their turn. Without looking at Deirdre, Theo rested his hand very briefly on hers, and then removed it to form a supplicant shape with both hands to receive the sliver of something that tasted like polystyrene.

They returned to their seats with heads bowed, and Ivy knelt once more. Deirdre followed her example, and prayed fervently to God to help her in this undoubted crisis in her life. She wished she had a cigarette.

As the joyful going-home hymn was sung, Deirdre risked a glance towards Theo, and saw that he was looking at her. He did not smile, but to her astonishment, he quite clearly winked. Twice she had been winked at this morning! She decided it was a sign, a definite sign from the Almighty that she was doing nothing wrong, harming nobody, and was, in fact, being a good Christian in spreading love and joy to all people. Well, maybe not to all people, but certainly to the Honourable Theo Roussel.

Beattie, still crouched in prayer in her pew at the back of the church, waited until she was sure Theo and the three women had left and would be on their way out of the churchyard. Her head was still thumping from the shock she had been given when Theo had announced his intention of going to church. He had appeared in her kitchen, washed, brushed and looking extremely determined, saying that they should be off now. There was just time to walk. He would go on ahead, and she could catch him up.

By running awkwardly down the drive, she had caught him up, and walked silently by his side until they reached the church. Then she had fallen back respectfully as they entered. As he had marched forward and she lagged behind, she had seen with a sinking heart the Bloxham woman, large as life in the front pew, her ridiculously dyed hair shining out like a vulgar wig on a woman for sale.

Now she walked slowly out of the church, shook the vicar's hand and hardly acknowledged his friendly greeting. She could no longer pretend that she was imagining things. Somehow those two had met in her absence. Not only met, she thought grimly, but restarted whatever had been postponed all those years ago. As she approached Hangman's Row on her way back to the Hall, she could see Theo talking to David Budd over his garden fence. She would slip by quickly, and hurry back to the security of her kitchen to prepare lunch.

She must find a way to stop all the goings-on that had so cruelly invaded her hard-won refuge. But not straightaway, she decided. It might blow over if she bided her time. If not, she would need to think some more.

Thirty-three

"I THOUGHT WE'D have our meeting in the summer house," Ivy said, greeting Gus and Deirdre in Springfields' reception hall. "It's a criminal waste not to make the most of the summer sunshine. If you ask me, the sunlight was sent for us to be out in it."

"If you ask me," said Gus, "which you haven't, of course, I would say fine, so long as there's a comfortable chair in that godforsaken summer house in the shadiest corner of the garden."

"Now, now," said Deirdre, bursting with good humour, "it's a really good idea of Ivy's. We can be private, and Katya can bring us coffee out there. Have we told Roy?"

"Still in the land of nod," said Ivy. "Mrs. Spurling wouldn't have him woken. And don't worry, Augustus," Ivy added. "I have asked for the summer house to be cleaned out and made comfortably ready for us."

"What did old Spurling say to that?" Gus said.

"Nothing," said Ivy serenely. "She made a funny sort of noise and slammed out of my room. Sometimes I wonder

whether she really likes me. Not that it bothers me," she
added. "People have not liked me all my life. I'm used to it."

Gus was tempted to ask if she had ever wondered why,
but instead said gallantly that *he* liked her, and Deirdre
liked her, and please could they get on with the meeting, as
he was venturing out for a short walk later.

"By yourself?" said Deirdre.

Gus raised his eyebrows and said he was sure a member
of staff would be found to escort him.

"Item one," he said, when they were settled, "minutes
of the last meeting."

"We haven't got any minutes," said Deirdre.

"Maybe we should have," Gus said.

"Oh for goodness sake, can we get on," Ivy said. "First
of all, let's hear what Deirdre learned at the Hall on Saturday." She looked meaningfully at her cousin, and nodded
her head.

"Well, as Ivy already knows," Deirdre said without hesitation, "it was all a bit of a waste of time. I turned up, as
before, and Rose Budd left me alone with Theo for an hour
or so. He was looking a bit peaky when I arrived, and said
he thought he was getting a cold. We talked for a bit, but
I could see he really wasn't keen on me being there. I tried
to introduce the subject of Beattie, but by then he wasn't
answering. Actually," she added with an impressive show
of compassion, "the dear thing dozed off. He went to sleep,
and in no time was snoring his head off."

"So did you wake him?" said Gus suspiciously.

"Nope. I gave up, and went to talk to Rose Budd. She's
a really nice girl, you know. Interesting to talk to, too.
We discovered I'd known her mother when we were both
young. And that little Simon," she continued, "is an absolute poppet. His dad brought him into the kitchen, and we
had a great game of—"

"Whoa!" Gus said. "Are you saying you got nothing out
of Theo Roussel, nothing about Beattie in the early days?"

Deirdre nodded. "Nothing at all, I'm afraid. Poor dear was obviously not feeling well. I'll try again next Saturday. He should be feeling better by then. Rose suggested telling him I would be back. Said it would help him recover more quickly, bless him."

"So what else is there to talk about?" Gus said grumpily. Perhaps he should recover more quickly himself, and get out of here and galvanise these two into some urgent action.

"Names," Ivy said.

"What names?" said Deirdre. She had never told so many barefaced lies before—white lies, an annoyed Ivy had called them—but felt relieved now that Ivy's reluctantly concocted plan had worked. Gus was looking distinctly cross, but he seemed to have swallowed her excuses.

Their discussion took a more positive turn, and Ivy filled Deirdre in with what she and Gus had gleaned from Roy Goodman. "We need to do some serious research into that news story of the missing woman. It's just a hunch," Gus said, "but Ivy and I had the same thought that it has something to do with Beattie. The connection so far is that ancient news story ringed in red. Must've meant something important to Roy's family. We need to know the exact name of the woman, and of the children she left, and what happened later. Now, the best research tool these days is the Internet." He paused, waiting for a reaction.

"What about the reference library?" Ivy said, who had an uninformed distrust of the Internet. "Nothing wrong with reference libraries," she said. She remembered from the distant past a woman from the local reference library coming to talk to Round Ringford WI. She had droned on a bit, and some members had had a refreshing nap, but Ivy had been interested.

Deirdre shook her head. "We haven't got time, Ivy," she said. "The police must be getting on with their investigations and I've seen Inspector Frobisher around the village

several times. We don't want Enquire Within to be beaten
to the winning post. No, Gus is right. I'm computer literate," she added proudly. "Why don't we all get together at
Tawny Wings this afternoon and start a search?"

"Better than a boring walk with a member of staff, especially if it's Miss Pinkney and not adoring Katya," Ivy said
slyly. "I agree with Deirdre, if you're up to it, Augustus."

They agreed there was no further business for the meeting, and went back to the residents' lounge, where they
found Roy Goodman doing the *Guardian* quick crossword.
"Morning everybody," he said. "Have I missed something?
Afraid I have only just got up. Sit ye down, and I'll read out
the clues. Keeps the Alzheimer's at bay, you know, exercis-
ing the old grey matter."

Deirdre quickly excused herself, saying she had to go
into town to visit her old lady. She would see them at Tawny
Wings at two thirty sharp. Ivy said that if anyone asked
her, she would say that crossword puzzles were a complete
waste of time, and anyway, she had some letters to write
in her room, which left Gus to keep the old man company.
Before she went, she asked solicitously if she should order
a taxi to take Gus to Deirdre's house, but he said the short
walk would do him good.

"Four across," said Roy, "six letters, one word, 'killer *or*
slang for a drink.'"

"Poison," said Gus. "Next."

BEATTIE'S HEADACHE HAD finally vanished, and
she had awoken feeling refreshed for the first time in days.
She was downstairs preparing breakfast when Mr. Theo
walked into her kitchen, a smile on his face.

"Lovely morning, Beattie!" he said.

She had thought endlessly about how she was to tackle
the new Theo Roussel, and had decided to go along with

him, being pleasant and encouraging. She had no alternative, she concluded. Her quarrel was not, after all, with Mr. Theo. It was with the Bloxham woman, and she was confident in her ability to outwit her without too much trouble. If only she was not so alone, she had thought in the middle of the night. There was one person who would understand, but she dismissed that thought immediately. A real friend, not necessarily a confidante, would be so consoling. But she had brought friendlessness on herself over the years, and she was not sure how to reverse this, now that she needed someone.

Rose Budd? No, she wasn't much more than a girl, and they had nothing in common. Miss Beasley at Springfields? But wasn't she a cousin of the Bloxham woman? No, that wouldn't do. Miriam Blake? Ah, now, there was a woman of her own age, and also in trouble. Some said real trouble, but Beattie had no worries about that. It might even give her a hold over Miss Miriam. And they had several things in common. They had both lived in the village for years, and from what she had heard, they had both been more than interested in Mr. Theo and in the future of his estate. She could even hint that they might come to some compromise over Miriam's rent.

"What plans for today, Mr. Theo?" she said with a friendly smile.

"Out and about, I think," he said. "Weather's too good to stay indoors. I shall be in for lunch, but possibly out for dinner. I will let you know later on. And you, Beattie, what have you got planned?"

"Oh, I thought I might invite a friend for tea, if that is convenient," she said.

"Ah, who would that be?" he asked. He could have sworn Beattie had no friends, either in the village or anywhere else.

"Why, Miriam, of course. Miriam Blake," she said.

*   *   *

AFTER A GOOD lunch of lamb chops, mint sauce, peas and mash, Ivy and Gus set off slowly up the road towards Tawny Wings.

"What a pair," said Ivy grimly, as she stumped along, rapping her stick rhythmically on the pavement for support. Gus also had a stick, but his was more for show than from necessity. He had a pang of conscience as he saw how determinedly Ivy pushed herself to use legs that would much rather have been idle.

"Nearly there," he said, remembering his childhood, when his mother had said those words every time they were on a journey, no matter how short a distance they had actually gone. "I am sure Deirdre will have a restoring cuppa for us both. I'm looking forward to our research," he added. "I've been thinking of getting a computer myself."

"What stopped you?" Ivy said. She knew how much computers cost, and was pretty sure Gus had no spare cash. Not that she was thinking of buying him one! Nor, for that matter, of lending him money.

His reply surprised her. His tone was serious when he answered. "Security. In my line of business, security meant everything. And even though I understand users are told their details are secure, I wouldn't risk it."

"What details?" Ivy said curiously. She had decided early on that Gus was probably exaggerating the importance of his "line of business." Maybe a lowly security guard, but nothing more vital than that.

"Oh, you know, personal details, bank account numbers, pin numbers and pass codes, all that stuff. As far as I can make out, you put all that secret information on a computer and it goes off through the ether to God knows where!"

"Don't blaspheme, please," Ivy said automatically, as they turned into the driveway and made their way to the front door of Tawny Wings.

Half an hour later, the three were ranged around Deirdre's computer screen. Ivy had to squint to make out the flickering words on-screen. "What's Google?" she said suspiciously.

"A search engine," said Deirdre blandly. She actually had no idea where the engine came in, but knew what Google could do for her. It could search miraculously until it produced undreamed-of information about any given subject.

"Right," she said, "have you finished your tea? Good, then let's begin. Best thing is to start with the name of the newspaper that Roy found. What was it, Ivy?"

Ivy looked blank. "No idea," she said. "He didn't say."

Gus looked smug. "I asked him later. *Suffolk Independent Press*," he said smoothly. "Folded in the eighties, but was once the most popular paper in the county."

"Good lad," said Deirdre, and typed the name in at speed. Ivy was impressed. "How did you learn to type so fast?" she asked.

"At the garage," she said. "Although Bert had all the necessary office staff, I liked to keep my hand in, and worked one day a week alongside the others. I miss it, but they wouldn't want me now."

"Ooh, look, it's doing something!" Ivy said, leaning forward.

"Yep," Deirdre said, busying herself with the gadget which she had explained to a puzzled Ivy was a mouse. "Let's download this archive website. Looks the most interesting."

"We've got the date," Ivy said, anxious to make amends for not knowing the name of the paper. "It was in the nineteen seventies."

"Let's hope it was a weekly paper," Deirdre muttered, not keen to sift through hundreds of dates in ten possible years. She read through some information on-screen, and said, "Thank goodness it was a weekly evening paper.

Now, what was the name of the woman who went missing?"

"Roy wasn't sure, was he, Ivy?" Gus said.

"No. But didn't he say it was something like Bentall. Katherine, or Caroline, or some such?"

Ivy nodded. "You know what," she said slowly. "I think we should have brought Mr. Goodman with us. All this stuff"—she gestured at the screen—"might have triggered some more memories from him."

"Well, we didn't," Deirdre said, annoyed at Ivy's defeatist attitude. After all, she'd hardly started on her search.

"You could go and fetch him." Ivy looked stubbornly at Deirdre. Gus sighed. Best keep out of this, he said to himself, though he did half agree with Ivy.

"Oh, all right!" said Deirdre. "And don't try touching the computer while I'm gone. You could lose everything I've got stored on there."

"There you are, then, Ivy," Gus said mildly, as Deirdre flounced out of the room.

"That's one of the reasons I haven't bought a computer."

Thirty-four

"HE'S RESTING, MRS. Bloxham," Miss Pinkney said sternly. "I'm afraid I cannot disturb him. Mrs. Spurling would be very cross."

"Blow that!" said Deirdre. "I'm cross!" she added. "I've been sent up here by Miss Beasley to fetch Roy Goodman, and I'm not going back without him."

Miss Pinkney was shocked. She had never experienced such an encounter before in all her time working in retirement homes. What was she to do?

"Oh, look, there he is!" Deirdre said. "Poor old lamb looks bored to tears, staring at the telly with all the others. He's as sharp as a pin, you know," she added to a rigid Miss Pinkney.

Deirdre walked into the lounge, went straight up to Roy Goodman, and said, "Hi, Roy! We need you. Can you come with me? I'll bring you back for supper. Ivy and Gus are waiting up at Tawny Wings."

"*Need* me?" said Roy Goodman. He got to his feet without assistance. "I haven't been needed for thirty years," he said. "Lead on, Macduff! Get my coat, Pinkers—I'm needed!" he said, and like an agile gnome, followed Deirdre to reception, where she helped him on with his coat and led the way out to her car.

Envious eyes watched as he left. The lounge had its inevitable share of men and woman who couldn't hear, couldn't see and some who could no longer care what happened to them, but had once been needed. And some who would have given all their considerable savings to be Roy Goodman, if only for one afternoon.

Ivy and Gus greeted him with pleasure, and he joined them round the computer.

"AH YES," HE said. "I see you've got a website up for that newspaper I told you about. What would we do without Google?" he said, turning to Ivy.

For once, Ivy spluttered and was speechless. Gus gulped. "Um, I see you're, um, er, computer literate, Roy? Is that right?"

Roy nodded. "Only in a small way," he said modestly. "Nice little Katya has been giving me lessons when the old dragon is out of the way. Pinkney doesn't mind. She's a good lass, really. Bark's worse than her bite. So where have you got to, Mrs. Bloxham?"

"Deirdre, please," she said. "We've got the right newspaper archive, but need to know as close as possible the date of the issue, and then remind us of the name of the missing woman, if you can still remember it."

Roy scratched his head. "Now then," he said. "It was in the seventies. I remembered that before, didn't I. The month would get us a lot nearer." He closed his eyes, and the others waited silently. "August!" he said triumphantly. "I know that, because there was a story lower down the page about the rotten harvest. Rained solidly for six weeks, apparently. Well, I knew that, of course, from our own farm, but friends who had all arable and no cattle had all their eggs in one basket. We had chickens, too!" He chuckled, pleased with his joke.

"August," said Deirdre, tapping away on the keyboard. "Ah yes, here it is. What was the woman's name again? Only the big stories would get into this archive by name."

"Bentall," Roy said. "Katherine?" interposed Ivy, feeling left out. "Or Caroline," said Gus, not wishing to be a silent partner.

Roy nodded. "Try Caroline Benthall," he said.

"With an *h*?" Deirdre asked, fingers poised.

"There's always an *h* in Benthall," said Ivy. "Surely you know that, Deirdre. With your secretarial experience an' all."

"Yes, with, I think," Roy said placatingly. "Try it with."

So Deirdre typed in Caroline Benthall, but with no luck. She tried again, this time leaving out the *h*. "Hey! There it is!" she shouted. "Look, Ivy! The picture and everything."

Suddenly everyone fell silent. It was the photograph. A woman in her forties smiled tentatively out at them.

"Ye Gods," said Gus. "It's her to the life. Beattie Beatty. Except, of course, that it must be her mother."

"So our Beattie's name is really Beatrice Bentall, not Beatty at all," said Ivy, confusing everybody. "Well, I don't know I'm sure," she added. "The woman looks happy enough. What could have made her run off, leaving small children?"

"Not all that small," said Deirdre, who had been reading on. "It says here there were two girls, one of five and the other fourteen. Both have been taken into care, and the police were treating the case as very serious, it says."

"What else does it say?" Gus peered at the screen.

"Not much," Deirdre said, and scrolled down the page.

"Stop!" said Roy suddenly. "Well I never," he muttered. "I'd forgotten all about that bugger," he said, and the others looked at him curiously.

"See that picture there." He pointed at the screen. "Isn't

that young Roussel? Right on the end of the picture. On a horse, at the county show?"

"Ask Deirdre," Ivy said drily. "She'll know."

Already staring closely at the screen, Deirdre shrugged. "Could be," she said. "But it could be any of those young twits who rode to hounds and all that stuff. I know he was a good rider. Won all the jumping classes at the show. I remember that. But couldn't swear that was him."

"Can you print it out, then we could look at it under a magnifying glass," Roy said. "I've got a really powerful one back at the detention centre. I use it for reading now."

"Back at the *what*?" Gus said.

Roy laughed. "S'what me and my old mate at Springfields used to call the place," he said, and his expression changed. "Dead now. He was a good old boy, was Donald."

Ivy reached out and patted his shoulder. "You still got some mates around," she said. "We three, for a start."

Roy began to hum, and then sang in a cracked voice, " 'We three, at Happydrome, working for the BBC' ... Can't remember any more," he said, and the others burst into spontaneous applause.

"Right," said Deirdre, sniffing a little, "I'll print out this page, and then we can all go back to the detention centre and put it under Roy's magic magnifier."

UNFORTUNATELY, MRS. SPURLING had returned unexpectedly, and had given Miss Pinkney the rough end of her tongue, which could be very rough indeed.

"They pay very good money to be in here," she had rasped. "And what for? Not to be let out on the loose with irresponsible people like those three! They come in here for protection, comfort and SECURITY!" The last word was shouted, and Miss Pinkney looked around nervously. She knew Katya was checking in all the rooms looking for

Mrs. Somerfield's spectacles. Hunting for lost specs was a regular job in Springfields.

"Afternoon, Mrs. Spurling," Roy Goodman said, leading the other three through the door into reception.

"My dear Mr. Goodman," she said, rushing forward and taking his arm. "Are you all right?" She glared at Ivy, who glared back.

"Of course I am," Roy replied, shaking her off. "Don't treat me like an old man, Mrs. Spurling," he said, "or else I must look for another detention centre with greater opportunities for parole."

"What? Did you say 'detention centre'?" Mrs. Spurling gasped.

"A joke," Gus said, stepping forward quickly. "We have taken great care of Mr. Goodman, and I think you will agree he is none the worse for a little outing."

Deirdre beamed. "Look at his pink cheeks!" she said. "Years younger, wouldn't you say, Miss Pinkney?"

Miss Pinkney nodded timidly. "I must see about supper," she said, and vanished swiftly.

"Ah, supper!" said Roy. "What's for supper, Mrs. Spurling? I could eat a horse," he added enthusiastically. This reminded him that they had to magnify a horse and rider before supper, and he beckoned the three to follow him to his room.

"If my ever-loving husband had not run off with the cook," Mrs. Spurling said to herself, "I would not have to stand here without support in front of a load of old loonies on the rampage." She grabbed the book she had come back for, and went out of the building with shoulders hunched and fury in her heart.

"HERE IT IS," Deirdre said, picking up a hugely magnifying eyeglass. Give me the paper, Gus."

He put it down on Roy's bedside table, and said she

should take first look. "You're the one who's likely to recognise distinguishing features and so on," he said.

Deirdre refrained from saying that the picture was unlikely to show the birthmark on Theo's right buttock, but looked seriously at the photograph.

"Oh my God," she said finally. "It's him. Look, see that hard hat he's wearing. It's got a couple of pheasant feathers tucked in the band round the crown. It was his trademark. It's him. I could swear it."

Thirty-five

THEO ROUSSEL HAD not come home for dinner last night, in spite of Beattie having cooked a pheasant in the way he liked best, in a casserole with white wine and apples.

She had tried telephoning him on his mobile, but it was switched off. Then she had thought of ringing the pub, but knew that if he thought she was checking up on him he would be furious. She had put the pheasant in the larder and made scrambled egg on toast for herself. As he was still not back at ten thirty, she had left a note reminding him to lock up, and went to bed.

Now, next morning, she heard him coming to find her, calling at the top of his voice. She was in the kitchen garden, cutting a lettuce for a salad lunch, and when she looked up to see him approaching, the sun was in her eyes, and for a moment she thought it must be some other man. This confident-looking stranger with dark glasses and an apologetic smile could not possibly be . . . But it was. Theo Roussel had spent half the night playing cards and drinking with old cronies in the Conservative Club in town, and had woken to find himself in the spare room of the town mayor, who had been one of the party. He had been touched by the genuine warmth of the welcome he received.

"Sorry, sorry, sorry!" he said. "Forgot to ring you about dinner."

"You did say you might not be in, but I expected confirmation. And I slept in a house that was not locked against intruders," Beattie said formally.

"Oh, come on, Beattie. A chap needs a little relaxation sometimes. Am I forgiven?"

It was quite clear to Beattie that he did not care whether he was forgiven or not, and she turned to pick up the lettuce. He had given no explanation, she noted. Not that he was likely to tell her the truth. He didn't need to, anyway. She knew where he had been. Tucked up in a cosy bed at Tawny Wings, that's where. Beattie could not bring herself to say the woman's name, even to herself.

"I shall be in for lunch," Theo continued, blissfully unaware of the ice in Beattie's heart. "Back about one. I have to catch up with young David Budd now." He walked off with a definite spring in his step, and Beattie glowered at his retreating figure.

THE BUDDS' COTTAGE was in its usual chaotic state, and when Theo knocked at the door Rose peeped out to see who was there. "Oh, blast!" she said, and called up the stairs, "David! It's the boss!"

"What, the very lovely Beattie?"

"No, it's himself. The Honourable. Can you come down quickly, while I throw everything behind the sofa?"

There was nothing wrong with Theo's hearing, and he laughed out loud. He tried the door and found it unlocked. Opening it a fraction, he called out, "Don't mind me, Rosebud. I just want a word with David."

Rose smoothed her hair down with her hands and went to the door. "Come on in, then," she said. "And look where you put your feet. Simon's gone for a nap after causing his usual whirlwind in the house. Ooops! Watch out for Thomas!"

"Who?" said Theo, looking around.

"Thomas the Tank Engine. Ah, here's David. I'll put the kettle on."

"Morning, Mr. Theo. Though it feels like afternoon to me," David said. "Bin up for hours! One of your ewes was in trouble. I could hear her, poor old thing. She was on her back and couldn't get up. All four skinny legs waving about in the air. You got time for a cup of tea? I missed breakfast, so I'll just have a bite to eat, if that's all right with you."

David realised he was talking too much, but it was such an odd experience, having the boss, the real boss, calling in to discuss farming matters. Something big must have happened up at the Hall. The man in front of him was like a kid let out of school, all smiles and bounce. He wondered how much Theo remembered about farming.

"Sit down for a bit," said Rose, brushing small garments off a chair and giving Theo a mug of strong tea. "You're looking well. Beattie all right?"

"Oh, I expect so," Theo answered. "Now, David," he began, and told him of new plans he had for the sheep. "And I think we should have a few milkers back in the cowsheds," he said. "I'd be keen to help with the milking, and we could use most of it ourselves and in the village."

"There's a lot to dairying now," said David, not fancying the extra workload. "Rules and regs without end. You ask any dairy farmer—if you can find one!"

"Don't worry," said Theo. "I'll take charge of all the bureaucracy. And I mean to look for a young student who could help you around the farm in general. I'm promoting you to manager, and we'll see if we can find a little extra for you with your growing family."

"How did you know?" said Rose, patting her stomach.

"I didn't," said Theo. "But congratulations! Do ask me to be godfather."

When he had gone, Rose and David looked at each other. "Deirdre Bloxham," said Rose.

"Then she'd better watch out," David replied. "Hell hath no fury like a Beattie scorned."

IVY SAT IN her room with the window wide open, taking deep breaths of the fresh morning air. She was thinking about Roy Goodman, and their researches into the Bentall story. It had happened so long ago, and if it hadn't been for Roy's excellent memory they would never have known. "Mind you," she said to her mother, whose ghostly shade seemed to have returned to listen to Ivy's innermost thoughts, "mind you, as he said, it's surprising how much you remember of the early days when you're old. Can't remember what happened a couple of hours ago, but the first day I started in the mixed infants class in Ringford is as clear as a bell."

"Talking to yourself, Ivy?" said Roy's voice outside the door. Ivy had left it ajar to get a good blow through the room.

"Come in, if you must," said Ivy. She had wanted to spend a good hour thinking out where they should go next to discover more about Beattie Bentall. She had a very strong feeling that if they knew what had happened to Beattie over the years since she was abandoned by her mother, then they'd be well on the way to discovering the murderer of old Mrs. Blake.

"I've remembered something else," Roy said.

"Go on," Ivy said. The old man had a twinkle in his eye, and she wondered if this was just an excuse to find her.

"Them children. Belonging to the missing woman, Caroline Bentall. There was a boy, as well. Beattie—if that *was* her—was a twin."

"It didn't say so in that article we got up on the computer," Ivy said doubtfully.

Roy shook his head. "No, it wouldn't. But we had this woman who trimmed cairn terriers—she used to breed them—and she came from over that side of the county. Came to the farm about every six months. Mother used to breed them. They were good working dogs, too, not silly lap dogs like they are now."

"So, what about the twin?" Ivy said, trying to get Roy back on track.

"Ah yes, well, I heard her and Mother talking in the kitchen. I remember it clearly, because I was home from school with chicken pox. Covered in spots, I was. But I hated missing school, and went back much too soon. Still got a couple of scars on my face—see?" He pointed to two tiny pockmarks beneath one eye.

Ivy sighed. "So, what about the twin?" she repeated.

"Sorry, Ivy," he said. "Well, this dog lady was talking to Mother about the missing-woman case. I was wishing she would hurry up and go, so I could cadge some biscuits out of Mother, while she still felt sorry for me."

"Roy!"

"Oh, yes, well, the dog woman said that what nobody else seemed to know was that the missing mother had had twins. It was a scandal at the time. Unmarried mothers were not so common then, although there'd always been plenty in the old days, when the squire and his sons had the pick of the maidservants."

He looked at the expression on Ivy's face and hurried on.

"Apparently the Bentall woman kept one of the twins, it was a girl, and had the boy fostered. So there's probably a man around somewhere who's Beattie's long-lost brother! O'course, he might be dead by now, or emigrated or summat."

Ivy frowned. "You're making this up," she said. "You wouldn't remember all them details from forty years ago."

Roy bridled. "I'll have you know, Miss Beasley," he protested, "that I can remember lying in my pram in the orchard at the farm, looking up at a bird on a branch and seeing it do a plop right on my teddy bear."

Ivy smiled, and then, because the memory was so ridiculous, she began to laugh loudly. She fumbled for her hanky, wiping her eyes. "All right, Roy," she said. "I'll believe you, tho' thousands wouldn't."

Roy beamed. "That's the first time I've seen you laugh, really laugh, since you came to this place," he said. "Well done, Ivy."

The door was still open, and as Katya passed by, she heard Ivy laughing and came back to look. It was such a rare sound in Springfields. Not many residents laughed out loud like that.

"Good morning, Miss Beasley and Mr. Goodman," she said. "It is a lovely morning, yes?"

They agreed it was indeed, and Roy suggested coffee and cookies would improve it even more. Katya rushed off, feeling that perhaps this job was not so bad after all.

"Now," Ivy said. "This business of the twin is important. I was having a think before you came in, and had wondered if one of us should go over to that place—was it Oakbridge?—and do some asking around." She picked up the telephone and tapped in a number.

"Deirdre? Can you get down here for a coffee with me and Roy. I can rustle up Gus as well. Something important has come up. What did you say? Well, now, at once, you silly girl! Coffee's on its way."

"Really," she confided to Roy, "you'd think my cousin was the busiest woman in Barrington from the way she goes on. She can spare half an hour, she says. Huh!"

Gus was in the kitchen chatting up Katya as she made coffee and prepared trays for residents who were staying in their rooms. He offered to carry one up to Miss Beasley, and noticed there were two cups.

"Mr. Goodman is visiting her," Katya said. "Will you be a visitor, too? Shall I put on extra cup?"

Gus thought how delightful was her version of the English language, and set off carrying the tray. He met Mrs. Spurling, who sniffed. "I have given up, Mr. Halfhide," she said as he passed her. "I have nothing more to say."

"Splendid!" said Gus, and turned his head to smile as she passed. Unfortunately, his foot caught in the rug, and he tripped, sending the tray load flying in her direction.

"Bloody hell!" she screamed, and fled to her office to write to the board of management to submit her resignation. Before she could begin, Gus's face appeared round the door.

"Get out!" she said.

"Just wanted to apologise," he said. "I'll be gone tomorrow. Your tender loving care has worked wonders, and I'm quite restored. Bless you, my dear," he added, hardly able to believe that this was the smooth, sophisticated Gus Halfhide speaking.

They were finally settled, all four, in Ivy's room, with a fresh tray of coffee brought up by a mortified Katya. "Mrs. Spurling says one more mistake, and I'm out on my ear. Is this right, or did I mistake her saying?"

"Don't worry about it," Gus said quickly. "She'll soon forget all about it."

He gently escorted Katya to the door and shut it firmly. "Now, Ivy," he said, reminding himself he was senior partner in this outfit, "perhaps you'd like to tell us what is so urgent?"

Thirty-six

"TWINS!" SAID DEIRDRE. "Are you absolutely sure, Roy?"

He nodded, pleased that his excellent recall had produced such a marked effect on the others. Deirdre was frankly disbelieving, saying he must have been dreaming last night and thought it was a genuine memory. Gus was not so hasty in his judgement. For one thing, his mind was focussing more on his scalded ankle than Roy's revelation. He dare not mention it to Mrs. Spurling. Perhaps Miss Pinkney would be more sympathetic and find a soothing balm. He would go looking for her after this meeting was over.

"You're quiet, Augustus," said Ivy. "Do you see what this means, if Roy's recollection is correct?"

"Of course," said Gus, snapping to attention. "It means our Beattie Beatty Bentall has got a brother. I wonder what he called himself? Maybe he kept his real name, and there's a mysterious Joe Bentall lurking in the shadows somewhere?"

"Miss Beasley has an idea for what we should do next," Roy said, and Gus looked enquiringly at Ivy, who said that she thought it was probably time for one of them to go to Oakham and do some asking around.

"Oakbridge," Roy corrected her. "I'll go, if you like?" he offered.

There was an embarrassed pause, and then Deirdre said gently that she thought perhaps one of the younger members of the agency should take on this particular assignment.

"On the other hand," Gus said, "Roy does know that area well."

"So do I," said Deirdre. For goodness sake, what was the silly man thinking of? Roy Goodman was very old, and totally unlikely to be able to trudge round a town, possibly in the rain, ferreting out snippets of information—or not, as was quite likely.

Ivy shifted in her chair. "If you ask me," she said, "Roy and me should stay here and keep our eyes open for what's happening here. Miss Pinkney had a chat with me this morning, and she was full of a story going round village about Mr. Roussel. He's been seen in the pub, apparently, and then out and about with young Budd. The gossips are having a fine time, as you can imagine."

"Well I never," said Deirdre, looking smug. "Amazing how people can change, isn't it?"

"Yes, well," Ivy said, frowning at her, "let's just get back to how you're going to start when you get to Oakbridge. Tomorrow, d'you think, Augustus?"

"Yes, certainly," said Gus. "Which brings me to an announcement." He smiled at Ivy, and reached across to pat her hand. "Much as I appreciate your offer to support me in my convalescence here," he said, "I am so much better now, really restored, and have told Mrs. Spurling that I shall be going back home tomorrow. Then Katya can have her room back. Whippy will be so pleased to see me. I've missed her a lot, and I get the impression that Mrs. Spurling will not be too sorry to see me go!" he added, but did not elaborate.

Deirdre said that was fine, and she would pick him up tomorrow morning, take him and his things back to his cottage, and then they could set off for Oakbridge straightaway.

"Good," said Ivy. "That's that, then. Now, I must be going."

"Where?" said Deirdre.

"To the shop," Ivy said. "I don't really need anything, but I make sure I have a short walk every day."

Roy Goodman cleared his throat. He said sadly, "So no more pontoon, then, Gus?"

Ivy looked at him. All the light had gone out of his eyes, and she realised he saw himself back in the lounge, staring at the telly with the others, this wonderful interlude finished.

"*We* shall play pontoon together, you and me, and Gus will be visitor, as Katya says," she said. "And you and I shall play cribbage, too. Must keep our wits about us, Roy," she added, "for what might happen next."

Thirty-seven

GUS LOOKED ABOUT him at his neat and tidy sitting room. "I didn't leave it like this!" he said.

Dierdre shook her head. "No, you didn't. But the fairies have been in and cleaned it up for you."

"It was you, I suppose," Gus said, and he leaned forward to give her a peck on the cheek. "Thanks a lot. Now, can I offer you a coffee before we start?"

Deirdre said she thought they should be off straight-away. "If we sit down now with coffee, you can bet some-one will arrive or the telephone will ring, and we shall be delayed. Come on, lad. Best foot forward."

Gus wondered whether to tell her about his scalded ankle, but it was much better today and he decided not. He had to reclaim his status as senior partner. A scalded ankle should be nothing to invincible Augustus, scourge of the criminal fraternity!

As they went back to the car, which Deirdre had parked outside the cottage, Gus turned and looked along the ter-race. A curtain twitched in the window of his next-door neighbour, and he saw Miriam's face peering out. On an impulse he waved, and to his amusement the face disappeared. Now she had seen he was back, he must expect a visit sooner or later.

Oakbridge was about thirty miles from Barrington, and in the big limousine they seemed to be there in no time. "I could get used to one of these," Gus said to Deirdre. "It's like riding in a feather bed."

"That dates you," said Deirdre. "How many feather beds have you slept in?"

"In this country, none," he said severely, "but overseas, I have slept in every kind of bed you can imagine. Feathers, straw, rough blankets on concrete, you name it, I've slept in it or on it."

Deirdre looked at him closely. "D'you know, Gus, I'm never really sure whether to believe you or not. What exactly was your work?" Gus gazed into the distance, as if to a far-off land where things were very different. "I'm afraid I am not able to say. You will just have to take me on trust, Deirdre. So let's look for somewhere to park and get on with our search."

"Duly snubbed! I get the message," Deirdre said. "What are we searching for, by the way? And have you any idea where we should start?" They parked the car in the municipal park, and started walking into the town centre.

"Newspaper office, for a start," said Gus. "Then the library, and then start accosting old ladies and gents in the street to see if any of them remember Caroline Bentall."

"That newspaper closed down years ago," Deirdre objected. "No point in going in the offices of the present *Blixton Advertiser*, is there?"

"Oh yes," Gus said. "This is the old newspaper building, and there'll be an archive of the old papers, as we know from the Internet. But they'll have a lot more in a dusty back room than came up on your computer screen. Come on, girl, in we go."

After half an hour trawling through well-organised old newspapers, they came across the one they'd already seen. "Let's see the next week. There might be a follow-up story," Deirdre suggested. They were rewarded by a couple of paragraphs on an inside page, stating that the missing Caroline Bentall had not been found, though the police were following up leads. The two children—again no names—were settling well with temporary foster parents in the town. There appeared to be no other relations who could look after the two girls. Police were appealing for anyone who had information to come forward.

"Right, well, let's look at the next week," said Deirdre. But unfortunately an explosion in a carpet factory on the edge of town, resulting in a huge fire that had darkened the sky, took up several pages, and the rest of the news was squeezed into a diminished space. There was nothing more about Caroline Bentall.

Deirdre looked at her watch. "Time to go, if we're to look elsewhere," she said. "It's like the proverbial needle in the haystack in here."

They walked down the High Street and followed the signs to the library. "I think we should say we're looking for a long-lost relative," Deirdre said. "They'll probably be more helpful that way. Shall I say she was my aunt?"

Gus shook his head. "No, not worth risking ramifications," he said. "Don't forget the unfriendly character who knocked me on the head."

"You mean you might be followed, bugged, all that?" Deirdre asked excitedly.

"Calm down, dear," Gus said. No point in alarming her. She was good company, and he did not want her to duck out of their investigation in fright.

"A Mrs. Bentall? Caroline, did you say?" The girl behind the library desk was young, blond, and wore glasses that in no way detracted from the fact that she was very pretty. Gus took over. "It was quite a sensational case in the seventies, I believe," he said. "We were interested in the history of Oakbridge, and came across this story. Curiosity was roused! You know how it is," he added persuasively.

The girl was used to men chatting her up over the desk, and said shortly that curiosity killed the cat, but she would ask her colleague, who was of an age to remember.

While they were waiting, Gus and Deirdre wandered round, looking at the book displays. "Here, Gus, look at this," Deirdre said suddenly. She pointed to a framed photograph on the wall. It was of a stalwart-looking man with a mayoral chain and stern expression. Underneath was a testimonial to his excellent work for the town during his term of office. His name was Geoffrey Harold Bentall.

"I see you've found Caroline's father," said a voice from behind them. A neat, grey-haired woman stood looking up at the photograph. "He was a popular man in the town. Responsible for all kinds of modern developments. Mind you, he was a builder himself, so some said he did pretty well out of all the new blocks of flats and terraces of small houses! Why are you interested in poor Caroline?"

Deirdre repeated Gus's story that they were interested in the history of the town—such an interesting old place— and had come across the story of the missing mother of two. They were curious to know what had happened. "Just curiosity," Deirdre said. "It must have been so sad for the two little girls."

The librarian frowned. "So what are you going to do when you've found out?" she said. She could spot a reporter from one of the gossip rags from twenty paces.

Gus thought quickly, and said that actually he was a novelist, and was always interested in odd stories. Not that he ever used actual names or places, he assured her. His plots always started with a curious happening, or character, or sometimes from a place, as in his last book, which had been inspired by an old church in the middle of a field, he explained, warming to his invention.

"How interesting," she said. "Well, if you like to come into my office, I could give you a few details."

"I WONDER HOW they're getting on," Roy Goodman said to Ivy, as they sat over the cribbage board. He had accompanied her to the shop, sat at the same table at lunch, and had stayed close by for the rest of the day. Now they were in the lounge, and the light was fading from the sky.

"Back home, I should think," said Ivy. She had known it was unlikely, but she had hoped one of them might have come in to report, or at least telephoned.

"And one for his knob," she said, counting up her hand of cards.

"Ivy!" said Deirdre, coming in on a cloud of expensive perfume. "Did I hear aright?"

"Don't be silly," said Ivy. "You know perfectly well I was counting up points. Is Gus with you?" she added.

"No. Feeling tired, he said, after our long day. He's gone home to bed. I put a hot water bottle in it, and he should be well away by now."

"And I suppose he said you weren't to tell us about your day until he could be here, too?"

Deirdre agreed. "Yep, he did say something like that. But I thought I'd just look in to say hello. How are you, Mr. Goodman?" she added. "Have you two been busy?"

Ivy raised her eyebrows. "Well, yes we have. But we can't say much about it until Augustus is with us. We don't really want to have to say everything twice, do we, Roy?"

Thirty-eight

"MY PLACE OR yours?" Gus had said lightly to Deirdre next morning. They were deciding where to meet Ivy. Deirdre had called in at Rose Budd's for some free-range eggs, and nipped along to the end of the terrace to see how he was feeling after all yesterday's excitement.

"I suppose we could go to Springfields as usual this afternoon. Still, there's more room at Tawny Wings," she answered. "Easy for Ivy to get to. She can just about manage to walk up, with her stick. She likes an outing."

"What about Roy?" Gus said. He had really liked the old man, and had not missed the disappointed look on his face when he thought he would be left out from now on.

"What d'you think? No harm in him joining us, if he can make it up to my house."

Gus said he thought the old boy would be quite an asset with all his local knowledge. "I'll call for him," he said. "They've probably got a wheelchair we can borrow."

"Dare you show your face at Springfields detention centre?"

Gus laughed. "There you are then," he said. "How could we leave out the old boy when that's how he thinks of it?"

"Answer the question," Deirdre said. "Dare you show your face to Mrs. Spurling after she practically evicted you?"

"I've dealt with worse than Mrs. S. in my time. Just watch me."

Deirdre said she would look forward to that, and departed.

WHEN GUS CALLED Ivy to tell her he'd collect both of them to walk to Deirdre's, he nervously asked if Mrs. S. would be on duty. She said he needn't worry because Mrs. Spurling had a day off to go to a funeral. "It'll be Miss Pinkney in charge," she said, "and for some reason she seems to like you. Said it wasn't the same without Mr. Halfhide keeping them all amused."

Gus sighed dramatically. "I can't help it, Ivy," he said. "I have this effect on elderly spinsters."

"Well, here's one who can resist," Ivy said tartly, and ended the call.

As Gus chuckled and put down the phone, there was a gentle knock at his door. He knew immediately who it would be, and thought of hiding. But no, he had to let her in sooner or later, so it might as well be now.

"Gus! How *are* you?" It was Miriam, looking really very presentable, and clutching a large box of chocolates. She thrust them at him and said she had been so worried, and not been able to find out what had happened.

"Come in," he said, trying to make it sound welcoming. "Have a seat. What lovely chocolates! Thank you so much. Shall we have one to celebrate my homecoming?"

Miriam relaxed. She had been nervous about calling on him, not sure how she would be received. Since her abortive visit to Miss Beasley, she had begun to suspect something was going on between Gus, the old girl at Springfields, and that smart woman at Tawny Wings. And Rose Budd was involved, too. As for Theo, he seemed to have taken leave of his senses, according to report. More likely he had come to them at last, Miriam had thought privately. Was there hope for her after all?

Then there had been that invitation to tea at the Hall, and Beattie had treated her like royalty. Bosom friends was what she apparently had in mind. Miriam's thoughts were in a whirl, and she hoped to gain some enlightenment from Gus.

"I do hope you weren't frightened by my tumble," Gus said. Miriam might have seen something from her watching position by the window?

"I think I must have been out," she said now. "I didn't hear anything, unfortunately. These old cottages must be more soundproof than I thought. The first I knew of it was after you'd been taken away in the ambulance. The whole village was buzzing with it next morning."

"I don't think I yelled. I was out cold when Mrs. Bloxham found me."

Miriam said that she was really sorry. She could have rescued him sooner, perhaps. "I could have tried that mouth-to-mouth resuscitation thing," she added brightly.

Lucky escape, thought Gus, but said kindly, "So what have you been up to? Are the police any nearer finding out who attacked your poor mother?"

Miriam looked suitably downcast. "They've been back asking me questions," she said, "but they won't tell me anything."

"What questions?" Gus said, and added hastily that he wouldn't like to think she had been upset by them at such a sad time.

"Mostly about Mother. They wanted to know things like how long she'd lived in Barrington, when she married my dad, if she'd worked at the Hall, an' on and on.

They wanted to know about me, too. Where I'd worked, if I'd had any boyfriends, all kinds of personal stuff like that. It's not fair, Gus. Not when I'm grieving for me dear old mum."

Gus looked at his watch as obviously as he could. Miriam took the hint, but said why didn't he come round and share a chicken casserole with her? There was plenty for two, and she'd made a plum duff for pudding. "I don't suppose you've got any food in the house?" she said.

As it happened, Gus knew that Deirdre had filled up his fridge for his return, but he was interested in what Miriam had been saying about the police, and so accepted her offer with gratitude. She was delighted, of course, and said he might as well come back with her now, and she would help him through the rusty old gate.

BEATTIE WAS ON her way to the shop when she saw Miriam and Gus disappearing round to the back of Miriam's house. Good heavens, the woman was insatiable! Not content with seducing Theo way back, now she had her claws into the Halfhide man. She walked on, feeling the ground shifting beneath her feet. It wasn't, of course, she told herself, looking down at her feet walking smartly over the potholed tarmac. It was an illusion, and she tried to convince herself that things were just as before.

But things *were* different, she knew, absentmindedly waving to Rose Budd at the end of the terrace. Theo was no longer willing to accept her judgements and suggestions. He wanted to see the farm accounts, the housekeeping records, even the orders for the shop. At breakfast, he had announced that he wanted her to buy everything she could from the village shop, keeping her purchases from the supermarket to a minimum. "'Use it or Lose it!'" he said merrily, quoting from a Post Office advertisement.

All her hard work and planning over the years had been

wiped out in a single afternoon, she reckoned, and then realising that he could have many more afternoons with Rose Budd's connivance. And now Theo had this ridiculous idea of reorganising the farm! It had all gone so smoothly, though admittedly the income from the estate had gradually diminished.

And that was another thing! Theo had said he wanted all the accounts, bank statements and cheque book stubs in his study. He would be buying a new filing cabinet to house all the financial documents relating to the estate.

"You've taken on so much over the years owing to my neglect and idleness," he had said, and added that now he intended to make recompense by relieving her of all those onerous tasks. "You must go out more," he said, smiling at her. "Enjoy yourself, Beattie. You've earned it."

She was left with nothing to say. Her blood boiled, and she was sure that he was having a great time making her suffer. His apparent concern was completely false. He knew exactly what he was doing to her, and it was he who was enjoying it.

She stopped at the foot of the steps leading into the shop, and looked at the seat placed there in memory of Theo's father. "To hell with both of you!" she said under her breath. "I'm not beaten yet. Just you wait, and that goes for you, too, Mrs. Bloxham."

"Morning, Miss Beatty," Will said, coming out of the shop door to put out the empty milk bottle crate. "Nice to see Mr. Roussel getting out and about again." He continued, "All due, I'm sure, to your tender loving care!"

Beattie would have spat at him if she had not spent most of her life grooming herself to be a lady. "I suppose you've run out of apples as usual?" she said sourly, and followed him into the shop.

Thirty-nine

DEIRDRE WATCHED THE oddly assorted trio walking slowly towards Tawny Wings. So Roy had scorned riding in a wheelchair. Dear old chap! He is a lesson to us all, she thought. No matter what happens to our crumbling bodies, it's the will to live, to keep going whatever, that counts. She must make sure that she remembered that. No lounging around in her luxury home. Perhaps she would learn to play that neglected piano. Or take up tennis?

They had reached her gate, and she went downstairs to welcome them. "You've done very well, Roy," she said. "Coffee's all ready. I'm sure you could do with a reviving cup."

Roy had given up drinking coffee a long time ago, on the advice of Mrs. Spurling, who said it was bad for the heart. Now he reckoned there wasn't much damage could be done at his age, and he sniffed the lovely smell of brewing coffee coming from Deirdre's kitchen.

"Bring it on!" he said, and allowed Gus to help him—in

fact, to practically carry him—up the wide stairs to Enquire Within's headquarters.

"Now," Gus said, as he saw Ivy drawing a deep breath ready to speak first. "Now, shall we report on our day's researches, Deirdre? You'll be pleased, Ivy, that our journey was not wasted."

Deirdre began, explaining that they had given up on the newspaper archive, but had then needed to go no further than the public library, where the librarian had been most helpful. She had been there for years, she'd said, and had seen many changes in Oakbridge, some of them not for the better.

"Get to the point, Deirdre," said Ivy.

Deirdre sent her a black look, and said that maybe Gus would like to carry on, if her account was not satisfactory.

Gus sighed. "Very well, then," he said. Never work with widows and spinsters, he reminded himself. "We had asked around for details of the Bentall family, but had no luck. Then Deirdre noticed a photo hanging on the wall. . . . Carry on, Deirdre."

"It was Caroline Bentall's father. Town mayor, chain an' all, and a very pompous look on his face. Anyway, the librarian then told us all she knew."

"And are you going to let us in on the secret?" Ivy said, with studied politeness.

Gus took over. "Apparently the family was well respected. Caroline was an only child, and the apple of her father's eye. She did well at school, but was not encouraged to go to college. Her mother was a mousy woman, so the librarian said, and obeyed her husband in every way. He wanted Caroline to stay at home and got her a job in the county council offices. To be fair, the librarian said, the girl had not wanted anything more adventurous. Boys was all she was interested in, and eventually settled for one totally disapproved of by her father."

"Mind you," said Deirdre, "I reckon no bloke would have been good enough for his precious Caroline."

"Agreed," said Gus. "Anyway, she wouldn't give him up, and then the inevitable happened."

"She got herself in the family way?" suggested Ivy.

"Correct," said Gus. "And was sent away in the good old-fashioned tradition, only to reappear months later somewhat slimmer. The twins were fostered."

"But she had a family eventually? Did she marry the bloke?" Roy had been listening avidly. "That was the whole point of the story, wasn't it? She abandoned her children. And what about the twins? Did the librarian say what happened to them?"

Gus looked at Deirdre and laughed. "Straight to the heart of it, Roy," he said. "Yes, she married later, but not the father of the twins. It was only after she'd had a child with her legitimate husband that she reclaimed one of the twins, the girl, from the foster family. The boy was left behind, and the librarian didn't know what had happened to him."

"Blimey," said Roy. "What a story! Like something out of *Peg's Paper*."

"*What?*" Gus stared at him.

"My mother used to take it. It was a girls' magazine. True life stories, she said, but even she didn't believe that. Lurid, they were, and she loved them."

"So who was the husband? Must've been a nice chap to take on the bigger girl."

"He was all right, but a bit short-tempered, according to the librarian. And he insisted that as the elder girl wasn't his, she should not have his name. So she kept her mother's name, i.e., Bentall." He paused, and then dropped the bombshell. "She was called Beatrice Bentall."

"So that's it," Ivy said quietly.

Roy agreed that Gus and Deirdre had done really well,

but probably the most important thing now was to find out what happened to the husband, and what he'd done to cause his wife to desert two perfectly nice daughters. "It was obviously his doing," he said confidently. "And what happened to Caroline? She seems to have vanished off the face of the earth."

"Perhaps he murdered her," Ivy said flatly. "Or someone else did."

The silence was prolonged. Deirdre shivered. "Shall I put the heating on?" she said. "It's gone cold in here. I'll go and make more coffee."

"Have you finished, then?" Ivy asked, quite oblivious of the sensation she had caused. "Is that all your friendly librarian knew about the end of the story?"

Gus nodded. "Yep," he said. "She went away to do her training around that time, and by the time she returned the whole thing had died down, and gossips were busy with a new scandal in the town."

"Let me guess," said Roy. "The town mayor had run off with his secretary, leaving his mousy wife to pick up the pieces?"

Gus laughed loudly. "You're a national treasure, Roy," he said. "I'll help Deirdre with the coffee," he added, and followed her down the baronial stairs.

IN THE KITCHEN, Gus stood watching Deirdre fill the kettle and put ground coffee in the cafetiere. "Are you thinking what I'm thinking?" he said, seeing her frown.

"What are you thinking?"

"That we've uncovered something so important we should probably take it to the police. Beattie must be on their list of suspects. Time to hand over to them?"

Deirdre turned to face him. "You must be telepathic," she said. "It was telling it all to the others, watching their reactions. Yesterday, somehow, we were so excited at finding out so much that it was like a game. You know, pass 'Go' and collect two hundred pounds. But now, well, I can see just how important it might be. What do you really think, Gus?"

"Haven't had time to think it out properly," he said. "Shall we ask the others? They'll be looking at it from another viewpoint."

"Right," she said. "I reckon Ivy might have a sensible suggestion. She often has, irritatingly! You wait, when we ask them, I bet she'll say, 'Well, if you ask me,' etc., etc., and produce the commonsense answer."

They carried the fresh coffee upstairs, and Deirdre refilled the cups. "So what shall we do next?" she said. "We reckon what we found out is really important. So should we go to the police or carry on investigating?"

"Well, if you ask me . . ." said Ivy.

Forty

"IF YOU ASK me," said Ivy, "I'd say we've got a long way off the track finding out who murdered Miriam Blake's mother. Good as your research was, you two," she continued, "it don't really shed any light on what the police are investigating. So I suggest *we* carry on investigating until we find some definite connection."

"Told you," said Deirdre to Gus.

"Told him what?" Ivy asked.

"Never mind," Deirdre answered. "Anyway, we haven't heard what you and Roy discovered yesterday. Your turn now, Ivy."

"Not me, it's Roy's turn."

"Oh, come on," Gus said. "Let's cut the politeness and get on with it."

"Right," said Roy, "I'll start and Ivy will interrupt."

"I'm sure she will," muttered Gus, and added loudly, "Off you go, then, Roy."

"Well, you remember Miss Pinkney told us about the

hot gossip in the village? About Mr. Roussel being seen everywhere, for the first time in years?"

Gus nodded impatiently, then began to speak.

Ivy interrupted. "Yes, he went to the pub and the shop, called in at the Budds and walked round the farm with young David. But most interesting for us, he called in on Miriam Blake yesterday, and stayed for more than an hour."

Deirdre and Gus chorused, "Who told you that?"

Ivy's biscuit had gone down the wrong way, and she choked into her handkerchief. Roy took over. "It was Rose Budd," he said. "Ivy and me went for a stroll down Hangman's Row, and she was in her garden. Full of it, she was."

Deirdre looked at the frail old man. "You walked all the way down Hangman's Row?" she said.

Ivy and Roy exchanged looks. "I pushed him," Ivy said. "He didn't want me to, but Mrs. Spurling stopped us on the way out and said Roy was her responsibility and she could not allow him to walk so far. She produced a shiny new wheelchair, and Roy is light as a feather. Nothing to him. So it was no problem for me to push. Better than a Zimmer."

"I'm going to get one of those electric shopping scooters," Roy said happily. "Never thought of it before, but it would be even better if Ivy didn't have to push."

"So you talked to Rose Budd about Miriam and Theo," Deirdre reminded him. She was extremely irritated to hear that Miriam had been closeted with Theo for more than an hour. "Doing what?" she asked.

Ivy shrugged. "How should we know? Rose didn't know. She doesn't have much to do with Miriam, and so couldn't ask her, could she? Mind you, if you ask *me*, they were up to no good. We know she was his fancy woman once before. Might have picked up where they left off, so to speak."

"Ivy!" said Deirdre. "That is pure speculation! I am sure Theo would have nothing whatsoever of that nature to do with Miriam Blake. Not after what the old mother told him about being brother and half sister!"

"And not when he had already taken up where he left off with you, Deirdre? I've got private doubts about the Hon. Theo. I'd hate to see my cousin led up the proverbial garden path."

"I'm quite capable of looking after myself," snapped Deirdre, and Gus decided it was time to step in.

"This is a really interesting piece of information, Ivy," he said, "and one we should definitely follow up. The question is, how?"

There was silence for a minute, and Gus thought that he should probably own up. "As a matter of fact," he said casually, "I had lunch with Miss Blake."

"When?" said Deirdre.

"Today. Before coming up here."

"Better explain," muttered Roy. "These girls will eat you alive if you've been consorting with possible suspects."

"Not *possible* suspects," Gus said. "Chief suspect. She said the police had been back asking more questions. Some new ones, and some old ones over and over again."

"Like what?" Deirdre said.

"Oh, about what she did before she stopped work to look after her mother. Whether she resented giving up a busy life. All that sort of thing. She was angry. Said it wasn't fair, they should leave her alone when she was grieving for her mother."

"Huh!" Ivy said. "For a grieving daughter she seems to have a lot of gentlemen callers!"

"Comfort and support, Ivy," said Gus, and laughed. "But in my case, a useful piece of information gathering."

"What else did she say?" Roy said.

"She talked a lot about Theo," Gus said, glancing apprehensively at Deirdre. "She was really upset, and said she could never find out why he suddenly broke off their weekly love-in sessions in Hangman's Row. I asked her if her mother had any explanation, and she said the old woman had been really cruel. Said Mr. Theo had found better fish to fry. He was a toff, she said, and toffs didn't get serious about farmworkers' daughters. He'd got fed up with Miriam, and no wonder, her mother had said. He could have the pick of the county. Miriam was just handy when he felt randy. She'd gone on taunting her, and Miriam had wept for days."

"And you believed all that codswallop?" Ivy said sharply.

"Sounded convincing to me," Gus said innocently. In fact, he had not believed a word of it. He had decided after an intimate lunch with Miriam that she was one of those fantasists who ends up not being able to tell the difference between truth and lies. It was what she didn't say that convinced him she knew the whole sordid story. Once or twice, when Theo's dad was mentioned, she had started a sentence and then broken off, as if editing what she was telling him.

"Well, looks like I'll have plenty to ask Theo next Saturday," Deirdre said.

There was an embarrassed silence. Ivy raised her eyebrows, and said that if Deirdre asked her, she would suggest asking the questions when she first arrived at the Hall, and then there would be plenty of time afterwards for this, that and the other.

"First time I've heard it called that," Roy said conversationally. Deirdre ignored him, and said icily if Ivy would like to make out a list of questions, she would certainly do her best to carry out her duties efficiently.

"The other urgent thing," Gus said, firmly changing the subject, "will be to find out what happened to Beattie's twin brother. Got any ideas how we do that, team?" he said, hoping to inject a professional note. Never again, he said to himself, will I work with geriatrics. Then he exempted Deirdre from this. He reckoned she was not much older than him, bless her. She'd been good company yesterday.

Now she made a sensible suggestion. "I think we should start by assuming that he kept the same name as Beattie, before she changed it. Bentall, I mean. We can look up all the Bentalls around Oakbridge first, then the whole county. There should be records of the foster parents, too, but you can bet your bottom dollar they'd be strictly confidential. Angry father of twins sent packing by Mayor Bentall, might seek custody, etcetera."

"We need to know who *was* the father of the twins," Ivy said. Once more there was a silent pause. Then she continued, "Any guesses?"

Deirdre looked at her watch. "Oh, my goodness!" she said. "I really have to go into town for a volunteers meeting at social services. While I'm there, I can ask about fostering rules in those days. Might turn up something. Would you like a lift back to Springfield?" she asked, looked first at Ivy and then Roy.

"We'll walk," they chorused.

Gus laughed. "I'll see them safely back," he said, and the meeting ended amicably.

Forty-one

MIRIAM BLAKE STOOD at the sink, looking out at her untidy back garden. When her father was alive, it was immaculate. He spent hours out there with his neat rows of vegetables and flowers to cut for the house. He loved flowers, but his wife didn't. She said they were all right for a few days, then they dropped petals all over the place and the water smelled awful. Without saying anything, he continued to bring them in and Miriam arranged them for him. It was a silent revolt, a conspiracy between father and daughter against wife and mother. Mrs. Blake's only defence was to throw them out after a day or two, long before it was necessary.

Now there were no flowers, and only exhausted perennials struggled through. Perhaps she could get Gus to take it in hand for her? Now he had been unable to resist her cooking, and, she hoped, her charms, she would feel quite happy about asking him.

What a week it had been so far! First of all, Theo coming in and buttering her up, reminding her of the good old days, asking how she was managing and whether she had decided to go back to work. She'd made him coffee, and he had been so nice and kind. But she saw now that it was all a ruse to soften her up. He'd got up to go, and then said he had nearly forgotten what he'd come to say. This was, of course, to tell her he had to put up her rent to a realistic level, same as the others in the terrace, but if she couldn't afford it, he would help her with housing benefit and see that she found an affordable council house. He had friends in high places, he had laughed. She had not seen the joke. It was clear that her new pal Beattie's promise to keep the rent low was now overruled.

Then, thank goodness, there was today, making it all come right again, at least for a while. Gus would champion her cause, she was sure of that. He'd had a lot of experience, he'd said, with bringing justice to people who'd been wronged. And the other way round! She was sure he had brought many a wrongdoer to justice. They'd had such a lovely talk. She couldn't wait until he called again. And if he didn't she would pop next door and see how he was getting on. After all, he'd had a serious fall, and it was the least she could do.

She dried up the dishes and put them away. The afternoon sun was still warm, and she decided to have a stroll to the village shop. It was taking her quite a while, she realised, to make use of her new-found freedom. She could go anywhere at any time. So long as she didn't leave the country! The police inspector had been firm about that. She felt the shadow of suspicion darkening her good mood, and shook herself. Fresh air and exercise, that's what she needed, and she locked up the house and stepped out at a brisk pace.

She met a couple of village people who'd known her for years and would always pass the time of day. But they looked the other way, and hurried on. She knew why, and tried to forget the snub. But then, when she reached the shop, it was full, and she had to stand and wait. The minute she had arrived through the door, silence had fallen. Nobody greeted her, except Will behind the counter, and even he looked embarrassed. The woman who lived next door to the shop, Mrs. Broomfield, was helping Will, and she studiously ignored Miriam when it came to her turn.

"Well," said Miriam loudly, plucking up courage. "I thought it was supposed to be innocent until proved guilty in this country?"

The huddle of gossips over by the DVDs for hire immediately began talking about their favourite film, and Will moved across to where Miriam stood.

"Good morning, Miriam!" he said. "Lovely morning!" He now had to make an important decision. Sadie Broomfield was going away for a week, and he needed to replace her. Now that Miriam was free, she would be the obvious choice. She'd done it before, and needed no initiation into the workings of the village shop. But although he had tried hard not to let it influence him, the fact that most people suspected Miriam of murdering her mother meant that the shop would be avoided for a week. Could he afford that?

Now she had made her remark about being innocent, and he made his decision. He cleared his throat and in a loud voice said, "Now then, Miriam, are you free next week to take over from Sadie? She's off whooping it up on the Costa Brava, leaving me in the lurch. Could you fill in for the week?"

Miriam felt the blood rising to her cheeks. She could have kissed him. With tears in her eyes she said of course she'd be glad to help him out. She'd come in for a pound of tomatoes, please. She was going to try her hand at a risotto, she said, for an important guest.

"Then you'll need some of my Italian ham," he said in an artificially jolly voice. "Gives it the authentic taste."

One of the gossips asked audibly if her friend had tried Farmer Jones's ham on the bone. "Fresh English produce is good enough for me," she had added, and left the shop swiftly, calling over her shoulder that next week she thought she'd go to the supermarket in town, just for a change.

Miriam drooped. "Are you sure you want me?" she whispered to Will.

"Quite sure," he said angrily. "I've a good mind to bar that woman from the shop."

Miriam shook her head. "You'd have to bar most of the village," she said sadly.

DEIRDRE HAD ARRIVED late at the social services offices, and crept into the back of the room. She was seen, of course, and the woman chairing the meeting welcomed her with exaggerated pleasantness. "*So* glad you could make it, Deirdre," she said.

After the meeting was over, there was coffee and chat, and Deirdre looked around for the person she knew could help her with fostering questions.

"It's a long time ago, I know," she said. "But would it be possible to look up records of who was fostered and with what family, dating back to the nineteen seventies?"

"Bit before my time," the woman answered. "In this area, was it?"

Deirdre said no, over the other side of the county, in and around Oakbridge. The woman shook her head. "Can't help you, sorry," she said. Then she brightened. "I know," she added, "there's a man over there—he gave us a little talk before you arrived—all about his experiences of social work in the old days."

"How old?" said Deirdre, beginning to feel like Mrs. Methuselah.

"Go and ask him," urged her friend. "He's a nice old boy, and I'm sure could help you. Go on, Deirdre, you know how senior citizens like to talk about olden times."

Well, nothing ventured, thought Deirdre, and pushed her

way through the chattering crowd to where a tall, heavily built man stood talking to a dutiful couple of social workers. He was probably in his seventies, and looked friendly. When she said she was sorry she had missed his talk, but wanted to pick his brains, he twinkled at her with a promising sparkle in his eyes.

"Oakbridge, did you say?" He was interested, and flattered that this attractive woman had sought him out. "Got my first job there," he said, smiling at the memory. "Just a young chap then, full of high ideals and hopes for a better future for mankind!"

"Did you have anything to do with fostering?" Deirdre said.

"Oh yes," he said. "We had to take in all the various departments. Are you trying to trace somebody?"

What a piece of luck, Deirdre said to herself. "I'm interested in a woman who disappeared leaving two children alone in a flat. Seems they never found out where she'd gone, and the children were taken into care. The only name we've got is Bentall."

"*Bentall*? The Bentall case? Good God, I certainly remember that. It was a real scandal at the time. The mother who disappeared was the only daughter of the mayor. Old Buster Bentall, we used to call him. Made his fortune out of speculative development. But that was a long time ago," he added. "What exactly did you want to know?"

Deirdre said that anything he could remember would be useful. It appeared he remembered the girl getting pregnant, going away and returning without a baby later on. Then she'd got married, he thought, and suddenly a child, a girl, appeared from nowhere, and she'd had another by the husband."

"What a memory!" Deirdre said.

"Photographic, the wife says," he replied modestly. "I can see old Buster Bentall now. Bit of a bully, red-faced and little piggy eyes. He'd not get away with it these days."

"With what?" Deirdre said.

"Making his money that way when he was in mayoral office. Had friends in the planning department. You scratch my back and I'll scratch yours. You know the kind of thing."

"Anything more about the abandoned girls?"

He rubbed his chin. "There was something. Came up later on, but I was about to start a new—Oh, I remember!" he said, beaming. "Although the mother never reappeared, the man she married was in the news a few years later. Robbery with violence. And he had form, apparently. Nasty piece of work, I reckon. No wonder she went missing!"

Deirdre held her breath. "Do you remember his name?" she squeaked.

"Oh, yes. He came from the worst family in Oakbridge. They were Jessops. Generations of no-goods, and he was reckoned to be the worst. Buster Bentall cut them off when they married. Wouldn't have his daughter or her husband in his house. His poor wife was heartbroken. The girl was an only child, you see."

"Now then, Deirdre," a loud voice came from behind them. "You mustn't monopolise our distinguished guest! Come along, now, I want you to meet my assistant. She so much enjoyed your talk."

"Sod it," muttered Deirdre, as they walked away. Still, she had probably found out most of what he remembered, and it was pure gold.

Forty-two

IVY SAT UP in bed, and felt a sharp pain in her lower back. She tried to ignore it, and swung her legs over the edge of the bed in order to stand up. The pain shot through her, and she gasped. Finally it subsided, and she managed to reach her chair to sit down. Well, what did she expect? She had insisted on pushing a wheelchair over rough paths and down a grassy lane. Roy had said he thought it was too much for her, but she had insisted.

Stubborn, said her mother's voice in her head. Always were and always will be.

"Go away, Mother," said Ivy, not noticing her door was ajar. A voice answered her.

"It's only Katya, Miss Beasley. Are you all right? You need some help?"

"Come in, girl, come in," Ivy said, wincing as she settled in her chair.

Katya came in, and saw at once that Ivy was not all right. She was pale, and frowned as she moved to reach for her handkerchief.

"Do you have pain," Katya asked anxiously.

"A little. Just a twinge in the back. Often get it," Ivy said, and added that old age was sent to try us, and she did not intend to let it get the upper hand.

"Shall I get Mrs. Spurling? Or Miss Pinkney? Would you like some painkilling tablets?"

Ivy eventually convinced Katya that she was perfectly all right, and if she could just sit quietly for a few minutes the pain would go. A cup of strong, hot tea would be just the ticket, she said. Perhaps she could have breakfast in her room.

She did indeed feel much restored after she'd eaten porridge, bacon and egg, and drunk three cups of tea, and even managed to dress herself without help. She knew from experience that the best thing to do with a painful back was to walk steadily for half an hour or so to loosen it up. She telephoned Deirdre to say she would be coming up for an early coffee. "On foot," she interrupted, as Deirdre offered to collect her. She was encouraged to hear Deirdre say with genuine pleasure that she must stay for lunch, and then they could have a good talk. "I've got something very interesting to tell you, Ivy," she said.

On the way to Tawny Wings, a Land Rover passed her slowly, then stopped, backed somewhat erratically, and the window was lowered.

"Good morning! Is it Miss Beasley?"

"It is," said Ivy coldly. "And who are you?"

"Theodore Roussel, and I've heard so much about you from your cousin. I thought I would just say hello. Perhaps you would like to come up to the Hall with Deirdre one day and have coffee with me?"

"Very kind of you, I'm sure," Ivy said. "Nice to have met you. Good morning." She bit her lip and limped on. Standing still, she had felt the pain again. Funny old thing, thought Theo, as he drove off. Not exactly friendly! And nothing at all like jolly Deirdre.

When Ivy was settled in a chair with a straight back, she explained to Deirdre that she'd got out of bed awkwardly. "Nothing serious," she said, "so don't fuss." On no account would she mention the strain of pushing Roy about the village.

"Well, now, what have you to report?" Deirdre said.

"Nothing much—except that I met your ex-boyfriend on the way up here."

"Theo? Where was he?"

"In a battered old Land Rover, cruising along outside your house, no doubt hoping to get a glimpse of you. He got me instead!" Ivy laughed grimly. "Anyway, he just introduced himself and drove off. Pleasant, I thought."

"That's wonderful!" Deirdre said. "He's really finally escaped the old dragon. Don't you think it's wonderful, Ivy?"

Ivy nodded. "Yes it is," she said. "But let's hope he doesn't go completely wild. You know what male dogs are like, once they're off the leash."

"He's not a dog! And he's certainly not a silly young man anymore. Did he mention me?"

"Oh yes, in passing," said Ivy.

"What did he say?"

"Invited me to come up to the Hall for coffee. With you, of course."

"Good-o! I'll give him a ring and fix a day. Calls are getting straight through to him now."

"So now we've got that out of the way, what's the interesting news?" Ivy said, shifting uneasily in her seat.

"Well," Deirdre said, "you know I was going to a social services meeting yesterday afternoon? Well, I happened to mention fostering to a friend who works there, and she passed me on to this man from Oakbridge who'd given a talk. I'd missed it, being late starting from here. . . ." And then she gave Ivy an entertaining account of her conversation and the information this man was able to give her, until the irritating interruption.

"So, what a piece of luck, eh, Ivy?" she said. "Now we know about Buster Bentall being a dreadful old Victorian father, and him cutting off Beattie's mother and the kids, and the criminal no-good husband and father of the third child. Oh yes," she added, "and the poor wife of Buster. Being cut off from her daughter and grandchildren broke her heart."

"Did he mention that there'd been twins? Or what happened to the boy? Or anything about the twins' father or the foster parents?"

Deirdre sighed. Trust Ivy to concentrate on what she had not discovered, rather than new trustworthy information. "No, dear," she said. "I was getting round to it when he was dragged off to talk to other people. But I did get his name from my friend afterwards, and his address and phone number."

"Well done," Ivy said, aware that she had been a bit grudging. If only these twinges would settle down. . . .

"So what shall we do next, d'you think?" Deirdre could see that Ivy was in pain, but knew better than to ask if she would like a pill. Best thing to do, she thought, would be to distract her. Poor old Ivy, she was determined not to give up.

"Another trip to Oakbridge, I suppose," Ivy said. "Now we know poor Caroline Bentall's husband was a Jessop, that's another important lead. There will certainly be records of him. Probably still some young Jessops in the town. Ask in the post office, Deirdre. You and Gus should go, and don't offer to take Mr. Goodman!"

Deirdre laughed, and went off to warm up a quiche for lunch. As she switched it to a low heat, an idea came to her. She walked back to the drawing room and was surprised to see Ivy on her feet.

"Two squirrels in your garden, eating the bird food." Ivy tapped her stick on the window and the squirrels scooted rapidly up a nearby silver birch tree.

"How's the back?" Deirdre said, and Ivy replied that it was much improved and she would thank Deirdre not to mention it again.

"Right," said Deirdre. "Now, I've had an idea. When Gus and me go to Oakbridge, why don't you and Roy come along for the ride? You've never been there, Ivy, and Roy could tell you about the town as we drive round. I can drop you off at a decent café, and you can have a bite to eat and then go back to the car. It's very comfortable, and you can listen to the radio or something. I could give you my spare keys," she added, warming to her idea. Then she looked at Ivy's face, and added quickly, "So shall we think about it and decide later?"

WHEN THEO RETURNED to the Hall, after an enjoyable session in the pub with some old village friends who remembered him as a young tearaway, he went straight to the kitchen and told Beattie he'd met Miss Beasley, Mrs. Bloxham's cousin, and had invited them both for coffee one morning. He would let her know which day, after he had spoken to Deirdre.

Deirdre is it now? fumed Beattie. But her new strategy made her say pleasantly, "That will be very nice. It is such a treat to see you out and about again. Lunch will be ready soon."

So *Deirdre* and Miss Beasley were coming to the Hall for coffee. Beattie bashed a piece of rump steak with the rolling pin until if meat could speak, it would have yelled for mercy. No doubt Theo would want her to wear cap and apron and bring in a tray set out with the best china on an embroidered cloth, curtsey and retreat backwards out of the room!

As she peeled newly picked cooking apples to make a crumble, she set her mind to find a way to turn the coffee party to her own advantage. After a few minutes, her face brightened. Ah yes, that would be the answer. She began to hum, and then burst into a cheerful if tuneless version of " 'All You Need is Love.' la de-da de-da." John Lennon would turn in his grave, she thought. When Theo passed by the kitchen door and heard an odd noise, he realised with surprise that it was Beattie giggling.

Forty-three

IN SPITE OF Ivy's protestations that it was a bad idea, she and Roy were comfortably tucked up on the backseat of Deirdre's luxury car, rugs around their knees, and a large thermos flask of hot coffee with beakers, sugar and chocolate biscuits in a basket between them.

When Deirdre had suggested it to Gus yesterday, he had not been keen, and said frankly that they'd be much freer to investigate whatever came up if they were on their own. "After all," he said, "we could find a lead in Oakbridge that could keep us there for hours."

Deirdre had agreed, but said they had to be very careful with Ivy. She could easily decide to give up the whole thing, especially with the back pain.

"She said it was quite gone when we turned up this morning," Gus had said sulkily.

"Yes, well, that's good. But she and Roy are very useful in this whole affair, and we don't want them to feel left out," Deirdre insisted. "Ivy has a talent for seeing straight through to the heart of things, and Roy in his best moments produces nuggets of vital local information. For instance," she had added, "there's that story of his about the recluse lady who'd lived in Springfields before it became an old folks' home. Who was she? And what about the woman who looked after her? I've never heard anyone speak of them before, and I've lived in Barrington quite a while now."

Gus had given in, and now they purred their way through country lanes and tunnels of overhanging trees. Gus had turned off his sat nav and asked Roy to guide them through a pretty route to Oakbridge. "Haven't been along here for years," the old man said now. "Look, Ivy, that's where my old Aunt Eliza lived. Dead now, of course, and the farm sold. Still, the old apple tree's still there—look at those Cox's!"

Deirdre saw a sign outside the entry to the farm, advertising apples for sale. She slowed down and pulled off into the farmyard. "Go on, Gus," she said, "go and buy us apples to munch."

He got out and muttered to himself that this was turning into an outing for the Darby and Joan Club. But he came back with a bagful of crisp apples and an old knife the farmer's wife had insisted on giving him. "She said some elderly people couldn't eat apple skin," he reported, handing the bag into the backseat. "We can return the knife anytime."

It was a much longer route than the main road, but even Gus began to enjoy the absence of traffic and the gentle landscape. Finally they turned into the car park in Oakbridge, and both Ivy and Roy said they needed the toilet. "Leave me the key, Deirdre," Ivy said. "We shall be fine. You might meet us in town, but ignore us. Me and Roy are determined to make the most of our parole."

As Deirdre and Gus walked off in the direction of the post office, Deirdre said, "So you see, Augustus Halfhide. And we still have plenty of time."

* * *

A YOUNG WOMAN behind the busy post office counter wished them good morning and smiled, obeying recent PO instructions to be polite to every customer, no matter how tiresome. She had a nice smile, and Deirdre was encouraged to ask her if there were Jessops living in Oakbridge.

"Are you a relation?" said the girl.

Gus took over and said no, but they knew someone who was, and were anxious to pass on a message.

"We have telephone directories for public scrutiny over there," the girl said, twinkling at him. "I'm sure they will give you the information you want." She pressed her button and the mechanical voice said, "Window number *eight* please."

"Dismissed," said Gus, as he, with Deirdre, headed for the telephone directories.

"Probably ex-directory, if they've followed their forbears into the underworld of crime and violence," she said.

"Pure melodrama! Come off it, Deirdre," Gus said, and found the right page. "Oh, my God, dozens of 'em! Where on earth shall we start?"

"Can I help you?" said a man's voice at their elbow.

"We're looking for somebody called Jessop," Deirdre said, smiling gratefully at him. "There's so many of them here."

"Is it the old man you want? Interested in his house? I saw it was up for sale."

"How old is he?" said Gus.

"Ooh, must be in his seventies now. We used to live next door to them until we couldn't stand them any longer and moved away!" He laughed, and Deirdre said she was sure that would be the Jessop they wanted. "We might be interested in the house," she said.

The helpful man nodded, pointed at the address in the directory, and wished them luck. "Better take y' bodyguard," he said, and chuckled as he walked away.

Meanwhile, Ivy and Gus sat in a chintzy café not far from the car park, happily drinking coffee and eating doughnuts. "Ivy, can I ask you something?" Roy said hesitantly.

"Depends what it is," said Ivy. Her heart began to thud. *Surely* not, not at their age?

"I've often wondered, since we met, why you're living in Springfields? After all, you're not infirm, and you've certainly still got all your marbles!"

Ivy sighed with relief, and thought for a moment. She was not accustomed to confiding her private feelings to anybody, but there was something gentle and reassuring about Roy.

"To tell the truth," she said, looking down at her plate, "I was lonely. One or two of my old friends had passed on, and another gone into a home in Tresham, and I could be in the house for a whole day without speaking to a soul. I was never one for relying on other people, but I began to feel—well—a bit lonely."

Roy had a good idea what this was costing Ivy, and reached out and patted her hand. "Just the same for me," he said. "Only I ain't got a lovely cousin Deirdre to rescue me!"

"I suppose she's all right," said Ivy, straightening up. "Better than I expected, really. Now Roy," she continued, "you've done very well, but I reckon we should finish up and get back to the car and settled down. We can watch people coming and going, and have a listen to *Desert Island Discs*. It's that nice whatsisname this week." With the immediate future organised, they relaxed and took their time.

"Excuse me," said a middle-aged woman, looking at the empty chair at their table. "Is this seat taken?"

"We're just going," Ivy said. "You're welcome to sit there."

Roy, who had spent years in the company of lonely old

people in Springfields, looked at the newcomer and saw the same hungry look in her eyes. Hungry for company, poor thing, he thought.

"Why don't we have another coffee, Ivy, before we go?" he said. "I am sure this lady won't mind."

Ivy looked at him in surprise, but the neat little woman said that would be so nice. Were they new to Oakbridge?

Roy said Ivy was, but he wasn't, and this was Miss Beasley and he was Roy Goodman. "And your name?" he said politely.

"Bentall," she said. "Renata Bentall."

Forty-four

DEIRDRE LOOKED INTO the front garden wilderness and up at the pebble-dashed semidetached house. "Looks neglected," she said, moving closer to Gus. "Is it empty already, do you think?"

Gus shook his head. "I saw a face at the window," he said. "Just a flash, then it went away."

"Man or woman?"

"Man, I think. Shall we go and knock?"

Deirdre took a deep breath and walked up the path to the peeling front door. She pressed a bell button, but could hear no sound.

Gus reached out and knocked firmly. "That should bring him," he said. "Or we could always yell through the letter box that we are police and he must open up?"

"Don't be daft," Deirdre said. "And anyway, there's someone coming."

Shuffling footsteps approached, and then the door opened a crack. "Woja want?" a gruff voice said.

"Mr. Jessop?" Gus said. The old man grunted, "Yes," and "So what?"

"We wondered if we could take a look at your house," Deirdre said, in her most persuasive tone. "It is for sale, isn't it?" They had noticed that there was no signboard outside.

"Why ain't you with the estate agent, then?" the old man said.

"Oh, we haven't got long in town," Deirdre improvised. "Just called on the off chance that you might be at home. It is Mr. Jessop, isn't it?"

The old man nodded, and said suspiciously that he never opened the door to strangers. How was he to know they wouldn't beat him up and ransack the house? "Not that there's anything worth having," he said quickly.

"We could leave the door open, so you'd feel safe?" Gus said. "But if you'd rather not . . . You've probably had an offer already?" This was cunning, as the old man had had no offers, and was canny enough to want a quick sale at this time of economic downturn. The estate agent had told him the housing market was dead.

"You'd better come in, then," he said, and opened the door wider. A suffocating smell of decay and damp assailed Deirdre's nostrils, and she gulped.

"In you go, then," Gus said, giving her a push from behind.

The old man shut the door, in spite of Gus's suggestion they leave it open, and motioned them towards the back of the house. "Better start at the worst bit," he said, and led the way into what might once have been a reasonably smart kitchen, but now resembled a rubbish dump.

"Have you lived here long?" Deirdre croaked, trying not to breathe.

"All me life," he said. "There's bin Jessops in Oak-bridge for generations. Well known, we are. We're a big family, an' before you ask, we ain't got nothing to do with that scandal about a Mayor's daughter what married a Jessop. Different lot altogether. So if you've come asking about that, you can scram. There's bin enough asking about that!" His raucous cackle alarmed Deirdre and she backed out of the kitchen. Gus stood his ground, and asked if the old man lived alone.

"Yep," he said. "But me son an' daughter-in-law live just down the road. I'm goin' to move in with them when this place is sold."

Poor things, thought Deirdre. But then it occurred to her that the money from the house sale would probably be useful to Jessop's son, if he could prise it out of the old man.

They continued on their stifling way round the house, with Gus and Deirdre asking innocent questions as they went. "Was your wife an Oakbridge girl?" Deirdre had admired the surprisingly high-quality dressing table set. Loot, probably. "None of your business," he replied, and then added reluctantly that when his wife was alive, the house had been a showplace. "Clean as a new pin," he said."You could eat off the floor."

Gus asked if he'd been an only child, or were there others in the family.

"Bit nosy, ain't you? You're not plainclothes, are you? If y'are, you can get goin' right away. Nothin' for you here."

"No, no," said Gus. "We live over the other side of the county, and are thinking of moving, that's all. Oakbridge seems a very nice town."

Mollified, Mr. Jessop agreed, saying that he had a sister who lived in the posher part. "Up Nob Hill." He cackled. "She's a widder woman now. Married later in life than the rest of us, and above her station. Rich family. Husband was a Bentall, distant connection to that Mayor Bentall an' all that rubbish. I don't see much of her now."

"Don't blame her," muttered Deirdre into Gus's ear as they came down the narrow stairs. There were holes in the stair carpet, and she stepped carefully, holding on tight to the sticky banister.

Finally, they were out into the fresh air, and Deirdre took long, deep breaths, as they walked back towards the centre of the town. "Phew! I think I would've passed out if we'd been in there much longer. Was it worth it, Gus? Did we learn anything? I could hardly think in that dreadful atmosphere."

"Oh, yes," Gus said smugly. "We learned something. I tell you what, when we get back to the car I'll explain it all in words of one syllable to you and Ivy and Roy."

As they approached the car park, Deirdre was relieved to see Ivy and Roy safely in the back of the car. "Well, at least they can't have strayed far," she said. She opened the door and was thankful for the scent of lavender water and subtle aftershave. "All well?" she said. They looked at each other and nodded. "Yes, thank you," said Ivy. "We managed very well. How about you two?"

Gus said they should all relax and have the picnic lunch, and then he would tell them about their interesting morning.

Deirdre poured out the coffee, and handed round the sandwiches on small disposable plates. She had remembered paper napkins, and Ivy used hers to dab the corners of her mouth in the genteel fashion taught to her by her mother long ago.

"We shall be swimming in coffee!" she said to Roy.

"Did you find a nice café?" Deirdre said.

They nodded. "Warm and pleasant," said Ivy. "And we had doughnuts." "Two each," Roy added. "So," continued Ivy, brushing the crumbs off her lap, "tell all."

Gus then recounted their morning's work, from discovering Jessop in the telephone directory to meeting the man himself in his sordid surroundings, and finally gleaning a useful piece of information.

"So," he said, "all we have to do is find his sister, the former Miss Jessop who married a Bentall."

"If she exists," said Deirdre doubtfully.

"Oh, she does exist," Ivy said, producing her surprise rabbit from the hat. "We've met her."

AS THE BIG car rolled along the main road back to Barrington, Gus spelled it all out for them. "Buster's daughter Caroline had twins by a man as yet unknown. They were adopted and she returned home. Later, she married one of the Jessops, but a different branch from our old man. Caroline's Jessop was unsuitable and violent. They had a girl baby, and Caroline was cut off by her parents. She retrieved her girl twin from foster parents and left the boy with them. No trace of him yet. Are you with me, everyone?"

Ivy nodded firmly, and Roy dare not say he was lost already. Deirdre said that Gus was explaining well, and to carry on.

"So," he said patiently, "we have Caroline and husband Jessop, with illegitimate girl twin and legitimate girl baby. From what we already know, Beattie was almost certainly the girl twin, and we don't know what happened to the legit girl. Clear as mud," said Roy, but added that he'd get the hang of it later. Ivy would help him.

"By the way," Ivy said casually. "We got her address and phone number. Lonely sort of woman, and we got on famously. She wants us to go and visit."

"Brilliant!" said Deirdre, pulling up outside Springfields. "Can we come, too?"

"Of course not," Ivy said severely. "She's not that lonely."

* * *

"HELLO, IS THAT Beattie? Miriam here."

"Good morning!" said Beattie, forcing enthusiasm into her voice. "How are you?"

"I'm fine, thanks," she said. "I was just ringing to see if you would like to have a cup of tea with me tomorrow afternoon?"

There was a pause, as Beattie thought rapidly how this would fall in with her plans.

"Well," she said, "I usually go to market on Saturday afternoons. . . ."

"Of course!" Miriam said. "I'd forgotten that. How about Sunday afternoon? That must be your day off!"

"Day off? What's that?" said Beattie. "But no, I would love to come tomorrow, thanks. Market day in town is not what it used to be, and I've been thinking of dropping it for some time now."

"Oh, good. Shall we say half three?"

"I'll look forward to it," said Beattie. After she put down the telephone, she sat for a while thinking out just exactly what she would do. First decision: say nothing about tea with Miriam to Theo. Let him think she would be off to market at her usual time, and tell him at the last minute about the change of plan.

IVY SANK GRATEFULLY into her comfortable bed and lay awake reviewing the day's events. She and Roy had returned safely with Deirdre, and Miss Pinkney had welcomed them back, saying Mrs. Spurling had gone home with a bad headache. She had said cheerfully that Miss Beasley and Mr. Goodman looked much refreshed after their outing, and arranged a tray of tea for them all in Ivy's room. They tried to map out what they would do next, but Ivy and Roy were tired, so the others had gone home, promising to think it all out ready for the meeting on Monday. Meanwhile, arrangements would be as usual for Deirdre to go to the Hall tomorrow afternoon to see Theo. And yes, she promised, this time she would be able to ask him all the necessary questions.

"I shall be prepared with some new ones, too, after today," she said happily.

Forty-five

THE KITCHEN AT the Hall was always warm, sometimes too warm in summer, when Beattie had the Aga turned up high for cooking. This morning, the weather had changed and a sharp wind blew around the stable yard.

"Lunch at the usual time?" said Theo, back to the Aga, warming himself. The Hall was a draughty old place, and he remembered his father doing exactly the same thing when his mother took over the cooking on staff days off. Perhaps Beattie should have a day off? He had never thought of this before. She was always so much in charge that he had just assumed she organised her free time to suit herself.

"Beattie," he said now. "Why don't you have a day off tomorrow? I can manage perfectly well. You can take the car. Maybe you could look up old friends in Oakbridge. Or explore the National Trust place nearby? I believe they've done a lot of work there. It would do you good," he continued, "you've been looking a little peaky lately."

And no wonder, thought Beattie. You try being up against a conspiracy! But she thanked him politely and said it was a good idea, but not tomorrow as she would need to make arrangements. Perhaps next Sunday. She would give it some thought.

After lunch, Theo wandered once more into the kitchen, sure that Rose Budd would be here any moment. To his dismay, he found Beattie, still in her working clothes, reading the newspaper. Usually at this time on Saturdays she had cleared away dishes, changed and tidied herself ready for market. He looked at his watch.

"Beattie!" he said. "Are you not feeling well?"

"I'm fine, thank you, Mr. Theo. Oh yes, of course, that reminds me," she said. "I shan't be going into town this afternoon. You'll remember I said how disappointing the market is these days. I thought I'd give it a miss today. Plenty of food in the larder, so we shan't starve."

She was delighted with his reaction, which could only be described as one of complete panic.

"But Rosebud? Won't she be expecting to come?"

Beattie shook her head. "I gave her a ring just now. She's quite happy about it. In fact, she sounded rather relieved and said how much she had to do at home. Rang off quite quickly, saying she'd tackle the ironing straightaway."

"I see," Theo said. "Well, it's your decision." He left the kitchen at a trot, and Beattie chuckled quietly to herself. Wonderful. Now, if she had timed it correctly, Deirdre Bloxham would be on her way.

IVY HAD WOKEN with the pain in her back returned. Mrs. Spurling said the wind was very cold this morning, and advised Ivy to stay in the warm. "We have a lovely lady coming in to play the piano for a sing-song," she had said. "I am sure you and Mr. Goodman will love the old songs."

As Ivy was well aware that a frog in full croak was more tuneful than her singing voice, she said she thought she would stay in her own room. She had a novel she wanted to finish before the library van came to the village next week. Then she had rung Deirdre to see if it was vital this time for her to sit outside the shop in the cold wind just to see Beatrice Beatty safely on the bus. Deirdre had said straightaway that she was sure all would go as before, and she must stay in the warm. She had not thought it necessary to tell Gus, and concentrated on making herself as attractive as possible.

Gus had forgotten to check on Beattie going off down the lane, but consoled himself that Ivy would be there to play her part as before. He kept a watch at the window, waiting for the car to go by, and smiled to himself as he saw Deirdre wave to him as she passed.

BEATTIE ALSO SAW the Rolls as it swept into the stable yard and Deirdre got out. She waited out of sight until there was a confident knocking. She paused for a few seconds, and then she opened the door.

"Good afternoon, Mrs. Bloxham. Can I help you?" she said, presiding confidently over her territory. Deirdre's expression was one of the most gratifying things she had ever seen.

Forty-six

"AREN'T YOU FEELING well, Mrs. Bloxham?" Beattie said, with mock concern. "You look as if you have seen a ghost. Do come in and sit down in my warm kitchen."

Said the spider to the fly, she added to herself.

"No, no, I shall be fine in a moment," Deirdre said, "I think someone just walked over my grave!" She made a brave attempt at a laugh, trying to organise her thoughts.

"I insist," said Beattie, taking her arm as if to help her up the steps. "Mr. Theo is very busy this afternoon, but I am sure he would be glad to see you in about half an hour's time. He is trying to finish an important letter in time for the post. Now, come along in, and I shall make you a nice hot cup of tea. I've been baking, and you shall have one of my special biscuits."

Deirdre did indeed feel a little shocked, and allowed Beattie to lead her to a seat at the kitchen table. Something had clearly gone wrong with their plans, and she supposed it must be that Ivy was not at her post, and therefore could not have raised the alarm.

"I had not expected to see Mr. Theo," she said now, her voice stronger. She could bluff this one out, and nothing would be the worse for it. Just a delay, that would be all, until next week. They would have to be more careful. She wondered what Beattie had told Theo. Surely he should have been able to make a quick warning call to Tawny Wings? She knew he had had the telephones fixed so that Beattie couldn't listen in.

"Have you come to see me, then?" Beattie said, pouring boiling water into a warmed teapot. "What can I do for you?"

"It was about the Women's Institute," improvised Deirdre, then thought, oh my God, what could I possibly want to know about the WI? "I was thinking of joining," she said, gaining confidence, "and I know you have been a member for years. Perhaps you could give me an idea of the kind of things you do?" If I have to go once a year with my single rose for the competition it won't do me any harm, she told herself.

A good try, but a lie, if ever I saw one, thought Beattie. "You'd certainly be very welcome, Mrs. Bloxham," she said. "Membership is dropping, even though we try hard to attract younger members, having more interesting speakers, all that."

"I'm not exactly a younger member," Deirdre said.

"Young at heart, though, Mrs. Bloxham. My poor mother used to say you are as young as you feel."

"Poor mother?" said Deirdre. She was rallying now, and thought she might as well make use of this mishap. "Is she still with us?"

Beattie shook her head mournfully. "Died years ago," she said. "After a long and painful illness. My sister nursed her until the end. So sad."

"And where did she live?"

"Oh, over the other side of the county. Local family."

"So you still have relations over there? That must be

very nice. I'm sure you keep in touch. Of course, I have my cousin Ivy living close by now, and I find it a great comfort. Since my Bert died, I mean."

"Ah, we seek comfort where we can find it, don't we," Beattie said. "Now, have one of my biscuits. Fresh from the oven."

"Oh, no thanks," Deirdre said, "I won't take your special biscuits."

"Mr. Theo's favourites," insisted Beattie. "He would never forgive me if you didn't have at least one. There are plenty."

Deirdre hesitated. They were small biscuits, wafer thin, and rather than argue she took one and ate it in three mouthfuls. It had a sharp lemony flavour, a little bitter. She refused a second. Let Theo eat the lot if he liked them so much.

At this moment the kitchen door opened, and Theo stood looking in. He winked at Deirdre. "Mrs. Bloxham?" he said. "What a lovely surprise. Beattie, won't you make us more tea and we can have a chat in the drawing room. You can bring me up to date with village news, De—er— Mrs. Bloxham. But first, Beattie, I wonder if you would just run down to the post box on the corner and get this letter off. I would like it to arrive tomorrow. Thank you, my dear," he said, and patted her arm.

As he walked off, talking animatedly to Deirdre, Beattie scowled. "Damn, damn, damn," she said.

DEIRDRE FINALLY LEFT the Hall just after three, having had two more biscuits and a second cup of tea. Theo had told her about Beattie's last-minute change of plan, and Deirdre had explained about Ivy not watching out for Beattie on the bus, and so they had had no warning.

"She's quite an adversary, our Beattie," said Theo.

"Never mind, we'll think of another way," Deirdre said,

rising and kissing him on the cheek. "Now you're out and about, there's absolutely no reason why you shouldn't call on me. I must go now, and bring Gus up to date, but I'll be in touch."

"My darling," said Theo, and kissed her hand.

BEATTIE SAW HER go off down the drive in the Rolls and looked at her watch. She would wait until Deirdre was well out of sight, then she would still be in time for tea with Miriam. She was almost certain that her plan would continue to work.

Gus, meanwhile, was surprised to see the Rolls slow down and park outside his gate. He rushed to the door. "What's up?" he said. "You're early, aren't you? Is he ill?"

"Let me in," Deirdre said. "I need a strong drink. Whisky, preferably."

Gus poured them both a dram of High Commissioner and they sat down. Deirdre gave him a dramatic account of her encounter with Beattie, and said it was a narrow squeak. "Nothing lost, though," she said.

Deirdre gulped down her whisky and Gus was alarmed to see her slowly turning a greenish yellow. "Ugh!" she said. "How long have you had this stuff? It's—" She got no further before rushing for the bathroom, from where Gus heard repeated retching. Then there was silence.

Gus frowned. What was the poor girl up to? He finished his own drink, and went up to the bathroom. "Deirdre? Are you all right? Need any help?"

Silence.

He knocked again, and when there was no answer he turned the handle and pushed open the door. "Deirdre?" He saw her curled up on the floor like a foetus in the womb, and he touched her cheek lightly. To his huge relief she moaned.

In an instant he had her up in his arms, and took her along the landing to his bedroom. "There," he said. "Got you in my bed at last." He could have sworn a tiny smile crossed her face. He put a rug over her and said he would be back in a couple of seconds. Water, he remembered, was the thing. She would be dehydrated from heaving up the entire contents of her stomach.

AN HOUR LATER, she was sitting wrapped in a warm rug, a cup of hot sweet tea beside her chair, which Gus had drawn up close to the fire.

"What on earth did you have for lunch?" he asked, as he settled in a battered old chair opposite her.

Deirdre shook her head. "Nothing out of the ordinary," she said. "In fact, I was a bit rushed, so I just had a boiled egg and toast. The egg was really fresh—one of the organic new-laid ones Will has in the shop."

"Is that all? No manky old banana, or curdled milk?"

"Nope."

"So nothing else to eat until you came here?"

"Ah," she replied, remembering. "Biscuits. Beattie had made some of her beloved Theo's favourite biscuits—yuk yuk—and insisted on my sampling them. I had three. She insisted on my taking the two iced with a star. But surely? They were wafer thin, and tasted strongly of lemon."

"An old dodge," Gus said.

"What d'you mean?"

"It's a cover-up. To obscure the taste of something nasty, you use a strong flavour of something nice, like lemon."

Deirdre was aghast. "*Poison*, d'you mean?"

Gus shrugged. "Could have been. That kitchen's pretty primitive up at the Hall, so I'm told. Could have been something put down for the rats, and still clinging to Beattie's hands. Or maybe designed to give you a really nasty bellyache, though unlikely. Anyway," he added, "you're not going home until you feel really strong enough. Tomorrow morning, if necessary."

"But the car . . . ? What will people think?"

"To hell with people. Think of it as a generous act to give them something new to talk about. Now, drink up that tea."

NEXT DOOR, BEATTIE and Miriam sat primly on the edge of their chairs, trying not to look out of the window. Miriam had seen the car arrive and park outside Gus's house, and had watched Deirdre hurry in. Then Beattie had arrived for tea, full of guesses as to what the big car could be doing there. Now they made an effort to talk of something else, but the subject returned inevitably to Mrs. Bloxham and Mr. Halfhide.

"Of course, you know she's anybody's? Anything in trousers," said Beattie. "She's been up at the Hall, pestering Mr. Theo. Honestly, Miriam, the woman is shameless."

"Does he know her, then?"

"Apparently. In the old days, when they were young. She seems to think they had undying love for each other, but as you know, Theo played the field. Like father like son, I say! But, do you know, Theo didn't even recognise Mrs. Bloxham when they met again."

Miriam blushed. Did Beattie know about Theo and herself? She couldn't remember how long ago Mother had stopped it. Had Beattie been at the Hall by then?

"So now she's after Gus Halfhide, d'you think? Shame, if he falls for it. He's a really nice man." And *mine*, she added to herself.

"As I said," Beattie replied tartly, "she's anybody's. And, of course, she's wealthy. That's an added attraction for the men."

Miriam wanted to say that she personally wasn't rich, but Theo had seemed to find her attractive. Instead, she said wistfully that even now, years later, Mrs. Bloxham was a pretty woman.

"Oh, I wouldn't say that," Beattie said. "But from the look of Mr. Halfhide, he would be after a few pounds in the kitty, never mind whether she was pretty or not. What is a still youngish man doing living in a farm cottage, seemingly hiding from the world?"

"He says he's been an investigating journalist," Miriam embroidered, and was shocked to see the change in Beattie's face.

"*What* did you say?"

"Oh well, I expect it's a silly joke," Miriam said quickly. "He laughed when he said it, but there is something about him, sort of secretive. I don't know nothing about his past or his family. And we have shared some time together lately. He needs looking after. I gave him a proper lunch, and he's had tea with me once or twice. But never a word about his parents, or whether he's got brothers or sisters."

She looked at Beattie, sitting so upright, so neatly and circumspectly dressed, and thought much the same could be said of her. Where had she come from? She just arrived at the Hall out of nowhere, mother had said, and had been there ever since.

They both said they must be getting on with some work, and stood up. Miriam caught a glimpse of the two of them in the mirror over the fireplace, and saw with a sudden jolt that they looked alike. Same high forehead, heavy eyebrows, slightly curving nose. Only their mouths were different. Miriam had full, generous lips, and Beattie's were thin and drawn tightly together. Good God, she thought. We could be sisters.

After she had seen Beattie off back to the Hall, she looked boldly at the car, still parked outside Gus's house, and then she glanced into his front window. It was not easy to distinguish the figures, but she was sure Mrs. Bloxham was sitting by the fireplace and Gus was leaning over her, straightening what looked like a shawl around her shoulders. Whippy was curled up on her lap.

Miriam's blood rose, and, beetroot-faced, she hurried back into her own house, banging the door behind her. "Who cares if he saw me!" she muttered. "He'll have to have a good explanation next time he comes to tea!"

Forty-seven

IVY WALKED SLOWLY down the High Street, conscious that the ache in her back was slowly fading. It had been quite an effort to leave the comfortable chair in Springfields lounge and set out with her stick. But now, after stepping out gently, she had reached the shop, and intended to turn back. Then she thought maybe she would treat herself to a box of Black Magic chocolates, and climbed the steps.

"Good afternoon, Miss Beasley!" Will said. He had just glanced at the clock and saw that it was nowhere near closing time so he might as well fill in time by being nice to an old lady.

"Are you still happy in our village?" he said pleasantly.

"No option," said Ivy. "Anyway, it's adequate for my needs now. Of course, at one time I was much more active and Ringford relied on me for all kinds of things." She wandered round the shop, reflecting that the one good thing about Barrington was that she had arrived as a blank sheet. All they knew about her was that she was Mrs. Bloxham's cousin. Had she still been in Ringford, where her reputation was of an upright, unrelenting spinster with a sharp tongue and frugal habits, her decision to buy herself a box of Black Magic would have set tongues wagging for days.

"There we are, then," Will said. "Don't eat them all at once!"

Shall if I like, Ivy muttered childishly to herself as she left the shop. She walked a few paces and then saw the town bus on its return journey coming towards her. Perhaps she would just hover and watch out for Beattie Beatty returning. The bus stopped, but as it moved on again, Ivy could see that Miss Beatty was nowhere to be seen. Puzzled, she turned and continued on her way back to Springfields.

"Ivy," said a soft voice behind her. Deirdre's car had driven up so quietly that she hadn't heard it. "Jump in," her cousin said.

Ivy was about to say that her jumping days were over, when she saw that Deirdre's face was pale and drawn, not at all what it should have been on returning from a visit to her admirer at the Hall. She clambered into the car, and they coasted on towards Springfields.

They settled safely in Ivy's room with a tray of tea, which, on seeing Deirdre's shaky progression up the stairs, Katya had prepared as quickly as she could. Then, in fits and starts, Deirdre gave a detailed account of all that had happened and Ivy sat silently thinking.

Deirdre wondered if she'd gone on too long, and exhausted Ivy. The poor old thing had been a bit middling herself. So she concluded her story by saying, "I suppose it might have been an infection, or something I ate yesterday. Gus seemed to think so."

Still Ivy said nothing, then sighed. "More like poison," she said.

"Unlikely, Gus seemed to think. What do you reckon, Ivy?"

"Could be poison. Rat poison, probably. They always have it around somewhere on farms. Young Budd could have trampled it in after setting traps. Just unlucky, maybe."

Deirdre did not believe it. She had reached the firm conclusion that Beattie was mad, and had tried to poison her with doctored biscuits. Or, at the very least, had meant to make Deirdre so ill that she would never set foot in the Hall again. But she supposed that she should not frighten Ivy, and nodded in silent agreement.

There was a knock, and Ivy said, "That'll be Roy. I said I'd be back around now, and he always pops in for a cuppa."

Does he, indeed! thought Deirdre. Romance among the oldies? It had been known to happen. Marriage even. She remembered reading recently in the local about a couple in their nineties who'd got wed. The picture showed them beaming out at the photographer, and she had thought, well, why not, even if it means only a couple of years' companionship and happiness.

Another cup was brought up by the ever-willing Katya, and Ivy debated whether to go over Deirdre's horrible afternoon again. She decided not, not yet, anyway.

The conversation turned to other things. Roy said he had had a visit, the first in three years. A young great-nephew who was driving through on his way to London had called in. "He asked tenderly after my health, when I know he'd rather have been asking tenderly after my bank balance." Roy chuckled. "But it was nice to see a young face. Our Katya was very attentive, dear little thing," he added with a smile.

Then he asked if Deirdre had had a nice afternoon up at the Hall, so the story had to be told once more, this time in an edited version. Roy was horrified, and said the sooner this whole business was cleared up the better.

* * *

GUS LOOKED OUT of his kitchen window and wondered if Deirdre had arrived safely back at Tawny Wings. He had tried hard to persuade her to stay, but she had insisted that she would be fine, and had to get back home. He had even settled Whippy on her lap, remembering that stroking a dog was supposed to comfort people and might encourage her to stay. But she had put Whippy down on the floor, saying she would be fine, and went off, wobbling slightly, to get into the car and disappear down Hangman's Lane.

The episode had shaken him considerably. Although he had not said as much to Deirdre, he knew now that they were up against something very nasty. Once more he thought of contacting the police, but after thinking about it for some time, he decided that this could precipitate more than a violent attack of sickness. If Beattie really did intend to get rid of her rival, a visit from the police might prompt her to panic and have another immediate go at Deirdre, and next time making sure of success. But if he did not tell the police, he was certain now that they had to move fast. They were close. He was pretty sure of that. The Bentalls and the Jessops were linked in a way they now understood, and the root of it all was back in another generation. If they could find out who had first made Beattie's mother pregnant and caused so much unhappiness, then the rest would fall into place.

He remembered suddenly with some excitement that Ivy and Roy had had that invitation to tea with Mrs. Bentall. That was it, he decided, and picked up the phone. He would cheer up Deirdre by telling her this, and then think of a way of discovering the connection between the Roussels and Beattie Beatty. He was sure now that she did not turn up at the Hall all those years ago out of the blue. There must have been a reason which had been kept quiet.

No answer from Tawny Wings. Gus frowned. Deirdre should be home by now, surely? Perhaps she had called at the shop. Yes, that would be it. He would ring again in half an hour or so.

As he watched, Miriam emerged into her garden next door, and walked up the path to her salad bed. She bent down, pulled up a lettuce, and turned. She was too quick for him to back away, so he waved. She returned his wave enthusiastically and mimicked opening the window. "Come in and have supper with me this evening," she shouted. "I'm having ham and salad. Got some nice rhubarb to make a fool," she added.

It's me that's the fool, he thought, but was so tempted by the idea of a good supper, that he yelled back that he would be delighted. Oh God, he thought, as he watched her skip girlishly back into her house. Why on earth did I ever decide on this village? Because it seemed quiet and remote, people getting on with their own lives and allowing you privacy if you wanted it. Ha! That was a joke.

Forty-eight

BEATTIE RETURNED FROM tea with Miriam to a silent Hall. Theo's car had gone, and she did not need two guesses to decide where it might be. Not too far away, and at a house with a stupid name!

She noticed that the light was fading outside in the stable yard, and thought with a sinking heart of lonely hours spent in the kitchen, when buried memories would return to haunt her.

She picked up the telephone, and dialled a number that she knew by heart. "Hello? Okay to talk? Right, well, here's the latest." She then relayed what had happened this afternoon, adding that she thought this was one battle she had won. "What? . . . Oh, some stuff I had lying around. . . . No, probably not. We shall see. . . . When? Oh, in due course. What about you? . . . Well, make it a better job next attempt. Miriam Blake thinks he's a mystery man, but then, all men are a bit of a mystery to Miriam. Yes, you were right! I have a feeling time is running short. Yes . . . what? . . . Oh, yes, but take care. Bye."

She replaced the receiver and began to prepare supper. Not that she expected Theo to be home for supper, but on the chance that he might be, she took a pheasant from the marble shelf in the larder and began to wrap it in bacon and herbs. She thought about her telephone call, and wondered if they hadn't perhaps got themselves in too deep.

Miriam had definitely said there was something mysterious about Halfhide, and had hinted that he was some kind of investigator. It sounded ridiculous, of course, but if she was halfway near the truth it could be an unforeseen and possibly dangerous development. On the other hand, why should anybody want to investigate them? Self-protection was all they were aiming for, and also, she had to admit, an insurance policy for the future.

Another thought struck her. How much did Miriam know about the past? From her conversation, it seemed her mother had kept her in the dark about a lot of it. She was a bit of an innocent, for all her reputation in the village. So was there more to it than being man mad? It might not mean much more than that she tried to lure every man she met into her bed and some she won, some she lost. She seemed confident that Gus Halfhide had already swallowed the hook. If this was so, would it be a good idea to bring Miriam into their confidence, and use her as information gatherer?

No it would not, Beattie decided. The more conspirators involved, if that is what they were, the more likely it was they would be discovered.

She put the pheasant in a slow oven, sat down in the sagging armchair by the Aga, and began to read the evening paper.

MIRIAM SET UP the small table squeezed into a corner of the living room, and spread a cloth embroidered by her mother. She had been good with her needle, and at each corner was a cutout butterfly which seemed to flutter as she smoothed out the creases. Miriam sighed. In some ways she missed her mother, but in others her death had been a huge relief.

She shut her mind to such thoughts, and switched on a dim reading lamp on the corner of the mantelpiece. The overhead light was much too bright. She switched it off. Next, she brought in home-cured bacon from the shop, bread that she had made earlier in the day, farm butter, and a fresh salad. She mixed English mustard from dry powder and vinegar, put it in the centre of the table and stood back to admire her handiwork. Paper serviettes! She opened a drawer in the sideboard and took out two. Gus probably wouldn't notice the holly and mistletoe theme, left over from a long-past Christmas. If he did, he would make a nice joke about it. He was kind that way.

But there was the matter of Mrs. Bloxham and the shawl. Miriam intended to get that cleared up straightaway, and then they could enjoy the meal. There was a tap at the door, and she opened it to let him in.

"I'm just collecting for the down-and-outs of Barrington," he said with mock humility. "Can you spare a bit of dried bread, or a bruised apple?"

Miriam collapsed. All her suspicions and anxiety vanished, and she roared with laughter, a real hearty bellow such as she had not produced for years.

"I can do better than that," she stuttered as guffaws continued to emerge. "Come on in, and have a drink. I've found some primrose wine that mother made a while ago, so it should be really mature."

Oh, goody, said Gus to himself, as his stomach protested in advance. A glass of primrose wine, well matured. He hoped it wouldn't have the same effect as Beattie's biscuits.

Miriam had started a tape of Frank Sinatra love songs, turned down low, and by the time they finished they had eaten every crumb and Miriam removed the plates to the kitchen. "Coffee, Gus?" she called. It was all going so well, with her telling him all about her early life—well, nearly all—and describing how her mother had changed from quite a jolly woman into a carping old dragon in her last years.

"How about your mother, Gus?" she said. "Were you an only child like me?"

"Goodness!" said Gus, looking at his watch. "Is that really the time? How it flies when you're enjoying yourself! D'you know, Miriam, I think I'll skip coffee and be off next door. It has been a really pleasant evening, and an epic meal. Bless you, my dear," he added, and waving a grateful hand exited from the front door and shut it gently behind him.

"Bugger it!" Miriam said. She scarcely ever swore, but now felt perfectly justified. In a few seconds she had scuppered all hopes of getting him to open up. Ah well, at least they had parted good friends, and next time she would be more careful.

THE HOUSE NEXT door was chilly and damp smelling, as usual. Gus turned on the lights and wondered whether it was worth lighting the fire. Probably best to fill his hot water bottle and go to bed with a whisky and a book. The primrose wine had been unexpectedly good, and he planned to ask Miriam to give him a bottle, if she had plenty. It had a wonderfully flowery aroma, and there was no doubt it packed a punch. All those years in the cupboard under the stairs must have given it real strength.

BED, HE DECIDED, and with his comforting fluffy hot water bottle he climbed the stairs.

Before he went to sleep, he reviewed the evening's

conversation. Miriam had given him very little useful information that he did not already know. Her nostalgic ramblings had been mostly about working at the telephone exchange, past romances and friends, and how much she had loved her hen-pecked father. Totally under her mother's thumb, apparently, poor soul. He thought of his ex-wife, and remembered her sharp tongue, and was reminded that he hadn't heard from her lately. Dare he hope that she had finally given up trying to get blood out of a stone?

As his eyelids drooped, a puzzling image floated by. While Miriam had been in the kitchen dishing up rhubarb fool, he had noticed a small photograph tucked behind the clock on the mantelpiece. The gilded frame caught the light, and he peered closer. Was it *Theo Roussel*? Not quite, he decided. But there were strong similarities. This was a man from another generation, wearing, as far as Gus could see, a tweed jacket and camel hair waistcoat. He was smiling, and he had Theo's smile. When Miriam returned to the table, Gus had asked her who it was, and she had said it was just a friend of her mother's and then changed the subject.

Forty-nine

IVY AND ROY had already arrived at Tawny Wings when Gus came panting up the drive. Deirdre opened the door to him, and he apologised for being late. "Blame it on the primrose wine," he said, though in fact the lovely stuff had had no ill effects. He had merely overslept, probably the result of a good supper and, touch wood, relief that his ever-loving ex seemed to have given up dunning him for money.

As they made for the stairs, he said, "You're looking very chipper, if I may say so."

"Feeling good," Deirdre said, with a smile.

"Ah. Visit from the squire on Saturday? Lots to tell us?"

"Wait and see," she said, ushering him into her office, where Roy greeted him enthusiastically and Ivy looked obviously at her watch. "Can we get going?" she said. "I have things to do later this morning."

Gus refrained from asking what an old lady living in a retirement home with all her wants supplied could possibly have to do that was so urgent. "Obviously no apologies," he said, "so shall we have the minutes of the last meeting?"

"Oh, for goodness sake, Augustus," Ivy said. "We can get straight down to business. Now Deirdre, it was reported to me that Theo Roussel's filthy Land Rover was parked outside your house on Saturday night until the small hours. And yes, before you say it is none of my business, I say it is. He is a prime suspect in our first case in my opinion, and being too intimate is unprofessional."

There was a stunned silence, and then Roy began to laugh. "Ivy, you are a gem," he said. "Who else could bring us back to order in such a wonderful way?" He reached out and patted her on the back of her hand, and she shook him off. "Well, Deirdre?" she said.

Deirdre was trying hard to be serious, and professional. "Ivy," she said, "I would never dream of telling you to mind your own business." For one thing, she said silently to herself, it would be a waste of time, like old Canute at the seaside. "No, I can assure you that any association I may have with Theo is purely in the interests of our investigation."

Roy once more laughed. "So what happened, Deirdre?" he said. "Apart from a spot of the other, I mean."

Finally Deirdre gave them an edited account of her return home after seeing Ivy, when Theo had turned up at Tawny Wings, again full of apologies for not being able to let her know that Beattie had not gone to market. "Apparently she told him just before she was due to go. He'd tried, but by that time I was already out in the drive, unloading shopping I'd done in the morning and ready to set off for the Hall. The old witch must've worked it all out very efficiently. Theo says she is a tough adversary, and I begin to see what he means."

"What else did he say?" Ivy said sourly.

"Well, quite a lot, really. For one thing, I was able to ask him where Beattie had come from, and why to the Hall. He told me where she'd lived, but not why she had arrived to housekeep for his widowed father. I suspect he'd not give me the real reason why, if he knew it."

"Glad you didn't swallow everything he said wholesale," Ivy muttered.

Deirdre continued: "Theo said he supposed she had answered an advertisement, and had got the job. She came from Oakbridge, and had good references, so his father said. Theo did not particularly like her from the start, and after his father died she gradually took over, not only the running of the estate, but Theo himself."

"He was hardly bound hand and foot, was he?" said a sceptical Ivy.

"It was a clever, gradual process, Theo said. He even came to believe he was ill. Not seriously, but enough to curtail his activities. In the end, he gave up and left everything to her."

"Until you came along," said Gus generously. "I hope he's duly grateful."

"He is," said Deirdre, with a dreamy smile.

"I wonder what was the real reason she came all the way across the county for a job, when all her family were back in Oakbridge?" Roy said.

"Didn't he give any hints, Deirdre?" Ivy asked. She considered that the Land Rover had been outside Tawny Wings quite long enough for dozens of questions and answers in the interests of the investigation.

Deirdre frowned, thinking back. It had indeed been a lovely evening with Theo. He had lit a fire for her in the long drawing room, tucked her up on the sofa under a soft rug, and sat with his arms around her, sympathising with her and making her feel like she hadn't felt for years. If ever!

"Not really," she said. "Theo did say something about Beattie spending a lot of time up at Springfields before it became an old folks' home."

"Less of the 'old folks,' if you don't mind," said Ivy. "Anyway, why would she have done that? Didn't you say it was lived in by a recluse lady with her companion, Roy?"

He nodded. "Never seen. Even the companion came and went in a car and hardly ever ventured into the village. People just let them alone, in the end. Villagers are like that. If a person wants to be left alone, that's fine with us."

"Even if they are living lives of quiet desperation?" asked Deirdre, remembering some of the isolated, lonely people she visited in her volunteer work.

"Nothing to do with us, if that's how they want it," Roy said cheerfully. "Up to them, isn't it?"

"So do we know any more about Beattie's association with Springfields in those days?" Gus had a familiar feeling, almost like Whippy when she got an interesting sniff and wouldn't leave it, that they were getting near something vital, something definitely central to the mystery.

"No, 'fraid not," Roy said. "Maybe when me and Ivy go to tea with Mrs. Bentall, she will be able to help us with that."

"Of course!" Deirdre said. "That's it, Roy. When are you going?"

"Tomorrow," said Ivy. "And don't offer to take us. We've already booked a taxi, so you'll have to wait until we get back to see what we've gleaned."

Deirdre's face fell, and Ivy felt a pang of guilt. Perhaps she was being unfair to her cousin, who, after all, had been a widow for a good many years, and deserved a bit of fun before she was too old. Just as long as she didn't get hurt by smarmy Theo at the Hall.

"Anything else, then?" Gus said.

"How about supper with Miriam?" Deirdre said, in a belated attempt at revenge.

"Good cooking, primrose wine, lots of girlhood reminiscences, but nothing useful to us. She's not so green as she's cabbage looking," he added. "Knows what not to tell, I reckon."

"Nothing else?" Deirdre asked.

"Well, I'm not sure it has any bearing on the murder, but I noticed a small photograph tucked away behind the clock on her mantelpiece. At first I thought it was Theo, which would have made sense, since Miriam had a fling with him years ago. But then I could see it wasn't him. Old-fashioned clothes, and a different look about him. Could've been the moustache, but not just that."

"His father," Deirdre said flatly. "There's pictures of him everywhere at the Hall," she continued. "Even one in the kitchen on the top shelf of the dresser. I noticed it on Saturday, as Beattie was busy trying to poison me."

Ivy had gone pale, and her hand was shaking slightly as she brushed a nonexistent hair out of her eyes. "Oh dear," she said. "You'd better go and make us some coffee, Deirdre. Hot and strong, there's a good girl."

Fifty

GUS HAD RETURNED home after yesterday's meeting, deeply concerned by Ivy's collapse. He was pretty certain that the old lady had had a slight heart attack, but she hotly denied that anything was wrong. Just a funny turn, she said. Often get them, she had assured Roy, who was upset, but full of dubious practical suggestions, like giving her neat brandy and wrapping her up in two duvets from Deirdre's beds.

In the end, Ivy had insisted that nothing was wrong. She had had a sudden thought, which was so serious that she had startled herself.

"What was it?" Gus had asked gently. But Ivy replied that until she knew much more, hopefully from Mrs. Bentall, she would not disclose what might well be a red herring. They had to be content with that, and after coffee Deirdre had insisted on taking her cousin and Roy back to Springfields.

"Are you sure you'll be all right to go over to Oakbridge tomorrow?" she had dared to ask Ivy, who had replied that she wished to hear no more about it. Deirdre had said that if that's how she wanted it, she must remember she had a mobile and use it if necessary.

Now Gus looked at his watch. The pair were setting off around three o'clock. The taxi should be arriving anytime now to collect them, and as he had heard nothing alarming from Springfields, or from Deirdre, he assumed Ivy had completely recovered. He would give anything to be a fly on the wall of Mrs. Bentall's best sitting room.

THERE WERE NO flies of any sort on Renata Bentall's pristine cream-coloured walls. Ivy was gratified to see that the house was clean, warm and welcoming. After all, she had said to Roy coming along this morning that for all they knew, Mrs. Renata Bentall lived in a down-at-heel, two up two down, workman's cottage in a back street of Oakbridge. But as they drew up outside, Ivy saw something that brought tears to her eyes. Not only was the house detached and large, but the discreet sign said "Victoria Villa," the same name as the solid redbrick house that had been her home in Ringford, her only home until she had ended up at Springfields.

Renata Bentall had seen them coming, and was standing with a big smile at the wide-open front door. "Come along in," she said. "I've been really looking forward to seeing you both."

Ivy, straight backed and without her stick, walked up the path as Roy reminded the taxi driver that they wished to be collected at precisely half past four. He leaned close to the driver, and said softly, "Don't be late, chum. She's a stickler for punctuality." The man winked at Roy. "See you later, sir," he said.

Renata had been baking all morning, and the tea tray was loaded with scones and jam and cream, and a perfect chocolate sponge, so light that Roy had two large wedges and even Ivy asked for just a tiny second slice. Their cups were refilled with fresh tea and diluted to requirement with hot water from a silver jug. Everywhere there was evidence of wealth, and Ivy relaxed. At least there was no danger for them here, no poisoners or conspirators.

"Do tell us more about your family," she said to Renata. "Other people's lives fascinate me. I was so confined in a small village all my life," she added, ignoring the truth that this had, in fact, been entirely her own choice.

"Ah, well, where shall I begin?" asked Renata.

"At the beginning," said Roy jovially. He, too, was enjoying himself. Goodness, what a difference Ivy had made to his life. He had been coasting along to a final wooden box exit from Springfields, when this wonderful new adventure had come along, and all because of Ivy.

Renata then told them about her marriage to Charlie Bentall, and his distant relation a generation back, known as Buster because of his initial zealous drive to bust through all the corruption he found at the town hall when elected Mayor. "His family were proud of him," she said. "O' course, my husband Charlie's parents were from another branch of the Bentalls, but the doings of the mayor's daughter were juicy gossip for all. Caroline was Buster's only child, and he doted on her. At the same time, she had no freedom and had to do exactly as he said, poor thing. My mother used to say no wonder she went off the rails."

"Oh dear," said Ivy. "How was that?"

"Oh, the usual," Renata said casually. "Got herself pregnant, no husband, nor any likelihood of one. Produced twins, had them parked out with a couple somewhere, then later on got married to one of the no-good Jessops. Our Jessop lot came from a northern branch of the family originally, and needless to say wanted nothing to do with the Oakbridge clan. So then Caroline had another baby girl, and reclaimed Beattie. That was the girl twin. They said

Caroline's Jessop husband beat her up, but we never heard the truth of that. Oh, goodness," she added, "this must be so boring for you! Do tell me more about yourselves?"

"So Caroline married a Jessop, and later on you married a Bentall?" asked Ivy.

"That's right. I suppose my Jessops and Charlie's Bentalls were like a Greek chorus standing on the side of the stage, watching Caroline's tragedy unfold."

Ivy made a mental note, and then said, "Go on, then. I've never met anybody related to a town mayor."

Renata returned to telling them of the rumours about Caroline and the terrible time when she went missing. "Never found, you know. The boy twin, Keith, stayed with his foster parents and was not heard of again in the family. It was difficult to trace him, as they were not official foster parents, just a couple of people on the make, paid by Buster. And they did a bunk at some stage. Nobody knows where they went, or Keith himself, for that matter. I heard he'd changed his name, though goodness knows what he calls himself now."

"So nobody knew who the twins' father was? How sad," Ivy said, trying her best to make it sound like a casual question.

Renata thought for a moment. "I don't really remember," she said, "except my mother said that there was a rumour that Caroline had been seen several times all dressed up, getting into a car driven by a good-looking man with a big moustache. The rumour died away, like they all do in the end, and eventually everything settled down."

"I can see it must all have been a big shock to the Bentall family at the time," Ivy said, trying to keep herself calm. "A bit like when my father died and we discovered he'd had at least three mistresses, all of whom came to the funeral!" And may God forgive me, she added to herself, for such black lies.

Renata laughed. "Do tell, but first you must have another sliver of cake. And you, Roy," she added. "I do think we should be on Christian name terms, don't you, Ivy? I am sure we're going to be great friends."

The rest of the visit passed very pleasantly, until at four thirty precisely there was a knock at the door, indicating the taxi had arrived. Ivy was irritated to see that they had a different driver, and although he was perfectly polite, more polite than the other man, she took an instant dislike to him. Oily, she said to herself, much too oily.

They drove away from Renata's house and Roy waved enthusiastically until they were out of sight. "What a nice woman," he said.

"And a very nice chocolate cake," said Ivy. "Shall you manage your supper?"

Roy laughed. "You had just as much as me, Ivy," he said. "All those tiny little extra slivers added up to my wedges, you know."

Ivy did not answer. She was looking to left and right as they drove through the town. "Is this the right way?" she said. "I don't remember that new supermarket over there. I am sure I would have noticed. Ugly great place, you couldn't miss it!"

Roy peered out of the window. Ivy was right. They were definitely on a different route. "Hey, where are you going?" he said to the driver, tapping him on the shoulder. "This is the wrong way out of the town."

"Got to make a call," he said gruffly, all his politeness vanished.

"We aren't paying you to make private calls!" Ivy said sharply.

The driver did not answer, but stopped the car and got out. They could see him making a call on his mobile, and it lasted a good five minutes. Roy said crossly that they did not need to stand for this, and he would walk back with Ivy and find another taxi. "Not far, Ivy," he said, "I'll give you a hand." He took hold of the door handle. "It's locked!" he said.

At that point the driver returned, and without looking at them or answering their questions about the locked doors, he drove off and switched on the radio at what sounded to them like full volume. Roy looked anxiously at Ivy, who was sitting up ramrod straight, with closed eyes.

"Ivy? Are you all right?" he said.

"I'm thinking," she said. After a few minutes she turned to him and whispered behind her hand, "He's one of them."

"One of who?" Roy mouthed back to her.

The driver turned his head and said loudly, "Shut up, both of you!"

After that, they said nothing, and Roy wondered why Ivy was looking so fixedly at the back of the driver's head. In fact, she was looking past his head and at his reflection in the driving mirror. It was obvious, and she was amazed Roy hadn't noticed it. The eyes and mouth were Beattie Beatty's. Even his voice had the same inflections, the same slight hesitation at the beginning of sentences. This was not surprising, she realised with horror, as the pair of them were twins.

Fifty-one

THE TAXI WAS going very slowly, but the radio continued at full blast. Ivy and Roy sat motionless, holding hands in the backseat. The driver hummed to himself, and when he knew the words, joined in with the blaring music. Roy reckoned they were about halfway home, though he couldn't be sure. It was an unfamiliar route, but he vaguely remembered that it ended up as a grassy track that led straight to the Hall.

Suddenly the driver switched off the radio. "Had a nice time this afternoon, did you?" he said, seeming more relaxed.

"Very pleasant, thank you," Ivy said. To Roy's amazement, she seemed quite calm and collected. "Now will you tell us why we are not taking the proper route back to Barrington. And why we are locked in?"

"Locked in for your own safety," he said. "Company policy. Sorry you don't like this way home," he added. "It is a bit longer, but much nicer landscape. And anyway," he continued, his voice changing back to its coarse rasp, "it'll give you time to put your twos and twos together. What is it you call yourselves? Enquire Within, is it? Very subtle. I know what I'd call it."

"We'd be grateful for any suggestions you have to make," said Ivy, and the driver frowned. Why wasn't the old bag looking scared? Well, give it time.

"Nosey Parkers Inc.," he said. "Pity you couldn't keep your nose out of our business. Still, we've got everything in hand. Just had to bring things forward a bit."

"How clever, Keith," Ivy said, and the driver twisted round sharply at her use of his name, causing the taxi to swerve dangerously into the path of an oncoming lorry. It hooted fiercely, and the lorry driver waved a clenched fist.

Keith laughed. "We get used to it in this job. Road rage, they call it, Miss Beasley. Beattie and me have a different kind of rage and have waited a long time to use it. Not you, nor your boyfriend there, nor Mrs. Tawny Wings Bloxham, nor the mysterious Mister Halfhide, are going to stop us."

Ivy said coolly that he could do what he liked, so long as he dropped Mr. Goodman and herself off at Springfields, as he was hired to do.

"No can do," he said, and switched the radio back on even louder. Nothing more was said until they bumped along over the rough track and arrived in the Hall stable yard. Ivy had signalled to Roy to keep silent, and now he glanced curiously at her. She had been rummaging about in her handbag, her hands busy inside its capacious interior. What on earth was she doing? Now she looked up, smiled at him reassuringly, and zipped up her bag. The car stopped, and Keith opened Ivy's door.

"Out!" he said, and then did the same with Roy. "Both of you, inside," he continued. "And don't try any funny business."

"Good God, what d'you think we shall do, man?" Roy exploded. "Do a runner down the drive? Disable you with a rugby tackle? You're talking to two old people in their dotage! You should be thoroughly ashamed of yourself!"

"Hear, hear!" said Ivy, and added that actually Mr. Goodman was not very strong. She was sure, she said, Keith wouldn't want to be responsible for anything serious that might happen to him. He ignored this and indicated that they should get out and go into the back door of the Hall, where Beatty stood waiting for them. He followed close behind.

"Good job you phoned to give me time," Beattie said to her brother. "So it was okay with the other driver?"

He nodded. "All fixed," he said. "Are the others here?"

Beattie nodded. "They think it's a social occasion," she said, and her laugh sent a shiver down Roy's spine.

Gus and Deirdre sat in the long drawing room, tiny glasses of sherry on a small table beside them. As Ivy and Roy came in, with Keith prodding them from behind, Gus took one look at them and leapt to his feet. "Ivy! Roy! What on earth has happened? And who are you?" he added, seeing Keith following.

"Are you blind, Halfhide? Long-lost twin, that's me," Keith said. "Beattie, pour coffee for the old gent. Don't want him snuffing it in the squire's drawing room. Then we can start."

"Start what?" Deirdre said. She had recognised the twin brother immediately.

"Start explanations," Keith answered impatiently. Beattie gave Roy his coffee, but Ivy reached in front of him and waved it away imperiously. "Probably poisoned. Don't drink it, Roy. Nor the sherry," she added, seeing that Gus and Deirdre had scarcely sipped theirs.

"Good thinking," said Gus. He admired the way Ivy had in those few words banded the four together. Four against two, Gus calculated. Should be child's play, even though he didn't like the look in Keith's eye. The two of them had clearly been plotting something for a while, he reckoned, and Enquire Within had got in the way. His thoughts churned on as they waited for Beattie to sit down.

Deirdre had begun to shake, and Gus took her hand. "Get on with it, then," he said angrily to Keith. "And anyway," he added, looking round, "where's the boss?"

"Out," said Beattie shortly. "Not back until tomorrow." Ivy noticed her glance towards the door in the corner, and did not believe her.

Gus unexpectedly began to laugh, and they all stared at him. "Blimey," he said. "You've been reading too much Agatha Christie. Here we are, gathered together under duress at the Hall, waiting for all to be revealed. So who's the murderer, and where's the police inspector? This is a total farce, and I'm off out of here. Come on, gang, follow me."

"Not s'fast, Mr. Halfhide," said Keith, the phrase causing Gus to laugh again. "Typecast!" he said delightedly. He pulled Deirdre to her feet, and then she screamed.

"He's got a gun!" she yelled, and the others froze.

"Keith!" Beattie said. "There's no need for that. Give it to me."

But he took no notice, and said they were all to sit down and listen. He added with a sneer that as they had not "enquired within" very far, he would oblige them by filling in the gaps in their investigations. "After all," he said, "you're not going to be around to do me any harm."

He levelled the gun at each one of them in turn and Beattie stepped forward. "Keith!" she said. "Put that thing down. Where did you get it? This is not what we planned at all! For heaven's sake let's just get out of here, and forget the rest."

Gus, completely serious now, motioned to Ivy and Roy to sit down, and helped Deirdre back into her chair. "Make it brief," he said to Keith. "You have very little time." His voice was quiet but authoritative, and Keith bridled.

"Bluffing will get you nowhere," he said, and began

his explanation in a strangely flat voice, as if reciting a prepared text from memory. It was a sorry story. Unkind foster parents and Beattie, his one comfort, taken back by their mother. He had been abandoned. As soon as he could, and still underage, he had left the foster home and made his own way, moving from place to place, sometimes living rough, and occasionally taking temporary jobs. "For a while, quite a long while, as a matter of fact," he said with a twisted smile, "I was the guest of Her Majesty. To put it another way, I was in the nick."

"And likely to go there again," said Ivy. Gus shook his head warningly at her. He had seen a few madmen in his time, and knew they were not to be trusted to act rationally. You had to humour them.

Keith lifted the gun and pointed it at Ivy. "Shut up!" he said. "Or else you'll be sorry."

He then continued, taking them through the time when he discovered that his mother and other sister were living in seclusion and under false names at a house called Springfields in Barrington.

"All cunningly arranged by my beloved father," he said.

"No need to mention that," Beattie said. "For God's sake hurry up, Keith."

His voice became a self-pitying whine. "I was not allowed out to see them," he said. "So I didn't find out until weeks later that Mother had died and my other sister had overdosed and gone the same way."

Beattie's face was set hard. "They were cremated," she said. "It was for the best."

"Why are you telling us all this?" Deirdre said, regaining her confidence with her hand held tightly by Gus. "It's nothing to do with us."

"Oh yes it is," Keith said. "Snoopers all, aren't you? Amateurs, of course. I could teach you a thing or two. Especially you, Halfhide. You had no idea I was in your house, waiting to put you out of action. You were first on the list, and lucky for you, I was out of practice."

"By what list and *why*?" Gus said. "Couldn't we cut the life story and get to the point?"

Again the gun was waved in his direction. "Shut up and listen!" he said, and his twin frowned. "Keith," she said gently, "would you like a drink? Don't get too upset, my dear."

Ivy took a deep breath. So the man was unhinged, she thought, and even Beattie was frightened of him. That was why he needed to tell us all this stuff, to show how clever he is. She crossed her fingers and hoped he was not as clever as he thought he was. Gus's calmness was reassuring, but she dreaded there would not be enough time before Keith went completely off his head and pulled the trigger. She found herself looking at her watch every two minutes.

He shook his head, and then rubbed his eyes with his free hand. He seemed to sway a little, and Beattie said, "Perhaps I could take over from here. Give you a bit of a rest?"

He frowned, but reluctantly agreed, and Beattie began. Then, before she had said more than a couple of sentences the door in the corner burst open, and Theo Roussel stood there. Keith snapped to attention and aimed the gun. Unfortunately for him, he took his eye off the others, and Gus, well trained, was on him in seconds, knocking the gun out of his hand and overpowering him. Beattie screamed and ran from the room.

"Well done, Halfhide," Theo said, rubbing his wrists. "The buggers had me tied up in that cubbyhole. Took longer than I thought to get out."

THEO TOLD THEM all to sit down and take deep breaths, while he fetched the brandy. "Better than sherry," he said. "Depressing stuff, sherry." Deirdre noticed admiringly that he was at once in charge. And all because of me, she thought romantically. Gus was still holding her hand and gave it a squeeze, reminding her he was there. He had not missed the soft look on her face as Theo came back with brandy and glasses.

"Shouldn't we get on to the police at once?" Ivy said. She was feeling a little shaky, and noticed that Roy's usually rosy cheeks were very pale.

"Of course, Miss Beasley," Theo said. "But don't worry. Beattie won't get far. First let's give ourselves a chance to collect our thoughts. And," he added, glancing venomously at Keith, now well secured, "there are one or two questions I'd like to ask this appalling villain here."

All except the now shivering twin relaxed a little. As Ivy listened to Theo asking angry questions and receiving grudging answers from Keith, she was shocked by the long years that had elapsed since this whole business began. How sad that Caroline's unwanted pregnancy had caused so much sorrow and so many unhappy lives. And murder? As Theo squirreled the truth out of Keith, she began to see what might have happened. The answer really did depend on who had fathered the twins. It was about money, she realised sadly. The root of all evil, right enough.

Theo had paused. Then he said in a low voice, "It was my father, the wicked squire, who took advantage of your poor mother. And she was not the only one, if village rumours were correct."

"Why didn't he marry her?" said an indignant Deirdre.

"Because he was married already to his lady mother," Keith spat out, pointing at Theo. "And the cruellest blow of all for *my* mother was that after producing Beattie and me and having us taken from her, only three weeks later Theo here, the legitimate son and heir, was produced to the rejoicing Roussel family."

"And the others you mentioned?" Gus said to Theo, remembering the photograph on Miriam's mantelpiece. Theo's father, of course.

"I have no idea," said Theo, but Gus knew he was lying.

"Oh surely, Mr. Roussel," he said politely, "I think you knew that old Mrs. Blake was another of your father's conquests, and poor Miriam was the result? He was a bit of a bastard, wasn't he?"

Theo shook his head in embarrassment and did not answer. Then Keith butted in.

"We were the bastards!" he shouted, glaring at Theo. "Me and Beattie. And yes, in due course your father made arrangements for Beattie to work here at the Hall, where he could keep an eye on her. He shoved my mother out of sight when she was finally found dying in despair, with my other sister looking after her. They might just as well have been entombed in that grim old house, too scared to go out or talk to anybody."

"Springfields?" said Ivy defensively. "It is in no way grim. The atmosphere in a house depends on who lives there. . . ."

She was about to elaborate when she heard a scuffling noise and the main door into the drawing room opened. At last! She breathed a huge sigh of relief. First into the room came Katya, the light of battle in her eye. She rushed across to Ivy, embraced her and uttered dramatic thanks to God that the old lady was safe. "You are so clever!" she said, kissing Ivy's cheek, "to send me text message! Our lessons not wasted!" she added, and kissed the other cheek.

She was followed by Beattie, mutinous and subdued, her hands cuffed to a policeman, and a neat, serious-faced man Theo recognised as the inspector who had asked so many questions after Mrs. Blake's murder. Frobisher, that was his name.

"Good God, man," he said sternly, "you don't need those things on poor Beattie. This is the man you want. Please release her at once."

Inspector Frobisher said frostily that they had met Miss Beatty running down the drive, and Mr. Roussel must leave him to know his own job. He added that he wished this gentleman and Miss Beatty to accompany him back to the police station.

"So no more explanations, then?" Gus said, thinking that Agatha would have spun it out for another hour or two. He was well aware that the full story had not yet been told. On the other hand, he did not wish to draw police attention to himself, and he nodded when the inspector said he would be in touch with all of them later. Then Frobisher led the policeman and the twins out, cautioning those left behind not to gossip around the village. "As if I would!" said Ivy.

Roy suggested they have more brandy, and Theo refilled the glasses. He had brightened up considerably, and twinkled at bright-eyed Katya. "Did you say Miss Beasley sent you a *text message,* my dear?" he asked.

"Oh yes, Sir Roussel," she said, and for one awful moment Ivy thought she was going to curtsey. "I have been teaching Miss Beasley the wonders of the mobile phone. She is willing student, I must stress."

"Huh!" grunted Ivy. "Wretched things. Still, I suppose they have their uses, my dear," she added gratefully, and patted Katya's small hand.

Fifty-two

IT WAS A sober foursome that left the Hall and made their way out to Deirdre's car. Ivy and Roy settled in the back, and Gus said he would walk the few hundred yards back to Hangman's Row. Deirdre sat still for a moment, not switching on the engine. "Don't you want a coffee or something with me?" she said tentatively to Gus.

He shook his head and smiled at her. "I'll ring you," he said, "but first I have to call in at Hangman's Row. Take care, all of you," he added. "As soon as I know more, we'll get together and wrap this whole thing up. Well done, you two," he added, feeling a sudden lump in his throat as he looked at Ivy, still so straight and severe, and little old Roy once more holding her hand.

The car purred off down the lane, and he walked slowly after it. He made a mental note of the answers they still needed, and by the time he reached Miriam's gate, he was ready for her.

"Gus?" she said, answering the door at once. "What on earth's been going on at the Hall? Was that a police car?

And *Beattie* in it? And who was the strange man? Come in, do, and tell me all."

Gus realised that she was excited, pleased at the prospect of upheavals at the Hall. "I could do with a glass of your mother's primrose wine," he said, looking at his watch. He followed her into the neat sitting room. The first thing he looked for was the photograph of John Roussel, and there it was. He could have sworn the old sod winked at him.

He decided to come to the point. "Miriam, did you know your mother was one of John Roussel's favourites?" Couldn't put it more tactfully than that, he had decided.

She grinned. "Of course," she said. "And like father, like son. Me and Theo, well, we were good pals, too!" Then her face fell. "Until Mum put a stop to it, o'course. Still, I could see it wouldn't do. He's my half brother, you know!" She giggled. "Sort of incest, I suppose you'd call it. Still, nobody else knew, Mum said, and made me swear not to tell. I didn't mind after a bit. It was just nice to know I had a brother."

"Did Theo know?"

Miriam made a face. "Mum said not, but I reckon he did, at some stage. She probably planned to tell him at some point to get a hold over him. When he stopped coming to see me, she said it was his doing, not hers, so maybe he'd found out somehow else. Not a nice woman, my mother. Shame really. You're supposed to love your mother, but I can't say I did."

"But you didn't kill her, did you?" he asked gently.

"O'course not! I wasn't there. I'd gone into the village, to the shop. Came back and found her dead, lying there with a knife stuck in her chest. One thing I'm really sure of, Gus. Theo Roussel didn't kill her. Wouldn't hurt a fly."

"So why do you think the police have taken Beattie in?" Gus knocked back his primrose wine in preparation for the worst.

"Goodness knows. Got it wrong, I expect. I'm just waiting for them to find out about me."

"What about you?"

"About me and Theo, of course. And that Mum had—oh lor, I suppose I have to say it—procured me for him, offering her one and only daughter for the amusement of the young squire. Why? Because of the money. I could be due part of the estate, Mum thought. That's what drove her on, I reckon, after Theo inherited, trying to get something out of him. She'd have been satisfied with a lump sum, she said once. She was not the sort to go to court."

Gus let out a heavy sigh. "Just as well," he said. "You weren't the only one, Miriam. The old man was the father of Beattie and her twin brother Keith. It was Keith in the police car. He's turned up only recently, mad as a hatter, but I reckon they were up to much the same as your mother. Choosing their moment to trap Theo, and get money out of him. Enough for their pensions, I expect. No doubt they, too, thought they were entitled to it."

"I kept telling Mum what I'd guessed about Beattie!" Miriam said hotly. "But she said she didn't care, and just went on her own sweet way, as always. Blimey, you only have to look at Beattie standing next to me! Sisters, no doubt of it."

"So your mother finally got in the way?" Gus helped himself to more wine.

"She got greedy, I suppose. Maybe threatened to tell all she knew about Beattie's background if she carried on?" She frowned, finally serious. "But I don't think Beattie would've done the murder, either. She's been quite nice to me lately," she added, as if that clinched it.

"So it could have been the brother, or maybe the two of them together?"

"Search me," Miriam said. "Your guess is as good as mine. Maybe we'll never know. D'you want to stay for supper? I've got chicken pie in the oven."

* * *

GUS STAYED FOR supper. He learned nothing more, but not needing to listen to her inconsequential chatter, he turned over in his mind all she had said in answer to his questions. He did not agree that neither Theo nor Beattie would have murdered the old lady. Either of them could have done it, and Keith, too. If they had planned it carefully, watching until Miriam set off for the shop and, knowing her propensity for endless gossiping, they would have had time enough to get in, stab the nasty old woman, and get out again, vanishing back up to the Hall, or into the countryside around.

Motive was another matter. It was more than probable that, as Miriam said, Mrs. Blake had regarded Beattie as a competitor for the estate and was blackmailing her, trying to frighten her off. This would have put Keith in jeopardy also, and the madman would have had no compunction about knifing his enemy.

Gus reluctantly came to the conclusion that Theo had no real reason to want the old woman dead. After all, many moons had gone by since his affair with Miriam. He had probably forgotten the whole thing, and carried on his merry way with other girls, other adventures.

Well, now the police had the whole thing in their hands, and there was no need for Enquire Within to do anything more. Had the agency been a good idea? They had never received the commission from Theo Roussel to pursue the enquiry for him. Things had just developed piecemeal, with no fat fee for them at the end of it. "Cheer up, Gus! The worst may never happen," Miriam said gaily.

"It already has," Gus said seriously. "Your mother has been murdered, Miss Beasley and Mr. Goodman have had the fright of their lives, and sad details of wasted lives have come to the surface."

"Ah, yes," Miriam said, "but let's look to the future,

Gus. You and me? That's possible, isn't it?" She looked at him lovingly, and got up to put her hand on his shoulder.

Anything's possible, thought Gus, except that! He patted her hand, and stood up. "Must be getting back," he said. "I'm dog tired, Miriam."

"Tomorrow's another day," she chirped. "Who knows what might happen tomorrow?"

Fifty-three

THEO ROUSSEL SAT in the now empty drawing room for a long time, thinking about the awful things that had been said and done in his family's name. When he was a child, his father had been his hero, so lively and dashing. And his pretty mother had been loving, worshipping even, to her handsome husband. Well, the old man had had feet of clay.

But was he, Theo, any better? Money and position, he supposed, had given him licence to behave badly. Poor Miriam Blake. Though, on reflection, she seemed a happy woman. Especially since her old mother died. A thought struck him. But no, he erased it instantly. She wouldn't have, not in a million years. A very softhearted girl. Always had been.

And now Beattie had been arrested, with that appalling brother of hers. A really nasty piece of work he was, too. He looked up at the portrait of his father, and noted sadly that Keith had quite a look of the Roussels about him. They all had, himself, Beattie and Keith, and Miriam

Blake. Ye Gods, what a muddle! He accepted without question that Beattie, with or without her brother, had killed old Mrs. Blake. Some kind of jealousy or envy, he decided, dismissing the whole thing.

"The only good thing that happened today," he said to nobody, "is meeting that delicious Polish girl from Springfields! What a poppet!" He must find out how long she was staying in England. Then, without a thought for the devoted Beattie, he cheered up at the idea that with the right approach, Katya might well take over the housekeeping job here at the Hall. He would certainly like to get to know her better!

He got up, shook himself, and walked over to the portrait. Maybe he would turn its face to the wall for a bit! But no, the old man wasn't all bad. Hadn't he left provision in his will for a memorial seat outside the shop? He'd had a strong sense of duty towards the village, hadn't he?

But there was something else he would do. He went into the study and lifted the portrait down from the wall. He opened the little safe door with the combination of numbers he had committed to memory. There it was, the lovely diamond ring that in a rush of enthusiasm he'd thought of for Rosebud or Deirdre, but had replaced, biding his time. He held it up to the light, and the fire within sprang to life, all its colours sparkling in his hand. "Yes, it should be worn," he muttered. "I might need it yet," he added, and smiled to himself.

He wandered over to the windows and looked out at the dark gardens, silent and reassuring. Continuity, that was the thing, he realised. It was his duty to keep the Roussel family name going here at the Hall. He strode over to the long mirror between the tall windows, and looked sternly at himself. A strict diet for a week or two would smarten him up. He still had a good head of hair, and his skin was good, in spite of years of incarceration indoors. Beattie had been responsible for that. Well, now she was gone, and he could look forward.

He turned and as he replaced the ring, saw something he had never noticed before. An envelope tucked at the back of the safe. He pulled it out, and was alarmed to see his own name. "Theo Roussel—for his eyes only." It was discoloured, and the flap of the envelope had come unstuck. He withdrew a small sheet of paper, and recognised his father's handwriting, large and flamboyant.

After he had read it, he walked unsteadily back to his chair and sat down and reread, anxious to make sure he had it right.

"My dear son Theo," it began, and continued, "I wish you to read this letter and then destroy it immediately. There is no need for anyone but you to know what it contains."

Theo shook his head, and his hands trembled. He read on. "You are my legal heir, and no one needs to know that my dearest wife was not your mother. Beloved Hermione was sadly barren. The two of us together, in total and loving agreement, decided that I should father an heir to the estate with a sweet orphan girl who worked in the kitchen here. You were taken away from her immediately after the birth, and she was to be handsomely rewarded. Sadly, she did not survive a difficult and long childbirth, and was laid to rest. You have been the light of our lives, Theo, and we could not have loved you more. Your loving father, John Roussel." After this, he had added the family motto: "Go forth and multiply."

Theo put back his head and roared with laughter. "The old devil!" he shouted delightedly. "Well, he certainly lived up to family tradition."

He found a box of matches, and holding the letter between thumb and forefinger, set fire to it until it was burning brightly, then threw it into the great hearth, where the dry paper quickly reduced to ashes.

So that makes us level pegging, he realised with amusement. Me, Miriam, Beattie and Keith. All by-blows of the wicked squire. He shut the safe door and replaced his father's portrait. "Father, my lips are sealed!" he said, and poured himself what was left of the brandy.

Fifty-four

THERE WAS NO chance of keeping the news from the village, and by the afternoon of the next day there were very few people who did not know that Beattie and her long-lost twin brother had been taken to the police station for questioning.

"Who'd have thought it?" Rose Budd said to David. "I mean, we all knew she was an old tyrant an' all that. But *murder*? Did you ever hear talk of a brother?" Little Simon had dozed off for his afternoon nap, and David was relaxing for ten minutes before going back to the farm.

He shook his head. "Never. He must have surfaced quite recently. Not long out of prison, so people say."

"But why, David? Why on earth should either of them want old Mrs. Blake out of the way?"

He shrugged. "I called in at the pub before lunch and people were guessing it had something to do with blackmail. Miriam's old mother was an evil old bag, so they said. The old chaps remembered a time when she encouraged

young Theo to pay court, and more, to Miriam. They reckoned the mother hoped to get something out of it."

"Like what?"

"Like money, Rosie. That's what this is all about. They
were guessing, of course, but there's usually a kernel of
truth in gossip."

"But Theo didn't kill her, for God's sake! We all know
that now."

"Apparently not. No, the old men remembered when
Beattie came to the Hall. They reckon she had something
to do with the Roussel family. It was all very hush-hush,
and no explanations given. She just appeared, and would
never talk about herself to anyone, though some of the WI
women had a good try."

"Long time ago, then. O'course, what I saw of Beattie
in charge, and her way with Mr. Theo, she worshipped the
ground he walked on. Probably had high hopes, even now.
Could have been something to do with that? You have to
feel sorry for Beattie, I suppose."

"I don't," David said firmly. "She was a dreadful woman,
capable of anything. Anyway, all will be revealed in due
course," he added. "I must get back to work. Mr. Theo will
be giving me orders from now on, I'm glad to say."

IT WAS ALL round Springfields, of course, in the mysterious way that gossip can travel round residents who have not
been anywhere all day, and have talked only to the staff.

"It can't be Katya," Ivy said. "She promised to keep
her mouth shut, at least for a couple of days until we hear
what's happening to the Bentalls."

She and Roy had escaped from the lounge after lunch,
fed up with all the speculation, and were sitting in Ivy's
room, mostly in thoughtful silence but occasionally talking
about yesterday's events.

"Oh, it'll be the cleaning women who come in every

day," Roy said. "And don't forget Miriam Blake. She has eyes and ears permanently tuned to the Hall. You bet she picked up the whole story."

"Ah, Miriam, yes," Ivy said. "Gus was going to see her, wasn't he. She probably wormed the facts out of him. He pretends to be tough, but he's a bit of a softy, and it wouldn't take many warm smiles and hot suppers to get him talking."

Roy smiled. "You're right, as always," he said. "Still, it doesn't really matter, does it? The police are in charge now, and we can retire from the case."

"Unpaid," said Ivy sourly.

Roy agreed, and said that next time they must make sure they get the fee up front.

"Sometimes," Ivy said, smiling in spite of herself, "I forget you're eighty-six. Have a chocolate."

UNACCUSTOMED AS SHE was to walking, Deirdre nevertheless strode out from Tawny Wings and set off for the village shop. The local evening paper arrived in the afternoon, and she was anxious to see if the Bentalls were in it.

Her head was still whirling from the scenes at the Hall. She had hardly slept, and when she did doze off, horrible dreams woke her up again, sweating with terror. After the last nightmare, when Beattie and Keith, standing like giants over her, brandished a knife and laughed as they forced her into a corner, she jolted awake, got out of bed, made herself a cup of tea and listened to the World Service on radio until it was six o'clock and a reasonable time to get up and start the day. Even the violent situation in the Congo could not alarm her as much as that nightmare.

Now the crisp air cleared her head, and she walked up the steps and into the shop feeling much more cheerful. After all, it was over now. The police were in charge, and Enquire Within could leave it to them.

The shop was crowded, full of chattering women, but when Deirdre walked in, all went quiet. "Morning everybody," she said. "Morning, Will. Has the paper come?" Then she noticed that all the shoppers had open newspapers. Will took up one from the pile, turned to an inside page and silently handed it to her.

The photograph had been taken as Beattie and Keith, arriving at the court in separate vehicles, had been escorted inside, both in handcuffs and with faces covered. Still in shock, probably, thought Deirdre. She started off for home, but changed her mind and went in the direction of Hangman's Row. She needed company, somebody who had been there, someone to read the paper with. Gus was the obvious choice, and as she tapped on his door she hoped he was at home. He was, and beckoned her in with a smile. "You don't look so good," he said. "Takes a bit of recovering from, doesn't it?"

Deirdre burst into tears, and sat down heavily on the sagging sofa. "Sorry, sorry," she blubbed.

"Primrose wine is what you need," he said. "I'm halfway through the second bottle. The old witch knew how to make a good brew." He filled a glass with the golden liquid and handed it to her. "Is that the paper? Let's look at it together." He sank down on the sofa beside her and handed her a tissue.

It was a short account, using the formal words of police routine in such a case. The two were remanded into custody, without bail. "Doesn't tell us much, does it," Deirdre said, sniffing. "I suppose it'll be a while before we know the truth of what actually happened."

"We know quite a bit," Gus said, taking her hand. "They had motive—money—and the opportunity. Miriam was out, Keith was ruthless and mad, Beattie was dominated by him and destroyed by old obsessions. We don't know which of them did the deed, held the knife and shoved it into the old woman, and we don't know if the police have any actual evidence that either of them did it. Fingerprints, that kind of thing."

"I suppose we'll just have to wait and see," Deirdre said, blowing her nose. "Fancy a pub snack this evening? I could do with a real drink later, and not this cat's pee."

IN HER WINDOWLESS cell, Beattie Bentall, as the police were now calling her, sat staring at a blank wall. None of it seemed real to her. The last twenty-four hours were surely a bad dream, a nightmare. She would wake up soon, wouldn't she?

She had been given a mug of tea, but when she began to drink, it was stone-cold. Her hands were also stone-cold, and she felt as if her body had turned to ice, frozen into an unfeeling state. She pinched her hand and felt nothing. Was she perhaps dead? Was this it, her punishment for helping Keith to kill Mrs. Blake? But she hadn't helped him. He hadn't needed any help. Could she have stopped him? No point in speculating now. Maybe she would have to sit here, alone and with no prospect of any relief, forever and ever. Death would be an escape.

"Now then," said a harsh voice, and the door opened with a crash. "You've not drunk your tea, I see. You must do better with this nice cod and chips. Shall I get you another mug of tea?"

"Yes, please," Beattie said, and realised it was the first time she had spoken since answering to her name and details in the court. So she was not dead! The smell of fish and chips was so good that she felt a pang of hunger.

Where was Keith? she wondered. He hated fish. Perhaps they would give him something different, though she doubted it. As she ate her cod with relish, she thought about Keith, and decided that whatever happened, when the time came for her to speak, she would tell the whole truth, the real truth. He was on his own now, and if what

she had to say incriminated him, then so be it. It was everyone for himself, as she had learned long ago. Surely, after
all those years apart, she was not his keeper, not responsible for him.

She saw his face, pale, thin and haggard. He was obviously not a healthy man. She had realised that as soon as
she set eyes on him. Judging from his perpetual cough,
years of living rough and an addiction to nicotine and God
knows what else had weakened his lungs.

Savouring the last potato chip, she thought of the future,
of the time when she would have to testify. It would not
be difficult to recall what had happened. The scene was
engraved on her memory. Winifred Blake, standing there
with a bread knife in her hand, fear in her eyes but on the
defensive, threatening to call the police if they didn't leave
her house. Then Keith had stepped forward and the old
woman retreated until she caught her heel in the edge of
the rug and fell backwards.

The worst thing had been Keith's bloodcurdling laugh.
She recalled her horror as he turned the bread knife round
and plunged it into Mrs. Blake's scrawny chest.

That wasn't what they had planned at all! They had
meant to frighten the old woman into giving up all her
claims on Theo, so that she would leave the field clear for
them. At least, that was what Keith had led her to think
they would do. She had realised then in terror that her twin
brother was unhinged, unpredictable and dangerous. When
he had calmly suggested they get out of the cottage as soon
as possible, she had feared for her own safety, and had
allowed Keith to push her out into the lane. He had disappeared then, off towards the woods, and she had returned
to the Hall, like a terrified rabbit scuttling back into its
burrow.

Then had come the lies to the police, protecting herself
and her mad brother. She was good at telling lies, always
had been, but from now on she intended to tell the truth.

She had no moral principles, just a strong sense of what was expedient. Looking after number one, her horrible stepfather had called it.

"Dear God," she said aloud. "Help me now. Keith is past help, so you might just as well concentrate on me. If I tell the honest truth, and they believe me, I could get off lightly. Is that too much to ask?"

She thought she heard a small voice saying, "But what about the poisoned biscuits?"

"Not meant to kill," she muttered, and walked over to the narrow bed. She stretched out and closed her eyes. "Not fair," she said quietly. "But then, it never has been fair."

When they came in to collect her plate, she appeared to be fast asleep.

SITTING COMFORTABLY IN a last shaft of sunlight slanting into Springfields' lounge, Ivy and Roy had been silent for several minutes. Then Ivy said, "Well, that's that, then. Do you feel the same as me, Roy? Sort of flat?"

Roy said he was sure it wouldn't be flat for long. "Shouldn't we have an Enquire Within meeting with Gus and Deirdre to wrap up the case?" he asked.

Ivy nodded. "Ah yes, that's it. No time like the present," she said and took out her mobile from her handbag. "Hello? Gus? What's that noise? Oh, Deirdre sniffing. I see. Anyway, this call is for her, too. Can you both be here for a meeting in fifteen minutes? Well, you can go to the pub afterwards! Good. Roy and me will be waiting in my room. Bye. Oh, and tell Deirdre to pull herself together, silly girl."

The meeting began with a brief roundup of the recent happenings, and then Ivy said firmly that it was time to put the Beatty case behind them, and start planning for the future. "And don't look at me like that, Deirdre," she added. "You'll soon get used to it. If you ask me, we've learned a lot on our first case, and I for one can't wait to get going on the next."

"Hear, hear!" said Roy, taking Ivy's hand.

"Well, as a matter of fact," Gus said, seating himself more safely on the edge of Ivy's bed, "I had a call before we left the cottage, and if I'm not mistaken, Enquire Within is back in business. . . ."

ANN PURSER

The Measby
Murder Enquiry

The author of *The Hangman's Row Enquiry* presents a brand-
new mystery, as cantankerous spinster Ivy Beasley finds that
spending her golden years in the quaint village of Barrington
won't be as quiet as she thought.

Ivy hasn't been in assisted living at Springfields for long, and
she's already found new friends, formed a detective agency
called Enquire Within and solved a murder. Now, as autumn
falls, Ivy and her team—Roy, Deidre and Gus—have more
mysteries to solve in between card games.

Enquire Within has been asked to look into a murder in the
village of Measby—a crime that, to Ivy's surprise, hasn't even
shown up in the papers. Similarly intriguing is the new
Springfields resident, Mrs. Alwen Wilson Jones, who claims
she was conned out of a large sum of money. But as clever old
Ivy discovers, Mrs. Wilson Jones, like everyone else in Barrington, has secrets—like a possible connection to the murder in Measby . . .

"Purser always comes up like roses." —*Shine*

CAN'T GET ENOUGH LOIS MEADE?

Don't miss the continuing adventures
of everyone's favorite amateur sleuth from

ANN PURSER

❧

CATCH LOIS MEADE SOLVING MYSTERIES IN
WHICH TIMING IS EVERYTHING . . .

WARNING AT ONE
TRAGEDY AT TWO
THREATS AT THREE
FOUL PLAY AT FOUR